AT THE RISING
OF THE MOON

for Maeve

AT THE RISING OF THE MOON

SHORT STORIES BY
DERMOT SOMERS

BÂTON WICKS · LONDON
THE COLLINS PRESS · CORK

Also by Dermot Somers:
MOUNTAINS AND OTHER GHOSTS
(Diadem 1990, now available from Bâton Wicks)

The ten stories in this collection were
written in the following sequence:
Cliff Hanger (1984. Published in The Irish Press, 1984)
The Fox (1985)
A Tale of Spendthrift Innocence (1986. Read to
  the International Festival of Mountainaineering
  Literature in 1990 and published in
  The Best of Ascent, 1993, and Orogenic Zones ,1994)
John Paul II (1986)
Blind Date (1987)
The Singer (1988)
Johann (1990)
Stone Boat (1991. Read at the International
  Festival of Mountaineering Literature in 1992
  and published in Orogenic Zones, 1994)
Kumari's House (1992)
Lightning in the Dark (1993)

Published simultaneously in Great Britain and Ireland in 1994
by Bâton Wicks, London and The Collins Press, Cork

Trade enquiries (except in Ireland): Cordee, 3a De Montfort Street, Leicester.
Irish trade enquiries to: The Collins Press, Careys Lane, Cork

British Cataloging-in-Publication Data
A catalogue record for this book is available from the British Library
ISBN 1-898573-05-0

Irish Publication Data
ISBN 1-898256-07-1

Printed and bound in Great Britain by
Biddles Ltd., Guildford and Kings Lynn

CONTENTS

LIGHTNING IN THE DARK

'Oh where's that place called Lonely street', Tony howled, flinging it accurately at the melody. Helen picked up the line on the flute, flicked it round, played it back. The Sherpa whooped, whistles from the porters, the omelette beamed up at Tony. But the tea-kettle spilled sulkily into the flames and no one but himself had noticed. He hadn't the energy to rescue it. He looked at Helen with marital affection and despair. She had blown the dinner again.

The sun slumped among the Annapurnas like a shot balloon. Sweat cooled, night-shadows gathered. Helen strained after the devious tune heard on the cook-boy's radio along the path below. She snatched harsh breaths between staccato phrases. At 14,000 feet music thins out. Rhythm falters like the heart. She sat cross-legged against a boulder. Eyes closed, her face was tired, smudged with the grime of a day's march. Rucksacks, porter-loads, tents, kitchen-gear littered the hillside hollow. Sleeping bags absorbed the evening sun. Sheltered by stones the big primuses hummed and flared.

Helen's tall figure was bulked out with a heavy duvet. At thirty she looked twenty-five in spite of fatigue. Striking – Tony judged her curls, eyes and broad mouth; there was a different image of beauty in his mind now. He closed his eyes and thought of Alice. It wasn't difficult; the moment his lids shut she shot into clear vision so abruptly he felt his face bulge with the impact.

She was naked, apart from incidentals – an open blouse? something clinging to her left ankle. His heart winced with desire. He began to sweat – opened his eyes. The cold omelette sneered up at him. Above Helen's head multiple Annapurnas gleamed against the sky.

A young porter beamed, bare foot hammering the ground. With a curved bow he scraped the Nepali tune from a homemade fiddle. Flute and dissonant strings charged the air with the raw gaiety of a crossroads dance. The music made a hedge against barren space. Ragged phrases flicked and teased like thorn-tendrils in a breeze. The cookboy crouched over his narrow drum, the sirdar stamped and swayed.

Before they left London for the Himalayas Tony had an affair. As sexual encounters go it was of the briefest duration, and the maximum impact. Its consequences increased with distance and altitude. Although she sensed the fall in temperature Helen knew nothing about it. Alice, the naked woman, was her closest friend.

' – How could you be in love with TWO people? It's ridiculous!
'Alice . . . Alice . . .' crooning her name, 'It's perfectly simple. You're irresistible – and I have lots of spare emotion. It's the way I am. When I was a child I was in love with the girl next door on both sides, *and* the entire Senior Infants class – ten of them were boys – '
'That's not love. That's a virus.'
'Alice! I've been in love with you since – I first met you. You ignored me completely. You talked to Helen all night, drinking white wine the way you do. You hold it in your mouth and laugh bubbles through it. You were funny, you were clever, you were sexy. So was Helen. I loved both of you.'
'THAT party – !' Derision. ' – I was drunk and depressed. That wasn't wine; it was turpentine. You bought it. I wanted to spit. I was having a period and I hated London. You're looking for an easy substitute for Helen. She's miles too good for you. If you think I'd betray – '
'Alice, we've had all this before. I love her; you know that. I happen to love you too.'
They couldn't help grinning; the recurrent absurdity, his intensity, the carefully tuned ho-hum expression on her otherwise interested face. They'd been having this conversation for weeks, in pubs, parks, coffee-shops, flats. The conversation was a relationship in itself. All that was missing was sex.

'. . . called Lo-onely Street?' he bellowed his line again, to general delight. Dorje threw an arm over his shoulder, echoed the phrase. Tony had been on trips where the staff and climbers were worlds apart. But Helen changed all that. Being Irish helped; she didn't feel superior. She was one of those seriously happy women who dressed in long, skirts because of Bezruchka's remark that female shorts were an affront to the Nepali culture. The skirts stopped three inches above no-nonsense trekking-boots. Stripped of this frightful uniform, which included head-scarves worn in the most unbecoming manner and foully tasselled Peruvian caps, his wife was a striking, strong, fit, woman. Talented. Compassionate.
She knew the staff, the names of their wives, how many children they had. She worried if someone was unwell, had a word with the sirdar and saw that loads were changed around for awhile. Among these openly familial people Tony was embarrassed to be childless. It felt

decadent. A lot of his climbing-friends had no children either. Independence, or selfishness? Musicians too; he glanced at Helen again.

Something was irritating her. He knew the signs, tension stated in the music, not just revision of the tunes heard during the day. The porters thought it was the usual party starting early. Tony was relieved the storm wasn't for him, though he knew he was the unacknowledged cause. As soon as the sirdar began to dance, arms swarming sinuously above his head, Helen stopped. Dorje was the problem. The fiddle faltered but the drum tapped on in deference to the foreman. Dorje stopped as soon as he could without losing face and called Shiba from his drum to tend the kettle. Across the valley the sun hit a notch on the Annapurna Ridge.

'What's the matter?'

'It's bloody Dorje. He's not paying them properly.'

'How d'you know? He says he is.'

'I asked them. They're not happy.'

Tony understood his own fatigue; he was used to mountains. A long, hard day above Ongre and the altitude had begun to bite. Nerves flared easily. He didn't want a row with Helen or a trade-dispute when things were going smoothly.

'They're happier than any porters I've ever had. He must be doing something right. It's his job to pay them. I don't think we've any right to interfere.'

He was equally disturbed by Helen's anger and the greasiness of his own response.

'That's insufferable Tony! You don't think we ought to interfere . . . ? Well I do! I'll have it out with him tonight. If you won't!'

'But Helen – '

'They haven't even got shoes. We're meant to provide shoes. We've given him enough money. How are they supposed to get over the high pass in bare feet?' She was inexplicably in tears.

'Helen, this is Nepal, not England. They have their own system. Shoes will appear if they're needed. No use getting yourself worked up!' The sting slipped out against his will; he resented her missionary attitude – as if no one ever understood porters before.

Her head snapped back; 'Worked up!? You just don't care, do you? About anyone! He could be charging them, as well as us, for the food. I'm going to find out . . .'

She struggled to her feet with a suppressed groan and marched towards the fire.

Dorje, fashionably clad, straddled the flames supervising the porter's rice. The young Sherpa, at home on the mountain, joked raucously with the lowland porters seated around him under coarse pixie-hooded cloaks. At Helen's approach the group fell silent, studying their toes. Rebuffed, oddly helpless, she veered into the darkness. Tony stamped angrily to his feet. Dorje left the fire at once, wiping his hands, smiling amiably. 'Some problem, Tony? Dinner Ok?'

'Dinner was good, thank you.' Conscious of the listening porters, as yet unfed, Tony considered tactful English, but Dorje could evade that, misinterpret it.

'We need to know how much you pay the porters?'

'I pay one hundred fifty rupees, Tony.'

'But they say they get one hundred and twenty, maybe less, so we wanted to know for sure what ....' straying into minor clauses, conscious of Helen listening in the shadows.

'Porters not speak English. Porters my job. If I pay everything now, maybe no porters for high pass. I pay full money in Jomosom, other side, Ok?'

Tony smiled in relief. They had till Jomosom.

Helen interrupted. 'That's good Dorje. We understand that part. Now, about shoes. We gave you money to buy these shoes. Did you give this money to the porters?' No doubt about meaning there. Tony saw Dorje squirm. But the friendly smile remained. 'In Chame I gave money, but they didn't buy ....' He shrugged with a broader smile.

'But Dorje, this money you paid, was this wages – money for work? – or was it extra money for shoes?'

Dorje was an accomplished dealer; he pretended not to understand, while yielding graciously to Helen's logic.

'They didn't buy.' What could one do with such porters? 'In Manang I will buy the shoes myself and give the porters. Ok?'

'Ok, Dorje. Manang.'

'Ok, Ok! No more problems? Porters eat dinner now? Ok?'

Tony giggled. 'You caught him there, Helen.'

'I don't trust him.' She was not entirely appeased. 'I like him, but I don't trust him.'

'They have to make a few bob, Helen.'

'I don't mind him trying to make it on us. Up to a point. But if he's exploiting the porters ....'

He steered her into the cold tent, saw her into her sleeping bag, fussing over her with affection. He lit a candle, wrapped her duvet around her feet and tied the sleeves, rooted out a bar of chocolate intended for the mountain. Helen pushed it away. Her face was grey in the candlelight.

'Tony, I felt dreadful today. Depressed, worried about everything, inadequate. I don't think I'll get to Base-Camp, never mind climb Chulu. I don't know what's wrong. I've never felt so helpless ....'

'It's just altitude, Helen. You'll soon get over that!' Deeply anxious he hurried on. 'You're pushing yourself too hard. You don't have to prove anything – we can't go any faster than the porters. For eighty rupees a day I wouldn't like to push them ....'

Helen's eyes were shut, her forehead the helmet-shape of a headache. Her lips tightened against the joke. He saw how she might look when she was older.

Helen had waited a long time for this trip, but as she waited its terms had changed. She had left Dublin at twenty-one with a music degree. London was to be the start of a world tour. But it had quickly become home, exciting at first, happy later, and then . . . comfortable.

It was during that comfortable stage, that uneasiness had surfaced, roused by the very lack of disturbance. The comfort was dull?, that it collapsed quickly under its own weight; it was like a kind of sleep, the drowsiness from which people rouse when it is too late to live. She almost decided, at twenty five, that it was time to have children, to renew her life at secondhand, but she remembered she hadn't travelled yet.

Tony would have had children straightaway and been a loving if inconsistent parent, inventing it as they went along. He grew up in a passionately irregular family, always on the move, coming apart to come intensely together again. Helen admired his odd tribe, and Tony was proud of them; they ran their relationships as dramatic theatre, disciplined by the principle that the show went on. He believed in opposites – contingency and the heart – and he was far from insecure.

Helen though, was sensibly afraid of two extremes; the traditional conservatism she had emigrated from, and the footloose disasters that passed as marriage in the two areas she knew in England – music and mountaineering.

She resisted children. She had sound, practical reasons, and many of her friends felt the same. Career, creativity, child-rearing in London, she wasn't ready! Tony accepted this with an ease that first relieved, and then unnerved her – considering his urge towards parenthood.

If she had loved him with a little more distance she would have admitted that he was even less ready. With the best will in the world responsibility would always devolve on her. Whenever Tony announced another major change at short notice, she looked at him with a quizzical silence that unsettled him till he put it down to a culture-gap. What occurred to her then, when his casual independence thinned the ground under their feet, was the narrowness of this relationship which didn't have to include both partners in the details of every arrangement. It would be so easy to break . . . .

Sometimes she thought children might solve this; at other times she knew they would aggravate it. In moments of strength she trusted her instincts but she always felt guilty at the inability to make up her mind about her motives.

Other people who actually got on with things seemed equally indecisive when she listened behind their language – they groped confidently in the dark. Many of her friends, who had made big decisions early, confessed that they hadn't reasoned at all, and saw Helen as the decisive one. She realised she couldn't trust anyone's opinion then; they were all confused – the practical ones who were too materialistic, and the idealists who were often dreamers. Was this uncertainty all that had been achieved? Having conquered the old repressive structures there was very little evidence of a new order; in fact, it was obvious people were rapidly reverting to roles they could trust for continuity.

Even Alice, who had always had a lucid scepticism, had turned broody now that she was in London. It must be the city. It was essential to get away to a fresh perspective. Tony injured his back in a climbing accident, nothing too serious but it lingered. He dropped out of an expedition . . . . Why not go out anyway, together?

It was one of those fictional moments like a marriage-proposal, when she could have been stunned, or victorious, or angry – a queen cheaply manoeuvred on a chess-board. Stand-in for a two-month expedition? It wasn't how she had imagined travel. And yet she jumped at it.

'Three months.' Bargaining for a little more.

'Six! And we mightn't come back.'

Tony folded his jacket into an expert pillow, sleeves packed either side to stop his head from rolling. Helen breathed unevenly beside him in the tent. He pressed appreciatively against her, closed his eyes and was invaded.

'You're not my type . . .' Alice argued, with the faint hint of desperation that provided his excuse. They would go on talking; it wasn't the words or the logic that mattered, but the emotion aroused.

'You're MY type. I'd be satisfied with that!' He played at teenage conversation with rapt absorption.

'I used to wonder about you,' she mused, 'before we met. Helen told me a lot, but she only saw the good side.' She frowned, clearly seeing the rest. Tony had a maddening itch to hear himself discussed.

'Not particularly handsome, but she found you attractive. She was right about the looks, but I can't see what the attraction was.' A grin twitched the corner of her mouth.

'You haven't seen everything, Alice . . . .' She raised a wry, eyebrow. It brushed the quick of his existence. Every move she made generated this erotic charge. Beneath his skin nerve-ends flicked in shoals. He was trapped. It was sexual hypnosis; granted, one had to be willing at first, but after that there was no choice.

When he thought of Helen it wasn't guilt he felt, or sadness. He loved her. He rejected the accusation of betrayal. It was as if he had been invaded; colonised by sex. And yet – it wasn't happening.

Tony was a teacher who never taught.

He had started with a degree in English and a Master's thesis – the Influence of Celtic Poets on the English Tradition. It left him out of work; people didn't care about crossbreeding in literature.

Helen did. Alice didn't, but that was later. Meanwhile, he concentrated on climbing and took an Outdoor Education Diploma in Wales to be near the action. Certain climbs – Thoor Ballylee, The Circus Animals' Desertion, date from that.

He was surprised that the course was inspiring in itself, even more surprised to find himself a P.E. teacher in a progressive school in London. The other staff ran football courses; Tony started an Outdoor Pursuits programme to loosen things up and provide an excuse for his own climbing. Trips away with canoes and climbing-ropes were so popular that he became an entire department – which undermined his own priorities.

He ran courses for his colleagues to show the value of the outdoors. They crept around cautiously, referring to themselves as being 'in Snowdonia', as if it was an exotic safari-park instead of old, worn North Wales.

But Helen was different. He met her at a time when all the London women he knew – maybe it was his fault – were either overwrought or sedated. Helen had talent and no neuroses; she taught music for a manageable number of hours, London animated her, and she loved North Wales.

Tony seemed quite accomplished himself – too many minor talents, as it happened, to develop a single one. Romance was inevitable. Alice didn't appear for six years.

She mightn't have appeared at all, except that Helen got homesick in the fifth year of marriage. She didn't want a lover, the usual solution, but she encouraged Alice to move to London, away from a crisis – got her a job in the Phonetics Department at the BBC. Tony had never heard of it; he had assumed whatever pronunciation the BBC broadcast became local usage immediately.

He hadn't met Alice; they bypassed so often it seemed almost deliberate. He knew her colourful career. She worked in Brussels to escape a relationship at home. She left Brussels to end an entanglement with her boss; returned to Dublin to another drama – and was on her way to London now.

He was disappointed by her; quiet, reserved, almost ordinary. He had looked forward to excitement – but at the same time he'd been afraid she might distract Helen from him; they had a history of shared experience which might exclude him like a hostile culture. In a reverse of the married itch Tony feared he was about to lose Helen a little, and he resented it.

Alice conversed intelligently, dressed calmly, was conservative – most of the new Irish were. She didn't harp on the past, and he and Helen didn't exclude her from the present.

Friends of theirs, disengaged males, queued to take Alice out, looking for someone like Helen. Everyone got on well; the social circuit hummed – a flurry of small dinner-parties, called anything but that, in little houses temporarily worth a fortune. All the things that could be done with brown rice . . . .

Helen played in a jazz-quartet on Saturday nights. Alice liked walking. Tony took her to the Lake District on a weekend with a couple of climbing friends. She went up over Scafell, down into Wasdale and they picked her up in the evening, pleased with herself. They found the remains of a wedding in a hotel-lounge and took it in turns to dance with her – the first time he'd seen her animated.

The little stoop was gone, shoulders swinging, classic body in motion, slender waist, breasts tangibly imaginable through the blouse, narrow hips, legs that gave eloquent rhythm to the beat. When she whirled on her toes the hood of black hair lifted, her eyes opened wide, full lips blew invisible bubbles at the ceiling.

Gazing intensely he was startled by the exquisite lines of cheekbone, jawline, elegant neck – every few seconds he saw a lightning sketch of pure grace. He kept peering to catch it again, couldn't tell was it imagined or real. Twice she caught him staring, his own jaw hanging stupidly. She tossed her head – there it was again, that fleeting grace – his eyes went off like a flash-bulb, missed it . . . .

There were ways of making it happen, triggering the sudden dazzle. He experimented with animation. Talk could never do it. Surprised laughter could. Anger made her look unpleasant – her eyes got mean. A car-horn behind her, a slammed door, elbow grabbed in a shop, all could induce the exquisite flash, or not – even retain it if he handled the follow-up right. Soon, he didn't need the secret stimulus anymore; even when she looked bland and shallow the vision was fixed in his mind's eye. He was in love.

Thursday nights Tony went down to the leisure-centre. Helen had a rehearsal later.

'Alice, why don't you try the pool? You used to love swimming. Tony will give you a lift.'

In pursuit there are no coincidences.

When he skidded in after pumping his muscles solid on the climbing wall, she stood on the tip of the diving-board in a marginal bathing-suit, springing rhythmically, arms raised. Her dive cut the water, barely a splash; it hit Tony's pumped blood so hard he thought he would haemorrhage through the ears. To his horror the result was a massive, adolescent response. He tumbled into the water to drown it. He floundered, swallowing water. Alice sliced through the blue pool, polished, pure, impersonal. Under a tight, white cap her face was naked and austere.

Embarrassment convulsed him; to think he had chased in to show off – the choppy stroke that drove him through the water, blunt as a tug-boat.

She got a flat near the pool. Helen said; 'Maybe you'd give her a hand to sort that place out. It must be depressing to move into ....'

He was a bona fide social worker then. Years of happy marriage had left him without any skill in seduction. He hadn't fooled Alice at all. He tried brushing warmly against her, but she moved coolly away. He embarrassed himself dreadfully with *double-entendres*.

Lying on his back in the kitchen, fighting a pipe-joint, and thinking of nothing else, he heard her say; 'Okay, let's sort this thing out. Now!' He sat up – whacked his forehead off the sink. Alice, in a mercurial change thought it hilarious. Instead of having to slink out the door he clutched his head and moaned comically, 'look how I suffer for you!'.

With that change of tone came open acknowledgement.

'What do you expect, Tony? That I'll betray Helen?'

'Betray? I wouldn't betray Helen; I'm her husband. I love her. Betray means hand over to the enemy. You're not the enemy, for God's sake!,

'That's why I can't betray her ....'

'Alice, listen to me. We're going away. For a long time. Six months, maybe a year. Helen's been looking forward to it for ever. It's got to be special. For her! I mean it! For her.

Alice, something has to happen or it'll be a disaster. I can't leave you like this. I don't mean.... Something has to happen. It'll be over when I come back. Maybe I won't come back .... No, it won't be over. It couldn't. It's too strong ....'

'This is ridiculous, Tony. You're ridiculous! How can you do this to Helen?'

'I'm not doing anything to Helen. I love her! She knows it. Damn it, I sleep beside her every night. I miss her if she's not there. I'm not going to tire of Helen. That isn't it! You must understand, for God's sake? This is something completely different. It's between me and you. Damn it, Alice, can't you see something has to happen. You're not indifferent to me – I know you're not – you needn't pretend. I can feel it.'

She didn't look at him, stared straight ahead, eyes wide and blank. He felt the moment shift, as if he'd found the secret button. He leaned on it. His voice wasn't his own now. Desire spoke hoarsely; he heard what it said.

'If it wasn't for Helen, you and I ... it's not presumptuous. I know we would. So do you. And I know we can't. We can't! I want to go away with Helen, and be what she needs me to be - which isn't much, because she's everything in herself. But Alice, I can't leave this! I'm not fit for anything. Anything! I'm out in empty space, completely seized up. I can't think of anything but you. I can't do anything, go anywhere. I can't work properly. I'll be the same when we go away! What good is that going to do Helen, for Christ's sake ...?'

The moment moved again, rocked on its base, a panel shifted. 'What am I supposed to do ...?' Alice's tone was shaken, troubled. Tony felt his chest swell and constrict. Hard to breathe. The new air flared in his lungs, his heart beat so hard his body hung onto it for fear of being shaken off.

'Alice! Alice – it's simple. For me it's simple. I need you. I've got to ... how can I get out of this? ... It's not just sex ... it *is* sex, but it's everything else as well. I love everything about you. My mind, body, emotions, everything is trapped. I've got to get past it. For everyone's sake! I need you now, Alice – I need what you are. Otherwise, I'm stuck in this ....'

'But that wouldn't fix anything, Tony. You'd be the same afterwards.'

'NO! No, I wouldn't! I'd be gone away. Time to heal, to get over it. You'll have someone when I come back. That'll be that! But I wouldn't have this terrible ... feeling – not just a feeling, it's a paralysis ... incompleteness, a curse! This thing has to be finished, Alice; certain things have to finish properly, or else they haunt everybody ....'

It didn't matter what he said anymore. He had arrived. The welter of sexual emotion spoke for itself. Desire and impending consent. He could wring consent out of the air like juice ... whether he had seduced it into being, or whether its prior existence had lent the sexual tension to his babbling was irrelevant. He rose abruptly to his feet, reached, but didn't touch her. Every word, every move was explosively spontaneous, yet he knew he was directing it.

She sat still, elbows on her knees, face hidden in her hands. 'Alice!' She didn't move. 'Alice ....'

She turned nasty. Sentimental fierceness sharpened the rejection. 'If you ever hurt Helen you'll suffer for it, Tony ....'

Back to the starting-line, but not disqualified. He had won ground. Her anger was not for him; the harsh look on Alice's face was directed against herself.

Jomosom, Nov. ?

Dear Alice,

... We should have done this years ago. Maybe we left it a bit late – that teenage thrill is gone. And Tony knows the place so well of course; we waste no time. But it takes some of the discovery out of it. This must be the most beautiful place on earth. I'm still shocked by the poverty. He gets a lot of mileage out of my innocence. The contrast between the country and the city seems acute, although there is poverty everywhere and the slums show it up more clearly than the hillsides

We've climbed two (2!) mountains now; both 20,000 feet. The first one was a mini-expedition. I couldn't believe the work involved just to get to the foot of it. And then the climbing! We had a base-camp, a high camp, a gear-stash, a midnight start, crampons, axes, rope, an ice- col, snow slopes, steep bumps and humps, a *'mauvais pas'*, an *'a cheval'* ridge, a summit, a Himalayan sunrise, a tumbling descent .... A week later we took the second peak like an afterthought.

The staff are astounding. Dorje, the Sherpa, does everything. I didn't trust him at first – which shows how far you can be wrong. He works twenty hours a day if he's let. Even though his job is foreman and guide he does most of the cooking and seems to work for the porters as well.

We crossed a high pass a few days ago, 17,000 feet. Dorje accompanied us over it, starting at 3am, carrying a huge load himself. He saw us to the foot of the mountain we were climbing, produced our lunch chapatis and cheese – out of his rucksack before we left. Then he went back over the pass to pick up a load left by one of the porters who got sick a long way back. He crossed over again and descended to Muktinath, with a double-load which took all day while we were climbing. He arranged accommodation for us down there, and then came back up to meet us so he could carry my rucksack down. And all with the kind of cheeky grin that cheers you up no matter how ruined you are.

Oh yes – the chapatis; he'd cooked them himself that morning, along with the breakfast-porridge. He's twenty-five and he owns a small herd of yaks. Alice, I think I've found the man for you ....

... I don't know where Tony is at the moment but he sends his love.

Tony woke to the sound of Kathmandu rasping like a glass-cutter at the hotel window. The last traces of darkness were being scraped from the city releasing the exact cacophony sleep had drowned the night before, as if day were a nonstop affair in the street which never actually ceased, but was subdued by bouts of darkness. He had formed this impression on his first night in the city years before. His jaw had swollen twice its size and a brutal abscess throbbed all through that September night. It was the tail-end of the monsoon, before the city dried out, and tiny stukas strafed the room. The torn window-mesh was designed to let mosquitoes in and sieve sanity out. He thrashed on a hard bed for hours hallucinating on pain and pain-killers. The sheets clung to his skin in a suffocating poultice. Traffic, voices, music maintained an insane crescendo in his skull.

He had longed for Helen, the only assurance in a demented world. Next day he sent her a shaky postcard; 'Abscess makes the heart grow fond.' Since then, never quite fooled by the charm of the city, he tested morning gingerly before trusting its strident undertow. But there was nothing at all unpleasant out there, apart from the slick currents of the trekker-trade, and if any of those were abroad at 7 am they were on the way to take flight to Thai beaches, where they would drawl stories of great heights gained, and icy dangers undergone in search of a braver beauty than sand and sea.

Tony yawned and decently wished them well. In most cases - he stressed the exceptions - their form of wandering is a fashion. When the time comes that affluent youth, whether hippies, yuppies, or some new breed of pup, discover that the great caves of Guinea are the current place to go they will flock there in droves and engender the local version of a tea-house culture, with chocolate-cake and potato-chips. Tony yawned again with the contentment of superiority; there was nothing to that form of travel but the pursuit of indolence in the guise of curiosity. By comparison, mountaineering was a semi-respectable excuse. Helen was still asleep. He resisted the urge to wake her. She might not be pleased. He found her overwhelmingly desirable, a long, languid shape stretched out under thin bedclothes, nothing showing but dark curls.

For distraction he separated the noise outside into strands of raw sound, listened to them individually as she had taught him to do with music, and then let them merge again in raucous ensemble. He heard the voice of the city and understood it. No longer foreign or frightening it was universal. Horns blared incessantly as taxis threaded the streets in short bursts of speed. A violent rumbling, directly below their first-floor room stirred Helen but didn't wake her – the steel shutter rising on a souvenir-shop. Cycle-rickshaws massed outside with loose chains and rattling wheels. A solid, chugging approached; no need for a horn – the third world tractor, tough, simple engine on two wheels. After it a brief vacuum, then the calls of bike-renters, rickshaw-men, and Tiger Balm boys, 'Hallaw! Hallaw!' assailed unseen passersby, and Tony caught their curt refusals.

The flute-seller arrived. He was in expressive form – long, graceful cadenzas, every note perfectly pitched, a flute he would certainly never sell, probably the only one ever made without a bum note of any kind. He kept it in an inside pocket, while the rest – nearly a hundred of varying lengths and thicknesses – grew on a flute-tree, a long pole butted on the ground. Thin, wooden spokes sprouted from the tree, each branch inserted in the core of a flute.

Later he would tire of virtuosity and play with one hand only, three fingers on the top notes squirting endless triplets like variations on Three Blind Mice. Must be more effective, Tony reasoned; supermarkets don't play Mozart before announcing a bargain; they use electronic chimes with the repertoire of a doorbell.

Helen was awake. Tony knew that slight change in her breathing. He couldn't check without turning his head but he thought she hadn't opened her eyes yet; the rhythm of her breath would change again.

Twin single-beds, ridiculous arrangement. Of course not everyone was married, or even intimate if they were. They made their own arrangements. Stretching, Tony considered the advantages; no disturbance on restless nights, no contagion during illness. Hardly convincing arguments. But lots of marriages lived apart and only came together for convenience; separate beds, separate rooms – a development of affluence. You had to be able to afford the space. If you could move that far apart it must be easy to move further . . . .

. . . He knew that Helen and himself – no matter how intimately their skin touched, how searchingly their eyes met – were separated by his dreams. She didn't recognise it yet, but Helen was locked out of his imagination and he had moved another woman in. The fact that Alice would resent a further role in which she yielded anything she had wanted to withhold, made him deeply uneasy. To what extent was her image her own property? His imagination was using her, he was helplessly aware of that. But he had lost control. It was as if every move bred further infidelity. Had he any choice at this stage, he wondered? He fled the consequences in panic.

'You awake, Helen?'

'Mmmmmmmm . . . .'

'Nice to be back, eh?'

'mmmmmmmMMMM!'

'Sleep well?'

'z-z-z-z-z-z-'

'Helen?'

'Sh-sh-shhhhh . . . .'

'What next, Helen?'

An exhalation, unlettered, 'Breakfast . . . ?'

'I mean, what next in a general sense. Breakfast isn't a choice. Breakfast is a function – like getting up, or going to the loo. It's important to get them in the right order, that's all. Although, breakfast and going to the loo can be simultaneous if you eat in the wrong place here . . . .'

'Damn it, Tony – ' she spat the fringe of rug out of her mouth, 'you've woken me up now.'

'That's the idea. So what next, Helen? Want to go to Thailand with the nouveau-hippies? Lie on the beaches, take in a hill-tribe or two, a tan? I see you've already got one. Lovely . . . .'

Helen was on her feet, stretching. 'We'll price a flight to Bangkok. If it's cheap we'll go, if not we won't.' She settled it without much interest. 'Are you getting up for breakfast or not, after all your talk?'

'Not. Let's have a closer look at that tan!'

As his arms closed tenderly around her his eyes closed too. At once he felt the familiar impact as the naked body cannoned out of his imagination onto his retina.

After a breakfast of coffee and croissants, delicious in Kathmandu though it would have been third-rate in Europe, they strolled fondly downtown.

The city was still new to Helen. It had been a blur of heat, noise and colour a month before when she dropped from the sky and bounced off the tarmac onto the mountains. On the edge of Thamel, the tourist-enclave, a beige heifer lay chewing the cud in the middle of the street, undisturbed, too bony to look placid. In a closed garden there were tall, dusty trees festooned with bats as big as pigeons.

The street became a wide boulevard with a pavement so high you could break a leg if you fell off. There were traffic-police on duty at the junctions directing the chaotic taxis, cyclists, rickshaws. Neat young men from a standard mould, their well-pressed trousers were tucked into white gaiters over small boots, they wore a blouson-style jacket with a little fur collar, a flat peaked cap white on top, and a belt to accentuate the typically slender Nepali waist. The taxi-drivers, no angels, accused the police of corruption, but their pleasant faces and toyshop uniforms looked remarkably innocent to Helen.

They turned onto sophisticated Durbar Marg in front of the palace gates.

'A bit like a moon-shot,' Tony dismissed the king's modern residence, 'a concrete rocket.'

'Meaning if it doesn't look like Buckingham P. then it's not a proper palace?'

'It's a palace alright. Could be the Palace Cinema, somewhere like Brighton.'

Helen ignored him. Even when it was a deliberate tease she resented the tendency to dismiss anything that was not British. Tony knew he wasn't like that, but her reaction could provoke it in him.

A man whose arms and legs were boneless stalks, a head and torso with rubber tentacles, lay belly-down on a trolley and propelled himself along the pavement, chin close to the concrete, singing.

Helen stopped aghast but he seemed reasonably jolly, going about the business of charity as if he had just rolled in after a late breakfast and had work to catch up on.

'I remember him!' Tony said, 'I gave him ten rupees three years ago in the exact same spot.'

'I'd say he has it spent. Give him another instalment.'

'But he'll expect it then.' Tony rooted In his pocket, 'It's like foreign aid. He'll be dependent. You wouldn't want that?' He dropped a handful of notes in the tin.

By contrast with the homemade trolley, Durbar Marg, a wide, fashionable street with some of the city's top hotels, was lined with airline offices, established trekking-firms and jewellery stores. The standards of each airline, Tony pointed out, were showcased in its office. One or two of the smaller ones were like dressed-up Portacabins, suggesting one boiled sweet and two lumps of cotton-wool, while the office of Thai Airlines, its uniformed staff seated like pilots behind computer-consoles, seemed just short of take-off to an exotic location. That it stopped short of this, that it gave no twist of orchids in silver-foil and served no gourmet dinner in reclining seats, that it could turn down human need without apology and land it flightless on the pavement was proof of the hard magic of the dollar and the power of market-share.

Kathmandu to Bangkok was booked solid, months ahead, they learned. An Australian in the queue broke down at the news. As if it was an in-flight movie Tony sat back to watch.

'But I hev a tickit!! I pide for et ... !'

'Madam, you may have ticket, but it is not possible you fly without Confirmed Reservations.'

English jargon spoken by a Nepali has a satisfying ring of finality, pronunciation polished, head thrown back as the phrase is efficiently fired.

Arguments broke out in the queue.

'There's a frightful sense of escape about' Helen breathed, 'as if the glaciers might engulf Kathmandu? I'm tempted to stay!'

Wide-eyed, in wordless agreement, they slipped outside.

'That settles it' – Helen was determined – 'I didn't want to leave.'

'You didn't!?! I thought you ....'

'I thought *you* ....'

'Why didn't you tell me?'

'You never asked!'

'It's your holiday, Helen,' he affirmed with an emotional rush 'we've had my bit.'

'Your bit!? That's what I came for – snow and ice and altitude and scenery and culture – '

'Headaches and diarrhoea.'

' – and I'd like more of the same. I've been reading about Solu Khumbu. Island Peak, Everest in winter – '

Next door, the Annapurna coffee-shop had the feel of a coffee-lounge in any solidly unoriginal western hotel; a lot of decor and service, ornate uniforms, busy little managers in tight suits, and not much on the menu. They poured Helen's coffee with a plate under the pot so that it didn't dribble into the saucer from the universally useless spout, but the coffee tasted much the same as anywhere else. Tony was exultant. 'TWO mountains! The most successful trip I've ever had – the only successful trip I've ever had. It's thanks to you, Helen.'

'I don't think I can take the credit. Except for keeping them easy. If I wasn't here you'd be swinging from an overhanging sérac ....'

'See what I mean? Thank Christ you're here.' He clasped her hands unconditionally across the table. Life was so simple. The cups rattled and a busy little manager flourished a waiter forward again.

Immediately, as if he could no longer sustain simplicity, Tony's brain surged with caffeine and doubt. Could he justify her expectations? Could he endure a familiar mountain area with his hands in his pockets? Would it be a relief? And if it was, how would he live with a failure of motivation and nerve? Weighting those concerns was a heavy sense of time to be bought hour by hour until he emerged after a lifetime and found Alice again. Four weeks apart and no relief – he wouldn't get over her now. He wouldn't break down either, go into a mourning decline or openly distress Helen, but the pain and desire would increase with the monotony of minor addiction. Through the mask of a relaxed grin he looked miserably at his wife, drinking her coffee with innocent satisfaction, smiling back as she stole crumbs of chocolate from his plate with her finger.

Helen, not Alice, was the real problem; she had never caused anyone anything but happiness and deserved the same. He could live with loss and absorb it, but he knew he couldn't endure Helen's pain if he hurt her. Was that concern for himself, or her? He knew he was guilty, and that the fault would continue. And yet, he was certain that he loved his wife in a predictably continuous kind of way that had temporarily – he hoped it was temporary – lost its joy.

'How'd you like to go home now?'

Her eyes widened – 'I'd hate it! I was about to get more coffee – '

She leaned forward with sudden concern, alerted by his stricken eyes.

'What's wrong, Tony?'

He pulled himself back, terrified by the brink he trod.

'Let's get up there quick, Helen, and make the most of it. We've got the acclimatization so we can fly into Lukla and save four or five days' walk. We could be well up into the mountains two or three days after leaving here.' Briskness would become enthusiasm if he maintained it. He whipped out a pen and notebook: 'Let's see; a rest-day at Namche, a short day to Tengboche, another to Dingboche, four days, we could be at Island Peak base-camp a week from now; give us four or five days – a week if we like, – to climb the mountain and recover. That's about two weeks, right? We've all the time in the world – ' a stab in the heart, ' – back down to Dingboche, easy day, round to Lobuche, that's another short one, three lodges there, you're right up under Everest then, just a couple of easy hours to Gorak Shep, lodges there at the foot of Kala Pattar, everyone climbs that for sunset shots of Everest – ' no pause for interruption or consultation ' – then back to Namche whatever route we like. You'll be interested in the monastery at Tengboche – home of Sherpa Buddhism – '

'It burned down, Tony. Don't you remember?'

'What! When? I stayed there three years ago . . . .'

'No one is blaming you, don't worry. I showed you the headline at the time, WORLD FAMOUS MONASTERY UP IN SMOKE. An American foundation installed electricity as a gift. It burned to the ground. No one died, but they lost priceless relics. They're rebuilding. I'd love to see it anyway.'

'Electricity! Is nothing sacred? McDonalds at Base Camp? So that's two or three weeks to climb Island Peak and get back to Kathmandu. A bit colder, not so many tourists, what do you think?' He sat back, flushed with recovery.

Oblivious to the spate of detail Helen watched excitement wipe the tension from his face. His blue eyes focused fully on her for seconds at a time, sparkling brightly against bleached eyebrows and golden skin before darting forward to the next detail. His eyes had seemed dulled for days as if sunglasses and constant squinting against sun and snow had given them an inward cast.

Since leaving the high mountains his face had become unusually drawn and tense but now it reflected the lively thrill of a new plan. Still barely listening she looked at his mouth as he spoke; the lips were full, undiminished by sun and wind, but somehow the tenderness had toughened – perceptible not by feeling but by a subtly painful comparison of memory. The light fell sideways on his handsome head and she examined next the eloquent lines that curved around the sides of his mouth giving his grin its rakish edge. Now that he smiled less, perhaps from unacknowledged disappointment, those elegant lines often held a thin trace of shadow and defined a lean, new face where the boy had lost the struggle with the man. Helen had fallen originally for his determined sense of youth, smooth and tough. When at last she marked the future making stealthy raids, first on his face, then on his hair, she was relieved to find she loved that too, in a realistic, unromantic way. This new affection was sharpened by something approaching pity for the shocks his resistance must absorb. And there was a premonition of fear, probably for herself, that he would not accept the demands of time and would involve her in his struggle. She knew that his injury had undermined him more than he admitted, and suspected that he was suffering now from the lack of a serious objective to test himself. There might be an unclimbed ridge they could try together? It was tempting to fantasize in a coffee-shop but she knew they would never make an expedition partnership. She liked summits rather than the climbing itself and would choose the simplest route. She had no intention of regretting this.

'When you say Island Peak is easy, do you mean easy as in E-A-S-Y, or just not horrific?'

'Easy as in A-B-C. A bit of steepish ice near the top, grade 2 perhaps, and the rest is scrambling. The views should be sensational – right under Lhotse, looking across at Makalu. We can skip the peak-fee and save $300 . . . .'

'That's illegal, Tony, and immoral.'

'Illegal, yes, but a lot of people do it. I'm thinking of bringing a school group out here soon. Put this down to research. What would you like to do now, Helen?'

'We'll come back to the permit later. I want to drop these cards in the Post Office. Let me finish this letter to Alice first. Have another bun or something.'

'Alice!? Can I see?'

'There's nothing about you in it at all. Your secret is safe.' Teasing, she rejected his grab, but her smile was puzzled. He grinned awkwardly, flexed his arms behind his head, threw them nonchalantly on the table, leaned forward to arrive six inches from her face.

'I might . . . send a few cards from Namche,' he yawned. 'I never write letters – except to you. That's why I brought you out – to save on postage.' He had slammed so fast through conflicting emotions before hitting subterfuge that the process had scorched him like electric shock. He was eye to eye with Helen in a moment of outstanding clarity, lightning in the dark. It had flashed on her side too because she was no longer smiling, her eyes were darkly vulnerable and he saw her exactly as a stranger, a doctor at an accident, might . . . victim; early thirties, soft flesh hardening on the facial contours, skin wrinkling, hints of grey above her ears, no external wounds.

For the first time he realised people had to have ways of loving when desire failed. Trust and friendship had to be built – romance did not last. But he would change too; he saw it in Helen's face. In that startled mirror he recognised his future, and pulled away. Not ready yet. He would have said it like that if the soldiers came with handcuffs – 'I'm not ready!'

But the strain of late-night music was gone from under her eyes and her skin was a rich, healthy brown. And although she had changed she would never be ruined by decay; her fine flesh would tighten and grow spare with a gentle austerity that would look wonderful at a piano. Perhaps there was an interchange where the spirit overtook the importance of the body? It must be rough for lovers who didn't coincide.

A warm, protective feeling diluted the remorse in him. He took her hand; 'I love you, Helen. I haven't regretted one second of this trip – you've been wonderful. If you weren't here I'd be wishing on falling stars and writing every second day. I'll never be able to go near a mountain again without missing you.'

So what do I want Alice for – he almost asked it aloud?

The answer was simple. It had nothing to do with Nepal, nothing to do with mountains, or marriage – it was the exact opposite; a month with Alice in a bamboo-hut on a moonlit beach in Thailand, exotic cocktails and meals, languidly chasing coloured fish underwater during the day. Not a trace of rigour in sight – except the pacing of sexual energy.

Alice at sea-level, in her element, golden sand between her toes, wet hair flicking jewels of water. She stood laughing in the foam at the edge of the waves, face tilted to the sun, wreathed in a haze of summer, and the light that belonged in an azure gloss upon the water danced in lazy, blue gleams in her sheaf of sloe-black hair. Whatever vantage-point Tony held – he seemed to lie flat on his back in soft sand – he could see nothing on the horizon, no hills, no mountains whatsoever, nothing but sweet, monotonous sea; nothing distracted his vision of long, dancerly legs naked in sand, utterly remote from snow and mountain-boots, and the spiked rat-traps for climbing ice.

'I think I've missed a period, Tony.'

'Oh? ... when ... that's not unusual when you're travelling, Helen? You're often ... well, you're not exactly regular ...?'

'I suppose not. It's not that unusual. Still – '

'I'm sure it's just a delay, sweetheart.' He beckoned the waiter abruptly with a scribbling motion for the bill.

Tony led the way, drawing Helen in his wake with a brusqueness that startled her, ducking among pedestrians and diving across wide streets thronged with traffic. She registered occasional landmarks for the future; the Bir Hospital announcing a full body-scan, an ornamental lake opposite the teeming market-streets, the military parade-ground, scorched grass and review-stand in curving concrete.

Royal Nepal Airlines occupied a large building facing the parade-ground. From a distance the main tower was richly decorated in the traditional style, with Newari wood-motifs, but on closer inspection it was shoddy, painted concrete. Helen reminded herself guiltily that cost must be a massive factor in third world design, and as for wood-carving – timber was a precious resource in Nepal. 'They must think it grows on trees!' Tony remarked when they saw it burning lavishly in the hills.

Inside, under an enormous and ghastly mural not even Helen could excuse, they queued for tickets to Lukla. The line, mostly patient Sherpas, was static. Behind the counter a severe Hindu lady examined her nails and picked invisible threads off her cardigan and sari. A boy brought her tea. Tony fidgeted, looking at his watch. He leaned across the counter and enquired in a manner that always amused Helen – the tone of a Briton who thinks he is eminently reasonable, 'Is it possible to buy tickets to Lukla, please?'

She regarded him with cold patience, the power-failure obvious, tapped a teacherly nail on the extinguished screen beside her; 'The computer is down.' The clipped precision implied – any idiot can see that. Though sorry for Tony, Helen smiled inwardly; she knew the feeling.

'Wonder if there's anything in *Poste Restante*?'

'I doubt it. They haven't missed us yet. Still waving in the street and spotting us in the pub – "Saw ol' Tone 'n Helen down the King's 'ead last night; never go anywhere. Course she 'as 'er music. Gawd knows what keeps 'im goin'." '

'So where's *Poste Restante*?'

'Are you expecting something?'

'Alice might have written.'

He steered her numbly out of the main cavern of the Post Office into a separate area. Tourists crouched over trays of mail laid out on a big table. Helen headed for her own initial – greeting familiar faces from the trek. Perhaps the slowness of the post had held it back; but if Alice's conscience had got the better of her it would have come on wings. He shuffled through his own tray, hoping she might have used their joint surname, a forlorn hope thinking back over her slapdash, occasional post. He speeded up in case Helen finished first and came to look. He had to find it. But the pettiness appalled him – he couldn't accept what he was doing. His attention balked, snagged on postcards, torn envelopes; "interfering with the post" – he wouldn't steal the damn thing if it was there. If a crisis was forced he would face it now. He looked down the line at her intent head to confirm the decision; love might have wavered but respect stood firm. She straightened up gaily and waved a blue envelope.

She went on riffling, rapidly, carelessly, in case there was more. Tony sweated, fingers slipping, he thought he saw, shuffling back ... his own name, familiar writing; he fumbled, Nepali postmark, local stamps ....

Ripped it open, single notebook-page ... 'Beloved Tony,' ... a heartfelt message, and her signature – 'with love, Helen.'

He gaped in her direction; her face ducked out of sight. Three weeks before, from the first post office they reached, at Chame, after a few days trekking, to record her joy at being there together. That was all – an affirmation. He looked again. She had opened her letter and was avidly reading. He pushed down to the end of the table and, bending, kissed the back of her neck intensely. She shivered with pleasure, and through her hair he saw Alice's vigorous scrawl slide back into its envelope. Pushing through the crowd he could not catch her eye; at the door he took her elbow; outside he searched her face for pain or anger. None, but an anxious crease between her eyes.

'Helen! – Thanks for that. Thanks for ... everything.'

She took his hand, squeezed it. Helen always remembered; flowers, presents, birthdays, anniversaries, no fuss, sincerely celebrated.

'How's Alice?'

'I don't know. She doesn't say. It's a strange letter, hello/goodbye. Doesn't ask for you at all. Did we fall out or something?' She glanced at him strangely, almost in sorrow.

'Probably scribbled in a hurry to get something in the post. She'll write again.'

'I'm relieved she wrote at all. She resented us leaving while she was in London. Alice could take that as desertion. She won't let us off easily.'

'Sort of a grudge, you mean ... ?'

'She ignored me once for a whole year, her best friend, something she thought I'd done ....'

'You never told me ... what did you do?'

'Nothing. Not what she thought anyway.'

'What did she think ... ?'

'Nothing, Tony, nothing – ' About to get angry she thought better of it.

'We were very young – sixteen, a lot more innocent than we knew. She fell in love with someone – a medical student. She was always falling in love but I suppose - well, he was pretty special. Unfortunately, he fancied me for some reason, and I was flattered enough to go out with him until I ... had to slap his face. Alice wouldn't have done that. He'd made the wrong choice. He was her first big disappointment; I think he set a trend. She didn't forgive me for a long time; I don't think she ever believed I turned him down.'

'I'm not sure I believe it myself – tell me more about this old flame.'

He felt mean, luxuriating in her minor embarrassment.

Tony had his own unsettling memories of their last hours in London. He had woken to ideal conditions for departure. At 7am heavy rain streamed down the bedroom window as if the leaden sky over Islington had collapsed with the weight of winter. The curtains shivered, and the scraping that had woken him was a tendril of unleaved creeper clawing at the glass. Alice! Yesterday –

He sat up in a flux of excitement and dread. A streetlight beyond the garden swam into view, a cold, drowned moon. Lights were on in all the West Indian homes across the road. England was sinking fast beneath wet waves; what sunny shores had those warm people abandoned to sail the world in this storm-tossed ship. Nearer, my God, to Thee?

In a single day he and Helen could turn the seasons round and touch down in exotic, hot Nepal. He could smell it already in the sodden London dawn; the aromas of Kathmandu – fruit, spice, sackcloth? – poverty and plenty; the fragrance of pine-resin and dust along the trails; the thin air of altitude, its very purity a scent in itself just as snow is a colour . . . .

'Alice! – ' She had detached herself from his embrace on the couch, straightened her clothes and turned away. 'Alice! – ' In despair he groaned it. Striding to her bedroom door, he had flung it open – she stood up like a sleepwalker, moved towards him smiling vaguely, still not looking. She tried to pass him in the doorway, walked into his blocking arm at breast-height. He brought the other arm behind her.

'My heart . . . Feel my heart, Alice!'

It thudded violently against her arm. Her head drooped to listen. The smooth, black hair and pale neck were under his lips, but he held his head back in the doorway as if making room for a stranger in a narrow space.

'We're off!' Helen absorbed him in blissful celebration, 'We're off today!' The rain streamed down.

Within her passionate embrace Tony found himself helplessly making love to a memory. He surged in its intimate rhythm.

Alice saw them off at Gatwick. She wore a yellow raincoat of shiny plastic, a grown-up version of the garb worn by children with fair skin whose mothers carry transparent umbrellas.

Tony, already in clashing cotton for the sunshine, found it deliberately antagonistic. He remembered she hadn't been at their wedding. Now, in the departure-lounge, it was as if she were participating in the ceremony she had missed. After hugging Helen she held her at unsmiling armslength and then handed her formally towards Tony. As she moved abruptly away he put out a drowning hand to detain her. She took it in her own, shook it like a final decision, then handed his shocked arm towards Helen – who failed to take it as if she hadn't been rehearsed. Tony was left swaying between them, a misplaced prop. In a new kind of silence they moved to the departure-gate on the very last call.

The Pakistan Airline jet, alcohol-free but for the private supplies of passengers, left England drowning; smooth and sedate as a submarine it swam towards the surface over northern France and broke out of the European waters on the edge of Asia.

Throughout the journey, behind the strained chatter, Tony pursued that silence; it was like unwinding a long bandage to arrive at a hidden wound – it uncoiled right to the heart of their union where secrecy had cut between them. All he could do was change the dressing; try to make up in manner for the loss of meaning, and hope Helen wouldn't notice.

In thoughtful silence they walked back a short distance from the Post Office, took a turn or two, left the traffic behind and dived into a swarming alley – houses tottered, ancient facades patched with crumbling plaster, wooden balconies nodding together across the street. Small shops wide open to the world were crammed with goods for local shoppers, racks of trousers, dresses, jeans and jackets, cheap shoes and sandals; food of every kind, groceries, cigarettes, acres of fruit in baskets and trays spilling lavishly onto the street; magnificent vegetables – big, fresh, clean, colourful – spreading down lanes and alleys, in and out of stalls and doorways, draped on bicycles, heaped in shoulder-baskets. Everywhere, clamouring crowds sifted and sniffed, selling, weighing, buying, hawking, shouting, spitting; old women mummified in wraparound shawls; beautiful, fine-boned girls; slim, vivid boys in jeans; dark-skinned fruit-sellers with doleful eyes; chubby, runny-nosed children; no space anywhere – every inch occupied by a product or a service; ten-geared bikes racked tight as teeth in a comb, shining pots and saucepans stacked ten-feet high in dwindling sizes; in primus-shops huge, multi-burner stoves were stripped, brazed, refitted in a space where one man could hardly move but several worked; another stall fixed motorbikes, spare parts heaped in greasy corners, a Honda 175 spanning the entire space, handlebars locked sideways to decrease the length.

The lanes narrowed, grew tight and squalid, dwellings sagged with age, still no easing of the crowds. In open-fronted rooms too low for head-height Helen saw craftsmen squatting in shadow, hammering meticulous rhythms into metal. At intervals these sub-floor hovels were abattoirs; cheerful women hunkered on a square yard of floor in a bleeding mass of offal chopping sinewy flesh with cleavers. From outside it looked as if they must hack away their own limbs in the spreading, sprawling gore.

Tiny cafes were tucked in there too, stoves flaring under cauldrons of rice and curry, disposable leaves for plates, table-tops gruesome as butcher-blocks. After the magnificence of their vegetables it distressed Helen deeply to see these peaceful people wallowing in slaughter, much of it gruesomely graphic – skin delicately stripped from skulls and carcases, the choicest flesh folded pinkly back to seduce the buyer. Tony, despite taking casual pictures and revelling in his own composure, was equally relieved to steer back towards the sanity of pottery and fabrics, vegetables and fruit.

'Let's have dinner in K.C.'s Helen!'

'But you hate that place. Tourist-imperialism was what you . . . .'

'You're right. I know! But I'm not going – ' Tony argued shamelessly ' – because I like it; I'm going to see who's in town. It's a practical visit!' After all the years it amazed and gratified him that he could still trigger Helen so predictably.

'Sounds more like hypocrisy!' she humphed. 'You can despise the expatriate club but you still have a good reason for eating there. What's the difference between you and the ones who worship it? I'm sick listening to them, up and down the trails, drooling over K.C.'s, all the fat trekkers whose only other topic is Thailand.'

'The difference' Tony teased, 'is that I know what it means – Romans in the vomitorium. But it's no good ignoring all the people we know just because they're not as enlightened as us. Don't worry, Helen; I won't have a drooling steak – something suitably penitential instead. Salad? On the other hand,' he mused, 'maybe I will have a steak. No point in a principle if you don't break it now and then to remind yourself – otherwise there's no sacrifice. That's why you have the odd cigarette. You suffer even more after it. Yes, let's go to K.C.'s and eat steak and chocolate-cake! It will be a truly moral experience – afterwards. And a drink in the dreaded Rum Doodle too, to wash down the remorse.'

'You've certainly knocked the good out of it for me . . . .' Helen was indignant until she caught the quiver of a grin in his voice and her indignation focused on his teasing instead. 'Englishmen think they're being moral when they're only uncomfortable,' she attacked with obscure accuracy.

K.C.'s was crowded. Its grey decor reminded Helen of a set for a Behan jail-play. To Tony's chagrin they were forced upstairs to find a table. The ground-floor was packed with all the people he had hoped never to see again after the Annapurna trail, and others who would probably inspire the same response in Solu Khumbu. The Frenchmen from Manang, who had scattered an old woman's goats to get a photo, were there guzzling steaks and beer. Grease glistened on their plump cheeks and the sweat of gastronomic dedication dewed their balding foreheads, but they smiled and waved at Tony in friendly fellowship. Waiting for his tomato-soup Tony shuddered with enjoyment. He was a fiercely social being. Meeting old friends was what he liked best in the world - meeting enemies ranked only slightly lower. The soup was magnificent, hot in taste and temper. Garlic stung the lips and tongue and black pepper seized the back of the throat. Hiccupping, he took Helen's hand in the candle-light to toast their success in soup.

' 'Allo, 'Allo!' A clamour of British voices, thunder on the stairs like double-boots on a bridge –

'Steve!!'.

'What're you doin' here?'

'What're *you* doing here?'

'I asked first – '

'I was here first!'

'Oh, you know – been on a little trip, Tony, spot of climbing with the boys. You've met Stevie haven't you?'

' Course I have. Hello Stevie – '

'Hi Tony. Hiya Helen – '

' ... and Stephen here, this is Stephen, he's American ....'

'Hi guys – '

'Well – ' Tony was expansive but Helen detected anxiety, 'two's company but Steve's a crowd, eh? Going or coming, lads?'

'On our way back.' Steve admitted casually. A flat pause told Tony everything. Helen watched him brighten. They hadn't done it.

'Ama Dablam, was it?' He could afford to remember, 'Be-bop-alamma-bamma-Ama Dablam!'

'Yeah, new route, West Face, did it in three days – ' Steve's evenness was almost plausible, but Stephen's Mormon-jaw dropped.

'Bad luck, lads,' Tony sympathised. 'Weather, was it? Too much snow about. Séracs and all that?'

Steve sat down, grinned, 'Yeah that's it, the usual. So what're you two doin' here? Thought you'd more sense Helen – nobody gets up anything with old Tony.'

'Seems you can't get up without me either!' They grinned amiably, biffed each others' shoulders. 'We're meeting the Kusum Kanguru lot here' Steve explained, 'Dave North and his mates, seen 'em yet?

Tony shook his head.

'No – no luck either,' Steve responded to Tony's quizzical look, ' they all got the shits in Lukla. Didn't even get up the ordinary-route in the end. Fancy a go at the Curtis-Ball next year, Tony?'

Helen waved a hand for her husband's attention. 'It seems we're the only ones to get up anything. Tony.'

'You mean you're not trekking? You've been climbing?' Steve was startled.

Tony began a deprecatory gesture.

'Two. Two peaks!' Helen interrupted firmly. She had no patience with the games. 'We've climbed two peaks. So far. And done the Annapurna Circuit. In a month!'

Stephen was impressed. 'Two peaks. Gee! Guess I been with the wrong team – '

'Nothing technical,' she assured him, smiling with a luminous pride that Tony cherished, 'nothing like Ama Dablam – just good 6,000 metre mountains, snow and ice and Himalayan views and all that – '

'Wow, that's what I'll do next time I guess; move around and climb, and get a feel for the country – '

'He just spent three weeks dodging avalanches and squatting in Base Camp with the shits,' Steve explained.

'Sounds pretty bad,' Tony nodded in self-satisfied sympathy, ' – get anything done at all?'

'Oh, yeah, sure – ' quick to reclaim ground, 'we did some rock-routes, new lines. There's like an apron on the North-West Buttress where it comes out to the left of the west face at about half-height. It's just like the West Face of the Blat, big sheets of slabby rock, first-class except for the top. We did some great new-routes, man, good as anything in Cham.'

Tony looked impressed – you had to give concessions – as if he might rush off tomorrow for a second ascent; 'Sounds great! Any problems with the L.O.?'

' 'Ello, 'ello! None at all. Best Liaison Officer I've had. Followed us up the first route. He reckoned it was a bit harder than anything on the army-crag in Jomosom. There was a 6a slab in the middle. I gave him a tight rope – brought it down to Severe . . . .' Sensing disapproval he dropped the bragging; 'How'd you find the climbing, Helen?'

'Hard going, but – '

'Helen was brilliant – ' Tony boasted, ' – carrying like a horse and looking like a beauty-queen!'

'Better than this lot – ' Steve was dour, ' – looked like horses and carried like beauty-queens.'

The stairs thundered again. 'That'll be the Daves.'

They tumbled in, a medley of small moustaches and once-shorn temples; one carrot-haired, another dark, one brownish with a blonde splash, and one with a wrinkled, hardy face, hair grizzled, not with dye but age.

'Heroes of Kusum Kanguru,' Steve trumpeted, ' – the Four Daves!' They skidded into a curtsy, three of them, the grizzled fourth was already at the drinks-list.

'You're not a Dave!' Tony accused – 'you're Tim Brown as ever was.'

'I bloody know, Tony. They insist on calling me Dave – they say it avoids confusion.'

The new arrivals were still fumbling at the furniture, squinting for chairs through greasy hair and glasses.

'I reckon it's a great idea!' Steve addressed Helen again, as a jury. 'It's going to rationalise sport. I propose we drop the geographical club-structure, it's outmoded and inefficient, too many small clubs and splinter groups. In future there'll be a Steve-Club, a Dave-Club, a Nige-Club for the Oxbridge lot, one for the Tonys, and that's about it, I reckon – a few Micks and Johns maybe, no one else really, is there? Same for expeditions; simple really?!'

'What about the women?'

'Good question, Helen! I can see you're thinking; "What about the women, eh?" Good question. Simple answer! Deed poll: Marriage -

Take yourself; associate, card-carrying member of the Tony-Club, special rate for family-membership. Fact is women do very well out of this scheme. If you want to join the Steve-Club you've only got to divorce Tony here and marry one of us! Or, you could 'ave one of that lot – ' He sniggered; the three Daves, engineer, physicist, computerist, were still bumping into each other in the centre of the floor while two burly Australian girls, wearing shorts as loose as army-tents, had taken their table.

Steve had a squint downstairs. 'Come on, team! Cushions!'

Tony winked apologetically at Helen who had finally caught a waiter's eye, and joined the stampede.

Downstairs, deep cushions in an alcove around long, low tables created a sense of spacious intimacy. A group could spread itself out here with a sense of privilege and set its own standards – anywhere between indulgence and decadence. Platters of sizzling food flew around like frisbees. Clumps of beer-bottles, ice cold, rose and fell like automatic skittles. In the cosmopolitan buzz the Daves and Steves felt securely British, solidarity augmented by their status as climbers rather than trekkers or 'touroids'. Their volume increased and they stared around for approval with the excited pride of children on a birthday-outing, as if paper hats and flushed cheeks were a true sign of distinction.

Other races were equally festive though not so enviably seated. Australian women – there were so many about that there could be none at home – barged in and out, wearing three-man tents, kissing each other goodbye with loud lipsmacks, making assignations in Delhi and Bangkok.

'America!' a voice yearned in the distance, 'Gawd, America – where you can shower with your mouth open!'

'Americans!' Dave North snorted through a headcold, 'They do everything with their mouths open – ' He caught Tony's warning eye, seated beside Stephen who went on serenely eating.

'And the Dutch – ' Steve veered hastily.

'Oh my God!'

'And the Danes!'

'And the Swedes ....'

'They all speak that disc-jockey English you can hear miles away.'

'Yeah, but it's good,' Steve reconsidered, 'I wish I could speak a foreign language that good.'

'I wish you could speak English that well,' Tony jibed, 'and it's not good! It's slick, pop-culture idiom.'

'What about the climbers?' Helen was a little cross. 'They're a funny lot too.'

'Different kinds of climbers – ' Dave North began ....

'Them as keeps their mouths shut, and you lot.' Tim spoke irritably, hinting at suppressed tensions post-Kanguru. Dave North, expedition-leader leaned over, a concerned sneer on his face, put his mouth close to Tim's ear and bellowed, 'Are y'alright, Grandad? Is yer hearing aid switched on?'

Tim's rancour couldn't quell them – they were on a tribal spree.

Tony had a catalogue of types in his head; he launched into mimicry.

'There's a lot of these about – ' his face turned square, ' – the Hemingway types with heavy bones and mahogany faces. The skull is a traditional mansion and the brain lives solidly in the right wing. Life is a safari, they're looking for something to shoot. The nouveau-hippy might do – ' His cheeks thinned dramatically, ' – he wants to make it to Tibet, man. His, like, spiritual destiny lies in the high, wide, empty plains, not here in Kathmandu with us touroids. He's eating a plate of chips and tomato-sauce, none of that expensive tourist-shit you're eating. It's a rip-off, man! He's got a female counterpart – keep your fingers crossed they don't breed ....

' – And the Americans! "Dirt-cheap labour in China," sorry Stephen, we met a guy today, six feet wide across the shoulders, his skull was so narrow one eye overlapped the other. He wants to get into China for the business-breaks, exports to Texas, "Dirt-cheap labour in China!" He'll make millions.

'And the Brits – not us – public school army-types, think they own the country; "Damn it man, I asked for tea! This tea isn't coffee, it's cocoa! We taught you everything you know and look at the mess. What? Never in the empire? you are now, mate. Who d'you think we are? Foreign-aid? Good God, man, we're the Tourist-Empire ...." '

Helen's head was in her hands, groaning with reluctant amusement.

She knew self-righteousness would only provoke them further, and yet it was so difficult to resist. They were so consistently puerile in groups! And Tony piled in with such relish, no detachment whatsoever, quivering to the slightest whim of his peers. If anything, for all his qualities, he was growing less mature.

'What's next?' Steve asked her quietly, undercover, 'What're you two doing next?'

She sighed. 'We're going up to Solu Khumbu.'

'Oh yeah!? To do what?'

Tony fielded the question. 'Oh, this and that – we'll have a look round, see what looks good.'

'We'll climb Island Peak,' she interrupted wearily, 'that's what we decided.' Why did he take the good out of it?!

'Island Peak!?' Steve was mock-pensive, 'what's this you used to say Tony?'

'Island Peak' Tony defended with heated dignity, 'is a mountain of great distinction. It may not be a test-piece, but the term "trekking-peak" has nothing to do with trekkers. It applies equally to Island Peak and Kusum Kanguru ....'

'Not paying a peak-fee surely, are you? Not for Island Peak!'

'Maybe, maybe not ....'

'Oh yes we are!' Helen was resolute.

Steve's jaw dropped, 'Three hundred dollars! For Island Peak?'

'So?' Helen grew belligerent, 'a hundred and fifty each. We won't have to duck around, hiding and pretending, and maybe get barred from Nepal for years.'

'I think they've a bloody cheek,' Dave North was bitter, 'three hundred bloody dollars to climb a hill! And the extras!'

'You don't know what you're talking about – ' Helen's patience snapped.

Tony cheered, 'You tell him, Helen!'

'In the first place it's not a hill; it's twenty thousand feet, high as Kusum Kanguru, but you didn't get that high, did you? In the second place, and a lot more important, Nepal is a third-world country. Nepal needs – '

'Helen knows about the Third World,' Steve explained kindly, 'she's Irish.'

' – Nepal needs foreign currency to raise living standards. Lucky they've got the best mountains in the world. That means tourism, tourism should mean foreign exchange – dollars, marks, francs, pounds.

But tourism also means damage, destruction, change of lifestyle in remote areas, decrease in farming, lots of ugly little lodges, massive – and I mean massive – deforestation for firewood to feed and warm the tourists. Deforestation erodes the slopes – that means landslides, floods, loss of good soil in the mountains, rivers clogged up all the way down to India and Bangla Desh – and you know what happens there. On top of that – and this is the real irony – the bulk of the money we spend doesn't benefit the average Nepali at all; it goes straight out of the country, either as black-market money when you do a deal with some grubby little tout and his boss salts the dollars away in Hong Kong – ' they were listening now; they relished anything shady, ' – or, it gets spent outside Nepal on foreign imports to service the tourist. Imports! Imports don't generate any wealth in a weak economy. They bleed it! Work out for yourself how much of the stuff tourists use and eat in Nepal is actually made here. A lot less than you think. I'm not talking about dal bhat and rugs. Furniture, taxis – start thinking!

'On top of all that – a lot of tourists are like us, back-packers of one sort or another, whether we call ourselves climbers or trekkers, living cheap, trying to spend as little money as we can, as much as possible of it on the black-market. But we're the ones going into remote, obscure, vulnerable places, carving out trails, wrecking the ecology, turning farmers into innkeepers and Coca-Cola porters – and we don't pay our way; not that it can be paid for!

'I think it's perfectly obvious what the government should do – in their interest, not ours. I suspect they've started already. Cut down the number of tourists to minimise the damage. And keep the revenue up by taking more from that smaller number. You don't get in unless you spend X number of dollars – and spend it on worthwhile projects. And keep that income out of the pockets of middlemen. Plough every cent of it back into the country as a whole. It means increased peak fees and trekking fees, shutting down areas like Annapurna to let them recover – the Indians did it with Nanda Devi, it'll have to happen here too. Otherwise we'll ruin the country.'

There was an uneasy silence, as if a teacher had called a halt. Frustration too, because Helen was . . . protected from counter-attack. Her anger had reached other tables, drawing sidelong glances, covert grins. Tony cleared his throat as she simmered beside him, 'Remember that porter we had in '86 - ' he reminded Steve, 'same thing . . . Helen is absolutely right! I forget his name – ' he told the rest of the table, ' – we always forget their names. He was much older than the others. He wanted nothing to do with them, or us. This guy was barefoot, tough, detached. He worked in a harsh, grim silence. Okay, it was voluntary, he was reasonably well-paid, he didn't have to work, but, thinking about it now ... he was more like a prisoner on forced labour than a porter.

'The second night out of Dumre we stopped outside a village, some of us went in to look for beer. This chap was there before us, in the pub. We could see right off he resented us, and the local lads didn't welcome us either – sort of contagious – but we weren't leaving. They made us feel like invaders. I'd never felt that before – like a member of a garrison. The local lads in the shack were farm-workers – they didn't have much to gain from the expedition-trade.

'Our old boy was knocking back rakshi in a serious way. We sent him over a bottle of beer and he didn't touch it, wouldn't look at it – though it's a real luxury to the old chaps compared to the home-brews, chang and rakshi. Still, maybe it's like wine in a navvies' pub –

'He always wore the traditional kit, big loose loincloth and a rough sort of smock, no concession to the trousers and track suits most of the others wear. I have to say he looked uncouth, sort of neanderthal, not twentieth century anyway, but part of that was the anger coiled up inside him. I don't know whether I thought it then or later, but I reckon the ferocity was a sense of dignity betrayed. I know we talked a lot at the time – didn't we, Steve? about Eskimos and American Indians.

'Anyway, the old boy got worse and worse that night. He was mumbling away into his rakshi, clenching his fists and giving out these angry barks. Some of the other porters came in ... they were all bunched together in a corner fascinated by this monologue while we were down the other end pretending there was nothing on. I felt like an officer in the wrong place – the squaddies are off-duty and they're getting out of hand. Time to melt away. The others wouldn't leave – I don't know about you, Steve – they were a bit miffed at their evening being ruined by a rowdy porter ... you know how Mick is! The old man got really passionate, and just when he was steaming up to boiling-point – Alan laughed out loud. Some laugh he has! It was just nerves really, but the porter choked on it – his fist went up in the air like a cudgel ... and smashed down on this table loaded with drink. The others were all putting up rakshi for him, though they weren't having it themselves – he meant something to them alright.

'He smashed the table in two, a solid plank it looked like. You could lay his fist beside a lump-hammer and never tell the difference. There was broken glass and spilt drink everywhere, people jumping for cover, but he just crouched there staring straight ahead with a frozen look on his face like he was turned to stone. He was never going to do anything ... one of those cigar-store Indians.

'We took off sharpish – Mick was first out. There was a lot of talk about being murdered in our beds, some people wanted him sacked on the spot. He was a threat, not a physical threat, more like a cultural discomfort in the folk-paradise of Nepal ... like being spat at by a child-beggar in Kathmandu when you're on holiday – that kind of thing.

'Me and Steve were against sacking him. It didn't seem fair. He wanted to work, he hadn't done anything to us, he was drinking on his time off and it was none of our business – we should have left him to it.'

'He was a really strong bugger,' Steve interrupted, 'always out in front. The others were a lazy lot. He set a standard.'

'Not lazy!' Tony argued irritably, 'that's the whole point. Anyway – I asked Nima, the sirdar, to find out about him for me. Nima is a modern Sherpa from Namche, he's young and sophisticated; I bet he's working for the big expeditions now. Those guys are detached by their background from lowland Nepal. In that sense Nima is part of an elite caste; he could comfortably look down on the Dumre porter and laugh at the hopeless fatalism of it all.

At the same time they're all part of the same culture-crisis; Sherpas Tamangs, Newaris, Grungs – highlanders and valleymen – they speak completely different local languages, but they can all communicate in Nepali. In the long run they're all subject to the same political and economic squeezes too, like Helen said. Nima got the story bit by bit; in the long run he was just as interested as I was.

'The porter came from a small, remote community in the agricultural Terai, far enough off the main road from Kathmandu to Dumre to be aware of it, but unaffected. They had a language, traditions, architectural style, crop-system, irrigation-terraces that could have been there forever as far as they were concerned – and a future that would be absolutely the same as the present and the past. Untouched by the outside world. Nima made a big point of the fact that they'd never worked for anyone but themselves – never had to.

'Meanwhile – the twentieth century was revving up outside. To provide electricity for the villages sprouting along the highway a valley had to be dammed and flooded. Seemed like a brilliant wheeze – hydropower, grants from China, India, the West? It wasn't meant to touch these local people at all – they probably wouldn't even get work on it – but they were promised compensation if it did any damage, and of course they'd get power on a spur-line. It was sort of their area after all. Seemed a good deal all round.

Two years after the dam the electric glow of the towns could be seen on the rim of the night-sky. Our people still had no power. That didn't surprise them very much. Then their water dried up. Streams stopped running, wells disappeared. They lost one season's crops entirely before anyone official came near them. Obviously the drainage had been miscalculated and the scheme had sucked in all the local water. There was probably a subtle balance and it didn't take much to shift.

'There was no compensation. The community collapsed overnight – whole families moved out to live in poverty in town. Young people disappeared off to Kathmandu.

'Our porter lost his farm, his house, his animals, his future. The following year, in Kathmandu, one of his daughters died in childbirth and a son went to prison. Soon after, his wife died where they were living in the slums of Pokhara. She didn't know how to adjust. You could probably call it a broken heart.

'That's how he came to work for us.'

As the mountain-plane scooted up and over the foothills towards Solu Khumbu Helen felt gravity shear away from her senses with a lurch alarming as an air pocket. Tony revolved in his seat, camera squinting through the scratched perspex. She shrugged as he identified peaks in all directions, routes, ridges, first ascents. 'You're like a boy on a date naming galaxies, Tony. I don't want a lesson in astronomy.'

The girl on the date already knew they wouldn't be gazing hand-in-hand at faraway stars for long – he wouldn't be content to observe and share – he would lose himself in the distance of everything he saw. She could cope with that, if he came back to earth at intervals. She had distances to travel herself, inwards, towards the centre perhaps; a more important journey, though she wouldn't have said so.

She wouldn't have said it either, but she was increasingly aware that her journey had broken down, was going nowhere. The small motor of the heart was quiet, and in its place was the muffled roar of engines climbing the sky. The plane banked and she tugged his elbow to show a tiny village perched on a spur in the dizzy depths, houses studding the terraces, wisps of cloud in the valley below as if the village belonged halfway between earth and heaven. A few green trees and a golden crop against the planetary brown, the most beautiful colours in the world. Tony jigged, impatient for the plane to level and bring Gauri Sankar back to view. When he turned and kissed her absently, as if to shut her up, it was the excitement of his own dreams she tasted. She wouldn't follow him into that space and she would not be asked.

The small plane zipped through the rugged airspace as if it had been fired briskly aloft. Helen felt the uneasiness of this new beginning; it flushed through her in spasms of doubt. Gaining height, changing direction, the plane swerved and gambolled as if it might kick its heels, clap its wings in the freedom of flight. Helen strove for the same feeling; she would be in control this time; no longer a novice she knew the ropes. She looked at distant snow-slopes, gauged their angles and knew they could all be climbed - if necessary. It was a lonely feeling, no thrill of aspiration; there was nothing up there apart from challenge, and too many people of the kind they'd met in K.C.'s. Others too of course, like Tony . . . .

But her eye was constantly drawn down from the empty sky into the folded valleys and ridges in the blue-brown haze where people lived, conscious of mountains on the rim of their lives in the same way they were aware of stars.

Children down there, after dark, held hands and pointed out the planes that slipped between their constellations, inspiring dreams of Hong Kong and Kathmandu. Did they wish for love, and fame and fortune, with no idea of the cold, bare slopes where any dream can lead – on a mountain or a city street? A bitter taste, cold as disappointment, rose up in her throat. Appalling ground lunged up to meet her. The plane throttled back, braced itself, shuddering – not a level inch in sight. The view was a physical impact in itself; hostile slopes scraping by on either side, glaciation above, a river-gorge below.

Over the rim of the ravine, engines howling, Lukla slammed into sight; dilapidated sprawl, brash tin roofs, tilted airstrip strewn with stones, one end tipping into the gorge, the other climbing towards the town. The small plane lifted its beak, flexed its wings, stuck out its feet and landed, running steeply uphill to a halt.

On the scuffed clay runway Helen struggled with her pack, felt the familiar weakness of altitude. The air had a thin, sharp taste, hard to swallow, unexpectedly depressing. Fresh snow whitened the slopes above the tree line, and an edgy crowd pressed against the barriers in the passenger-shed. 'No flights the last few days,' Tony guessed, ' – bad weather. There's been a back-up.'

Lukla itself was more like a stagecoach stop than an airport town, an unplanned huddle dragged into being by the accident of a patch of ground on the edge of a ravine where planes could fall away into flight. On a good day regular flights reach Kathmandu in less than an hour. People depend on this. It saves four days walking, out to Jiri, against the grain of the land. But tickets are confirmed, in advance, for one flight only. On bad days, fog blinding Lukla, or snow on the runway – or smog in Kathmandu grounding the planes – a trap springs shut. All flights are cancelled, and today's passengers huddle disgruntled in Lukla's lodges. That night, tomorrow's passengers arrive, cold, miserable, fed up with mountains, and they have priority now, while the others retire to the waiting-list. And if tomorrow's and the next day's weather is bad, which it may well be – weather being a matter of unpredictable patterns, but patterns nonetheless – then the waiting-list grows and grows, disconsolate trekkers pile up in the lodges jerrybuilt round the airstrip for just these chances; they congregate every morning in the passenger-shed and grow hourly more querulous, bitterly resentful of Nepal's bureaucracy and weather, as if one is responsible for the other, and the innocent trekker is the victim of both.

Tony had seen fights break out between tourists and staff, more often between travellers themselves who had international connections to catch. A notice warned; *Please keep all knives, khukris and other arms in checked-in baggage.*

They lingered to watch as a crowd vied for seats on the plane going out. A big Japanese group, confirmed to the minute, mopped up all the places. The haggard waiting-list spilled round the counters issuing sardonic bulletins to keep their spirits up. They had whatever news there was even before the staff; strike in Kathmandu, smog, ten planes today, no planes today. Although she was being shoved and jostled by the crowd, Helen was glad of the distraction. She found herself watching avidly, yet coldly detached from what she saw. She observed every human detail with an almost shocking clarity, her own reactions numbed as if she was directing her intense attention away, feverishly away, from herself and her own feelings.

They spent the night in Lukla. Helen wanted to move on but Tony was keen to stay. He had been trapped there twice before on the way out from the mountains and he wanted to luxuriate in his freedom this time. Lukla, he said, was one of the great bottlenecks of human behaviour and it should not be missed.

'Have it your own way!' she snapped with such unexpected aggression that he was forced to defend himself with logic rather than yield.

'We wouldn't get anywhere useful this evening. If we leave early in the morning we'll make Namche in a reasonable day .... But if you'd rather ....'

Helen had already stamped into the nearest lodge. Standing outside in shock Tony felt a confusion of shame and the inability to express it. This new silence of hers was a kind of general denial, unspecific, like being ignored. Once identified, he recognised it as something he already knew intimately.

All evening, as they wandered round the village arranging porters, drifting in and out of lodges, he was full of humour and direct concern. He persistently linked her unresponsive arm and kissed her cold cheek on the principle that enthusiasm is contagious. Helen was unwarmed, untouched, still observing others with a cold fascination from which she drew no comfort.

She kept bumping, as if by design, into a tall, solitary girl from Leeds in a capacious denim skirt an ethnic cardigan on top. Her hair was probably blonde, but nobody would ever call her that. There was something decently, sexlessly British about the pleasant face and jolly manner. Her grey eyes were intelligent, but although she was alone she was not self-sufficient. Her manner was a brave attempt to make the best of things.

'You're lucky to have someone close to travel with – '

Tony had dashed gallantly off for further supplies of tea.

'Not that one needs ... independence has its own rewards.' She tried to look wickedly gay, too honest not to blush at the effort. Helen thought sourly that Tony was at his very best impressing strangers.

Then there was a bony young Scot with an inflated ego. No opinions, but a stream of anecdotes to show how cleverly he'd extricated himself from difficult situations. He had irritatingly innocent skin with raw, red-tipped ears that barely protected him from Helen's exasperation. His friend had no defences; an overweight American with bristly jowls, sentimental eyes and an unctuous sincerity that was doubly annoying for being real. He dropped his voice towards the end of every sentence into that crusty tone bad actors use for both weariness and awe, and made Helen scream silently. Tony mocked him openly and he focused on her instead, telling tales of Dublin bars where he'd had mystical experiences listening to old men talk – and then, a minute later he was flying helicopters with total awe in Alaska.

'Me an' my old camera here' he patted it, just barely not calling it Ole Betsy, 'we're gonna stay out tonight, mebbe take a moon-shot . . . .'

'Like the Apollo moon-shot?' Tony was in quick.

Helen sensed the bleak loneliness of the outsiders haunting the tourist-world in search of fulfilment. This evening they seemed to latch onto her, all these strays, as if they knew her. It was obscurely terrifying and brought out sparks of cruelty in repudiation.

Doug locked his Labrador-eyes on hers and in an attempt at a creative image patted Ole Betsy again, 'Good ol' camera. Had her twenty years now and served me well. Gotta couple screws loose in there now – airplane vibration, I guess – '

'Maybe it's you has a couple of screws loose!' Even Tony was shocked by her sharpness. The victim's jaw dropped and he slouched away.

Ignoring Sandra from Leeds she entered into passive conversation with a plump Nepali, Michelin duvet, who worked at the airstrip. From Kathmandu, he missed his family. He realised the mountains were beautiful, but beauty wore thin with long acquaintance; ' – and here there are no facilities, no transport, no nudes – ' it was "news", but it sounded better the other way in his precise, lipsmacking English with little runs of idiom sliding smoothly into the monologue to be derailed every now and then by grandiose eloquence, as when he remarked that the government could not afford to provide another airport in Kathmandu, 'surrounded as it is by hills and – ', his lips smacked on the juicy word, – 'hillocks!'

They slept in a crowded dormitory on separated bunks. Sandra lay nearby, her feet pointing at Helen's. Unused to altitude she panted and moaned fitfully. At dawn Helen found two shivering boys outside, the porters Tony ordered. One, at sixteen, was lean, seasoned, tough; the other, a year older, had the moonfaced roundness of a child. Helen decided to remain detached – these boys needed work. She gave them a silent breakfast of chocolate and woke Tony with a curt order to lighten the loads. Across the valley, Nup La, black rock gleaming with ice, hardened her heart with its reminder of a crystalline world.

A Norwegian family, Christian missionaries, set off with them. They nodded at Tony's cheerful salute. Helen had watched them the previous evening keeping coolly to themselves. They were on holiday – proselytising is not allowed in Nepal – but their very appearance was a lesson in dutiful Protestantism. Again, this morning, they managed a virtuous sense of family, shepherding their offspring as if nothing existed except for its impact on their principles and their children.

Helen was fascinated and repelled by the parents; the father tall and thin, with a distinctly bony skull, see-through hair plastered to its strong contours, pale eyebrows jutting over light-blue eyes which held an expression of slightly humorous scepticism that might have been a conscious lightening of his Christian severity. He had sunken cheeks and a thin-lipped, preacher's mouth. His wife, attracted to his principles rather than his presence, Helen thought had a clear, youthful face excessively exposed by the plain scarf that bound her hair back tightly. A teenage daughter walked beside her mother with a pale prettiness that made her almost invisible.

Then the younger children tumbled onto the trail. Helen felt an unaccountable stab of pain. The twelve year old daughter was young enough to be shy but not at all self-conscious; with her big eyes, her mother's wide mouth spread in a smile, transparent skin and long flaxen hair – a blue ribbon at the back of her neck – she had the devastating charm of innocence. A younger brother hurtled past, singing with excitement, sending his parents into a flurry of protective concern. The father's thinness reached its limit in his son's features, bone-thin with a razor-blade profile, dazzling eyes, a shock of loose hair tumbling down the left side of his forehead which would surely have been shorn off by its own weight if it sliced across the meridian of his lively face.

Helen walked alone. Occasionally she caught up with the children and chatted stiffly to them but they quickly deserted her for more exotic interests. An odd, unhappy weariness weighed on her senses, not quite a headache, not quite nausea. The trail meandered above the glacial torrent of the Dudh Khosi, crossing and recrossing it on flimsy bridges. She concentrated on the solid houses under a rash of shiny, tin roofs, the sturdy, fresh-painted chortens, the straggling farm-terraces where women in long, grey skirts toiled, bent double, feet and fingers rooted in the rich soil.

More and more this gruelling work was giving way to lodges and tea-shops. It seemed a precarious transition, thriving at the moment with the Everest Trail, and this might increase eventually to the wealth of a European alpine economy or it might collapse back into desolation further undermined by the abandonment of farming and the loss of delicate irrigation and terracing systems built up over generations of labour and maintenance. Tony was bursting to relate previous adventures on this track, to point out Kusum Kanguru, Kwangde, and other landmarks rich for him in expedition-lore. She refused to reassure him. It was hardly even a conscious silence; it simply didn't occur to her to talk. She was cut off by an instinctive pressure as if he was an irrelevant acquaintance. And yet they were entering what should be the most satisfying phase of their lives. When she thought of it like that she felt like an old wife at a wedding, confronted with her own unhappiness by the transparent apparatus of the dream.

Encounters confirmed her isolation. The Everest Trail was sufficiently busy that trekkers were embarrassed and bored by each other's presence – in some cases angry that they didn't have it to themselves. They often ignored each other, like tourists on a city street, who hadn't come all that way to see their own kind.

On the other hand some were completely oblivious to the locals and were relieved only by each other. Sometimes – Helen had excused it before – this was simply a feature of youth, the need to feel experience collectively – but now, sick of Goa, Thai beaches, and bus-roof marathons she recognised it as superficial character, the arrogant sense that culture was only a performance, relevant for as long as these people were passing it by. Instead of challenging their presumptions it reinforced their superiority.

'If ya wanna enjoy this country ya gotta block the people right outta your mind, man; they're rippin' ya off!'

She found it increasingly hard to concentrate. The sense of uplifting detail – smiles, flashes of colour, casual songs seemed to have deserted her, and the outside world had a closed, cold feel to it like the faces of the locals hurrying by on their invaded trails, indifferent to the visiting hordes.

Just beyond Ghat she found a small European girl, ten or twelve years old, with reddish hair and scrubbed, pink skin, sitting desolately on a rock surrounded by Sherpa women and children. The distress on both sides was palpable but there was no resolution; the child was frightened, the big, greyskirted, head-scarved women discussing what they might do, the wide-eyed toddlers who cry so little themselves, silent in the presence of tears.

They stepped back on Helen's arrival; here was the mother, no doubt. The child shrank away from Helen's flushed face.

'Are you alright? What's your name? Do you speak English?' The Sherpini giggled loudly – 'do you speak English??'

The girl faltered, still avoiding Helen's eyes; yes she spoke English, she was lost, separated from her parents on the way down from Namche. She thought her father might be ahead already and perhaps her mother behind. More tears. Helen soothed awkwardly, patted her shoulder, she was too curled up to hug – there was no problem if she stayed here, her father would come back or her mother would arrive -

Freckles, red eyes, sandy lashes, smudged tears, she couldn't be comforted – her parents were on a different trail altogether, fresh tears, and the women were upset again, crowding closer. Not the right mother – do you speak English!?

Helen persuaded reasonably that there was still nothing to worry about; they would obviously return to the right trail and find her. But the child had thought it all through and she knew the worst; 'No - my father will think I'm with my mother and my mother will think I'm with my father.'

Helen's heart dissolved at the fear that could express itself so clearly in a foreign language. Tears flooded her own eyes. She changed the subject for want of a solution. 'What's your name?'

The little girl didn't really think it was relevant and had to be asked again.

'Louise,' she admitted bleakly.

'French?'

'No.'

'Swiss?'

'No. Danish . . .' and that low, flat field of a peninsula far, far away at sea-level emphasised even more her predicament, lost, among the highest mountains on earth. Just then her parents burst through the crowd, together, in a flood of recrimination and concern. Helen, feeling inexplicably guilty, slipped away.

Further on, at Chumoa, a narrow wooden bridge spanned a stream in the permanent shadow of trees. The water below was frozen at the edges, and a small, intent boy in a frayed tracksuit held a plate-shaped chunk of ice in his fingers sliding it along the handrail of the bridge.

Helen paused, but instead of rumpling his hair as she meant, she reached further in abstraction, touched the frozen dish, and recoiled in shock as if her fingers had been burnt.

The child paused, stared up at her, his grimy face expressionless.

Beyond the bridge a water-driven corn-mill squatted over a stream, compact, stone-built, roofed with weatherbeaten boards. At a second mill upstream, a wizened old lady squatted on the floor feeding handfuls of corn into the wheel. The mills at Chumoa; as natural as if the landscape had thrown them up long ago to conspire with the people in the simplest possible existence. The old woman turned abruptly away, for fear of being photographed.

When, at last, beyond the ravine entrance to the Sagarmatha National Park the trail took off viciously uphill in tight switchbacks Helen's spirits lifted a little with the effort.

Sweating porters carried up bundles of planks and rested at every turn. The planks were lashed together into solid loads and carried upright, jutting over the head, slung from a headband. The powerful neck and shoulders took the carrying strain while the legs grappled with the climb. A cord, attached to the top of the load pulled it forward into balance when they bent over. These were long-distance, heavy-duty hauliers carrying double-loads and paid to match. To Helen's horrified eyes they looked as if they were playing an enormous, punishing instrument strapped to the back with the string in front of their noses.

Bushy, black yaks loaded for market, laboured up the zigzags, panting in short gasps, jaws open, pink tongues hanging.

'They're burning oil.' Tony passed her at a constriction where a convoy of yaks and porters were blocked by fallen boulders. They exchanged reluctant smiles before irrepressible energy took him up a steep bank overhanging a ravine. Helen knew she would find him at the next tea-shop. That had been his style all day, vaulting from lodge to lodge, greeting her with a quizzical grin as she plodded past.

Tin roofs. High houses with tin roofs –

Her first startled impression of Namche Bazaar, the Sherpa capital, was a horseshoe of high houses perched on a slope overlooking the abyss from which she had emerged. It stared straight out above the plunging forests at the shattered teeth of Kwangde Ri.

Namche bustled with prosperity, a medieval market-town in the twentieth century; hotels, shops, stalls, bank, post office. Sherpas and Tibetan traders strode about its lanes with the heightened excitement of cowboys in a frontier-town. Tourist, grain sack, plank – every incoming item was grist to the mill.

In the Lodge, still avoiding each other, they glanced into the dormitories and the dining room full of youth-travellers huddled round the pot-bellied stove as if it was theirs alone. Sharing a married grimace they rejected the dormitory and took a double room. Chunks of thawing silence kept them apart, although years of experience made the outcome inevitable. Casually Tony wedged her in the doorway and her withering glance had more to do with dignity than anger. Warmth stirred secretly within her. Soon, it would be difficult to remember what . . . .

They ate silent soup, meditative pizza, conciliatory dessert, ignoring the group – English, Australian, American, Dutch – who passed a guitar around the stove like a joint, performing for the girls who gave nothing at all, except advice about going to Thailand, having been in Thailand, and parts of Thailand being destroyed by tourists but if you got there before the rush – 'there will be', Tony giggled, 'still plenty to destroy'.

'Remember *Animal House* ' he reminisced with unnecessary volume, 'when Belushi took the guitar at the party, smashed it politely across his knee and handed back the two halves . . . .'

'Hardly a valid form of criticism – '

'You're missing the point. Sometimes decisive action is the only possible course. Why don't you take over, Helen? Play. Sing. You could turn this place upside down in ten seconds.'

'Because I don't feel like it!' Somewhere within was the echo of a snarl she would never express in words.

'What's the matter, Helen?' He was good at self-righteous crossness – 'this is what you always wanted. What's wrong? I can't get a word out of you. Is it altitude? A period? Maybe we shouldn't have come up so quick . . . .'

'Not now, Tony – don't bully me now!' The snarl was closer to the surface, and she added with a fierceness that chilled him; 'and it's not just me, so don't pretend it is . . .' furiously aware that she had no argument, couldn't put her finger on any event. Like accusing him of absence when he was always there.

Their room was a square cubicle of stout planks, privacy undermined by knotholes and warped joints.

Helen sat, unyielding, on the edge of the plank bed. He fussed pleasantly around her, humming his innocence, brushed out her tangled hair, kneaded her shoulders, fed her chocolate – as if she could be bribed!

Hm! – she thought dismissively, keeping it to herself, as he hooked his arm around her finally and drew her down to stretch out fully-dressed.

Boots clumped past in the corridor, the room shook, ill-fitting doors thudded upstairs and down. Music filtered through the building. Helen hadn't heard a note for days; her ear had switched off. A light came on somewhere – there was electricity in the evenings – it leaked under the door and through the chinks in the walls. Low voices came from both sides, and muffled laughter. Tony hugged her tighter, burrowed an arm around her waist to lock her to him.

Warm, wordless breath stirred her hair. His jaw settled against her cheek with practised assurance. At intervals, as if a specially fond thought occurred, he kissed her dry lips, being particularly careful not to scrape her with his bristle. Once, when she glanced up, he seemed to be gazing over her head, his eyes lost in shadow.

Now that she could almost answer, he wouldn't ask what was wrong.

Awkwardness was excluded from the circle of his embrace. Her mind floated; how to know you loved someone? More urgent – how to know she was loved?

No answer except instinct, and to take his word. It wasn't given as often . . . .

She came to depend on it, and when it was most important there was silence instead, or distraction.

Impossible to imagine anyone else in her arms – beginning all over again. Resenting the tight cage of his limbs she tried, defiantly. Images flickered, detached as calendar-leaves. Nothing. She lingered experimentally on a face downstairs – cleancut features, polished skin, beach-boy hair. Typically, he had a whining voice and a sawn-off, squat body. She kept him seated in her imagination, his mouth shut, until Tony stirred and shouldered him into oblivion.

Part two – she grinned cynically within. Tony knew her weaknesses and his strengths; she had never hid her feelings. Perhaps she should.

'You'll rue the day,' Alice had said once, with almost elderly bitterness, 'when you let them see you care.'

Too late now – he had already prised her shoes off with his toes. His arms were inside her duvet, she was slipping out of the sleeves, as if he had received a definite signal and gone to work with several pairs of hands – zips were open, and her legs were arching busily into view. Complying, she alternated between pleasure and anger as the tension seeped away and flooded back in sharp spasms. To be so reduced, so easily handled, switched on and off at a touch!

Capitulation so outraged her at the critical moment that she almost jerked her limbs away in stiff resistance – and yet she yielded. It was choice, not submission – knowing that whatever shadows melted briefly, they would return. Intimacy was essential; it wasn't any less addictive being used to it, although she knew the ordinary was there behind it all the time, as plain as old wallpaper, or the street outside.

But there was no street outside; this was Namche – crooked alleys and melodious lanes. A dream-world where nothing signified? She allowed reluctant sweetness to melt her limbs as if her blood were honeyed.

It was dark, a velvet blackness threaded with mysterious light, and there was an intensely preliminary silence, not only in their room but in the cubicles on both sides. Gradually her breath began to issue in short, involuntary gasps, audible to the others, just as she could hear their inhibitions fade.

There was nothing delicate about Tony's presence. He worked, she thought, like an outboard motor; head down, muscles clenched, inexhaustible.

Later, her breath seemed to come from outside her, in deeper, harsher gasps; she heard it from a distance, as if the night were breathing through her body. Eyelids twitched beyond control, eyes rolling, desperate to see where she would plunge within herself. Her spine locked in an arch that remembered every contraction it had ever launched. She could hang endlessly, humming like a bird in this starved pre-ecstasy when the suspension was right. A dream of flying – until at last she would float and swoop, pleasure building like speed and she vanished through some condition she could never remember after.

This time she would not yield and leave him churning smoothly wherever it was he went, towing her body with him, netted in seaweed and streaming hair. They would go down together. The rising arch of her spine prepared to break him.

But there was a relentless vigour there, as if he felt the challenge – no kisses, no whispers or caresses; powerful hands forced her hips back against the arch; not quite breathing now, but exhaling, in deliberate grunts, both, timed to the blunt impact, flesh on flesh.

A lonely flare of passion threatened to betray her; she cast around for cold bearings, thought of the butter-haired dwarf next door, and the rush subsided. Silence in the other rooms now, quiet river-banks, while Tony powered on, and Helen held him deep as a drowning breath.

All the while she knew. The body, the heartbeat, the hands were his, but Tony was somewhere else. If she shouted he might hear the voice – but not the question.

She knew; of course she knew, and was used to knowing – and would forget when she had to; and now he was urging her firmly towards the edge, and she had forgotten already – her head and shoulders out in unsupported space, limbs clinging to some root deep in the current. She would not go . . . until that came too; and then – in a tearing, throttled rush everything tumbled with her and was swept away in a flood of vacant sensation, frantic fingers grappling the foreign body spinning past her in the dark.

They came to rest drifting in the shallows and found each other again by touch. They rolled into an old, comfortable embrace, and, purged of memory Helen fell instantly asleep.

Tony lay wide awake, his body humming bitterly. Alice had been there in the dark. Just as he grasped her she vanished to the far side of the world. Helen stirred in the tender hollow of his arm murmuring sleepily. It might indeed be possible to love two people, he understood - but he could only be faithful to one.

Solu Khumbu   Dec 5th

Dear Alice,

We climbed another one yesterday, 20,000 feet. Today is a rest-day. Don't let this letter worry you – I just need to talk to someone. . . . The trip is terrific, but I haven't been all that well lately. Probably nothing much, altitude and so on, but if I tell Tony he'll take it too seriously and we'll get nothing done. You know what he's like.

Between you and me . . . .

I've crossed that out, but I'm sure you'll manage to read it anyway. It seems unlikely because we take no chances; it would be madness for me in these conditions.

All the same – oh, never mind, I'm addled with fatigue and altitude – I just need to say it to someone.

I won't bore you with the mountain, but it definitely deserves a mention. It's surrounded by enormous monsters, the biggest on earth, so it looks fairly handy. I barely made it to the top. The last bit was quite hard – hundreds of feet of ice, not my style at all, but it brought me close to an awareness of what the whole thing must be about. There's a thrill to climbing something steep and high which has nothing to do with the summit or the view or any of the obvious virtues. When you have to fight I can see the fight becomes a worthwhile end in itself. Maybe I'm becoming a climber at last, in a reluctant sort of way.

It's a lot to do with Tony, of course, though not entirely. I'd hate to be here and be a wandering distraction. We need to do things together –

that's why we came – but it's just as important that he should come down to my level as it is for me to move up. I'm not sure how often that'll happen. Maybe it's just the way I'm feeling at the moment, but aren't most of the fanciable ones like that – into achievement before sharing? Is it only the mediocrities that want to be equal?

Okay, I wasn't great on the bloody mountain; I was slow and sick, and I even cried at one stage, but I put everything I had into it, and won't have it ignored or dismissed. How can I get better without encouragement?

My performance yesterday reminded me of music, Alice – long afternoons in the practise-room when you were all out at games and I plodded away on that bloody piano. When I think of it – inkstained fingers, cheap nail varnish, ivory keys the colour of nicotine! You thought I had talent because I could rattle out dance-tunes blindfolded, but that stuff is programmed; once you know the pattern it plays itself. What I really wanted, and you thought a complete bore, was to play the likes of Chopin – from the heart, not from the page. I didn't have the expression. Too much rhythm, insufficient feeling. That's why I work in entertainment. You thought I'd found my vocation; I hadn't – I'd lost it.

Even now, thinking about it, my fingers ache to poke holes in a sonata, even thought I'd crawl out the far end with frostbite. Maybe it's a personality-problem, not a creative urge, because I think – I think I could feel the same way about mountains now. I hope not, but I'm afraid so. I'm hooked on the grand scale again. It'll be a lot to ask of Tony – to come down to my level. He's already looking for someone else to try something frightful called Taweche. Much too hard for me ....

In the lodge at Lobuje, the last settlement before Everest, a young Korean held forth to an amused company of Sherpas, trekkers, a Nepali army-officer – and Helen and Tony who were not amused at all.

The youth had nothing to do with the winter-expedition on Everest.

Attracted by its glamour he had come to climb in the same area, and he boasted feverishly of what he might do. His broad, flat face was inflamed with adventure, a young warrior in the final village vowing to slay dragons on the morrow. In ringing tones he told the villagers exactly what kind of hero he was, and the dragons he had already slain.

The Sherpas sniggered into their chang and the army-man mused on his role as liaison-officer, responsible for permits and climbing-fees. The Korean's new boots and gleaming equipment stood outside the door, ready to go.

It had threatened to snow for the last two days since Helen and Tony had returned from Everest Base Camp, where they walked up Kala Pattar, a pleasant little mountain without snow or ice.

Helen had seemed unnecessarily slow on the ascent. Tony allowed himself to grumble and she hardened into a familiar silence. At the top she stood on the highest boulders, and then – scrambling down, she slipped and fell.

There were no tears, no injuries, and although something collapsed inside Tony whenever Helen was hurt, this time concern was overwhelmed by irritation; it was almost as if she'd fallen on purpose, let herself go out of . . . because she didn't understand this climbing thing and wouldn't try harder while they were here – and wouldn't understand either the effort he was making to help, to choose things they could do together.

'Don't – ' he warned the Korean grimly ' – don't tell the Liaison Officer we're going to climb. We haven't PAID'

Helen slipped silently past. Tony put a hand out but she was gone.

The Korean hadn't quite understood, but he put a shh-finger to his lips like a drunk. Tony sighed and drew him round the back. The north face of Taweche hung like a gable against the grey sky. Kyoung Bae Kim made martial gestures at the direct line up the face. Tony, recalling all the idiots he had roped up with, checked the two snow-ramps escaping to the right.

'Tomorrow morning – 4 a.m!' He punched four fingers at the grinning face and went to pack his gear.

On the mountain the Korean was fast and fearless. Conditions meant nothing to him; old snow on rotten ice. Tony would have turned back from the bergschrund. Instead, he laboured onto the slope and scraped upwards. Before he had climbed twenty feet the youth was level with him, grinning with glee. The rope hung down between them, unattended, already snagging below.

Tony swallowed his anger and humiliation; they would get up the route, that was the main thing. A significant achievement, maybe even a new one. He began to phrase the description, but after a few judiciously heroic words he concentrated on the gruelling task in hand.

Throughout the morning he used every trick he knew to save energy. It was steep ground, unstable rock jutting through the ice. Kyoung Bae Kim was prodigal with strength; by afternoon he was tiring – twice his feet slipped and he hung on his axes laughing at the joke. They were only half way up. Like a dog on a lead with only one direction the Korean strained towards the distant summit. A couple of hours before dark, Tony took the escape-ramp. The youth clipped into his axes, untied without a word, threw him the rope and went on alone.

The escape and descent were perilous; a freezing bivouac on the ramp, his back injury returned, locked him in a rigid stoop inching downwards all next day in a snow choked gully, to a second bivouac. In the morning the valley looked desolate, as if everyone had fled under cover of darkness. When, at last a plume of smoke rose from a distant cluster of cairns he felt a flare of relief; the first sign of life below.

Back at Lobuje Lodge he looked wearily for Helen. Her sleeping bag lay spread out in the dormitory. At the sight of its solitary limpness he was deeply upset. Gone for a walk, maybe, or to another lodge – He returned to the smoky kitchen. Excitement congealed within him, turned to irritable hunger. He ordered dinner, ate it, looked outside again, finally asked the lodge-owner.

Yes, she remembered – black hair, she was here yesterday, not today.

Sick, she recalled, patting her stomach vigorously, very sick, maybe gone down . . . ?

Tony reeled. Impossible – her gear was still there, her sleeping bag. She couldn't be without a sleeping bag . . . .

The woman opened the order-book, found Helen's entry; 10 Black-Tea-No-Sugar – nothing else. She pointed to it meaningfully.

'Oh yes, I'll pay. My dinner too. How much?'

'No pay. No problem. When you come back, pay.'

She tapped the ten teas again. 'She no eat. No food. Very sick. Maybe gone down.'

'But her sleeping bag . . . she must have left word! A message?'

She shrugged, unable to help, turned to the fire.

He stumbled to the other lodges – uncomprehending faces – back to the kitchen again. A girl hurried in behind him, handed a note to the cook who glanced casually at it. Tony saw his name . . . .

12th Dec. 2pm

Mr Tony Waters,

Please come to the Clinic at Pheriche as soon as this finds you.

(Dr) Alan Lutrell.

Helen had woken to a numb sense of daylight, feet frozen in the bag. A persistent crackling – breath in her blocked airways. She sat up shakily. Nausea squeezed her stomach.

A silhouette at the far end of the room leaned into a pool of torchlight. Static spattered from a radio clamped to his head. A peaked cap jutted. Tony? No – gone . . . . As if struck in the chest the figure snapped to attention, stared at the radio then slumped. Seconds later he jerked to his feet and flung out through the door. Morning lit the room before the door swung to – boots on icy gravel, yak-bells –

Smoke from the kitchen seeped through the wall. Loud voices, rattling. Helen tested her throat. Ravaged. She needed tea.

Vigorous figures in the kitchen. Excitement palpable. Mingma stacked yak-dung in the stove. Tall, broad-shouldered, with even features and a generous mouth – a handsome Sherpa face. She smiled in welcome. Her sister, cheerful, plain, in full-length corduroy skirt, poured out black tea unasked.

Thermos-flasks held milk-tea, black-tea-no-sugar, coffee, milk-coffee. Expedition leftovers on the shelves; tins of meat, fish, fruit, cheese; packs of soups and noodles; bales of biscuits, bars, chocolate; labels, logos in every language; EVEREST in every shape, size, nationality. In an alcove, Mingma's bed, photos of the King and Queen.

There was something in the air; five Sherpas hunched by the stove. Stirring porridge, pouring tea, Mingma held forth, fine chin jutting, lower lip sagging sometimes in a vulgar lapse. Heedless of the smoke the men gave back long salvoes, thawing some ordeal into speech. Now and then a belly-laugh, the women too, showing big, white teeth.

– Can't be too serious – Helen thought and felt better; held her mug out. The door opened, closed before any smoke escaped. Silence fell. An oriental in down-jacket and pants sat into a space that melted for him. Helen knew the overhang of the cap from the dormitory. She saw a fine-boned, sallow face aristocratic in its superior expression. The chin receded, nose and mouth jutted, the moustache of fine hair gave a delicate, marsupial air. Not Japanese; too tall, narrow cheekbones.

Mingma presented milk-tea in a special cup. Silence continued, all eyes on the floor. Tension gathered in Helen's stomach, nausea renewed. Mingma brought more tea. She whispered, 'Sherpa dead on Everest.'

The mug lurched in Helen's hand. The moment of death on the radio. The winter-expedition. She'd seen the base-camp from Kala Pattar. Pan-Asian, various countries involved.

'How did it – '

A man leaned helpfully; 'High-altitude Sherpa. My friend. Coming down from high camp to base. Avalanche. Ice fell on him. Killed.' He smiled at Helen, pleased with his clarity.

Helen felt a fascinated revulsion for the sport she had adopted. Heads turned towards her, nodding, smiling. She dropped her eyes. Within an hour all the climbing-Sherpas clattered into Lobuche to fill up Mingma's kitchen; a dozen men, in their twenties and thirties, in duvets, canvas jackets, ski pants, breeches, boots, sneakers – Rucksacks heaped outside – they tumbled in, as if to a party.

Steam rose off them, talk and laughter bubbled. Mugs and mugs of tea, Mingma scolding, listening, ministering like a fond sister, while her own sister, bare-armed, flushed with important exertion, laboured at the chang, squeezing heaps of wet, sour rice, sieving the rich, white liquid into a plastic bucket. She churned it over with a ladle, not a lump or a grain, filled a kettle, dumped it on the fire to take the bitter chill off the beer. She shoved the men aside, no one seeing her except Helen because of her absolute lack of looks, and bustled out the door to return a moment later with an armful of logs, then out again with a five-gallon drum, brought it back full, slung by a rope on her back – she swung it round and filled a barrel near the fire, then out again for more – or maybe just a reflex ricochet out the door, nothing needed –

In the press of bodies and the swirling smoke Helen could hardly breathe. There was internal pressure too – she was ill; not altitude, she knew, but something worse by far. She couldn't return to the bleak dormitory, sleeping-bags scattered like loose skins. She wouldn't sleep, she would suffocate in the cold loneliness that lay around the corner, minutes, hours, a lifetime ahead. Whether it waited outside or inside her body she wasn't sure, but it was there, a miasma of sickness and misery.

Once, she pushed outside to vomit. She stumbled round behind the lodge, thought of climbing up the slope to see the north face of Taweche, but uphill was impossible and she pushed back into the choking warmth. More tea – she had to fight dehydration.

Seated between two Sherpas she was jerked to and fro in the vigour of the argument, jokes, laughter, loud denials. The one on the right, wiry and short in winter-clothes and boots, grinned apologetically with lively eyes, a crooked nose, a merry mouth full of broken teeth; 'Sorry, sorry . . . .'

He was first on the chang, gulping gratefully from a brimming glass, bouncing up and down, commandeering the kettle, sloshing out glassfuls for the others, insisting, expostulating, overriding refusals, slapping flat palms aside from the rims of tumblers, carrying on two or three arguments at once, while Mingma stood, arms folded, the lower lip dropped between raucous exchanges, surveying them all – Ang Nima in particular – with affectionate irony.

He gave Helen a dig in the ribs, a cheeky grin – 'Where you go today? Kala Pattar? Base Camp?'

'I've been there. Yesterday ... no, the day before. Did you come down from Base Camp now?'

'Yes, all here come down this morning.   Everest expedition. My friend – ' his own eyes beamed with life ' – he died last night. Is coming now. Down'

'Was it an accident, or was he sick?'

'Sick. Altitude! Many times to Camp four, above South Col, many times, quickly up and down. Then yesterday, Camp four, very sick, slowly coming down, no good, Camp one he died last night.'

He looked at her merrily, ' – Chang, you like chang? I pay!' leaning forward for the kettle.

'No – God, no – Your friend, where was he from?'

'Kumjung. Near Namche. Me also. High-altitude Sherpa, many expeditions. Also this man here, my friend, our Sirdar – ' He poured chang onto the tall man's fingers so that it splashed onto the floor; everyone laughed and the grinning foreman was forced to remove his hand and accept a refill.

'Sherpa-style,' he said ruefully to Helen, 'Say, "No, no, don't want," then take. You like some?'

'Just like at home ... .' For a while Helen had forgotten her illness. Another cup of tea. This was a wake.

'Was he married? Children?' She couldn't resist.

'Yes, yes, married. Two doctors – one eleven, one eight.' Helen translated the daughters. She felt sick again.

'You married?' he asked with genuine social interest.

'Yes, yes I am.' She even showed the ring. 'My husband was here yesterday. Back soon. Gone trekking with a friend,' she extemporised.

She needn't have worried; no opportunism in his manner – just curiosity and chat.

'And you? Married?'

'Yes married!' he grinned proudly, hoarse with amusement and self-mockery; 'I have three children, all doctors, one twelve, one six, one ten months old. Now I need a son.'

In another corner a sudden argument broke out, voices raised, between a Sherpa in tweed breeches and another with angry eyes and a curling lip. The liquid in their glasses looked sour and dangerous.

Mingma glared in mock-exasperation. Helen thought she might box their ears, and yet, when the angry man drained his glass and demanded more she poured it out at once.

The tone all round became aggressive then. Helen was ignored. A youth, face slack from drink, stood up, confused tears in his eyes. He was jerked down sharply by the jacket. Mingma's sister, bare-armed still, shuttled in and out with water.

A small, distraught woman edged in through the door. The raised voices continued - then, as she stood uncertainly, fingers picking at her apron, the noise dropped and a nervous shuffling began. Helen felt a nameless, hot ache pass over her as the woman tried to melt into a corner. She offered her seat, insisting gently. Ang Nima had the matter in hand, on his feet shoving, shooing, exhorting, until everyone moved up and a space was made. The small woman in the standard grey, back-pleated skirt with striped apron and grey jacket, her face lined and desperate beneath a scarf, sat on the edge of the seat and rocked back and forth in silence.

Mingma pressed a cup of tea into her kneading hands. The men were silent, heads hanging, staring into their drink. She began a bitter weeping as she rocked, and when she spoke, head bowed, her quivering voice rose slowly as in a ritual, keening words that were half-spoken, half-wailed and went on unbroken except for sobs of breath in a stream of grief. The untouched tea, was spilling on her lap.

Listening, understanding, no one moved except Helen who only understood the appearance and gently prised the cup from the knotted fingers before the stain could spread. Then the others, Mingma, Ang Nima, the sirdar, leaned in with words of comfort, disclaimers, promises, but to no avail; the widow's rocking and wailing continued. Helen heard an unbearable echo of children's voices, clear and sharp.

Someone pressed a glass of clear liquor – rakshi – between her hands; everyone and everything concentrated on making her sip for comfort and control, as if they had to prove to themselves that there was some cure for such distress. They even raised her hands with the glass between them dripping on her apron, but she turned her anguished face aside.

This was love, Helen knew; fierce attachment without romance or sentiment; the instinctive love that is always perched on the edge of pain.

Whenever the door opened as Mingma's sister hurried in and out the widow's yearning eyes swung to the opening as if someone else must surely enter.

The third time it happened she darted to her feet, pushing away the untouched glass, and stumbled out.

Then grief, as well as chang, went to the heads of all the mourners. All of a sudden they were drunk. Horrified, Helen understood. They worked under pressure, in a strange cause, in a bleak and deadly place. It was a gamble with death – someone would usually die; sometimes more. This season's victim was coming down now. There was a release of tension and a deep awareness of its cause.

The Liaison Officer – Helen recognised him – became the butt of their anger. A small man in jeans and a huge down-jacket his feet tapped the floor in a non-stop, nervous rhythm. The sirdar led the attack, drunk but eloquent, waving an arm too slack to be a threat while the mild L.O. stared at the floor, shook his head slightly at moments of particular vehemence.

There were other trekkers in the room now, avid eyes recording details. The sirdar switched to broken English to make his accusations public.

'That is one way ... but is not my way! Men sick on the mountain and the Lazy Officer laying down in Namche. Supposed to be in Base Camp to help our problems, not laying down in Namche. Lazy Officer and sirdar supposed to sign report of expedition – I will not sign. That is not my way. Men sick!'

And then, in a burst of increased emotion as if blows were coming –

'One day I come down the mountain, and my head is swelled like ... like a Pumpkin!'

Noise outside. Ang Nima whirled to Helen; 'He is coming. He is coming down.'

Draining their drinks they rushed out. Already, a big green tent had been erected beyond the river. Three men, one burdened, came hurrying towards it. Yaks grazed, the Norwegian children slithered on the ice, and Helen – through the silence and blinding light – heard the fat American from Lukla; 'Is it at all conceivable that he is being carried down in a foetal position on another man's back? Is that conceivable?'

Down by the tent the widow's slight figure stood apart, facing his arrival, and the mountain behind.

The Sherpas returned briefly to the kitchen. More than a team of workers they were a community. Mountains were their work. No one seemed to resent or blame the expedition. Mingma joked with the tall man in the peaked cap; all the climbers were tired – she would go to the top herself.

Before dispersing, aggression broke out again, on the verge of a fight. Mingma barged in to break it up. She turned away in a fine show of anger – and winked roguishly at Helen.

The day sank slowly, hour by hour. In the late afternoon Helen crept to the dormitory and lay shivering on her bunk. Her stomach cramped over and over again, staccato lines of pain stabbing the abdomen; giardia, she thought infected food – this must be giardia .... But she felt a deeper signal in the pain, barbarous, incoherent, shocking ....

Later, she wandered outside – moonlight and frost – and saw the glowing funeral-tent afloat, like a medieval barge upon the night. As if in a dream she waded slowly through the fluorescent dark, not towards the boat, but at a tangent of her own. Shadows shivered on the luminous walls, bells tinkled within and tiny drums thocked.

All night the lamas were busy in the tent of the dead.

Helen thought of the other solitary men suspended in that darkness at the end of the world; Christophe Profit on a pinnacle of Lhotse, Tony on Taweche. She dreamed of blood, and felt it, out of control within her. There, in the cold moonlight she knew what was wrong – she had been alone for months.

Behind his very presence he had left her quietly, and she knew now where he'd been. Scored by bells, and drums, and the violin-whine of pain, the thread of circumstance was clear.

Later, wisdom settled on her like cold ash. It was over. She knew it was over – if only because she had discovered it. They would wander on together, upright in their lives, but damaged beyond repair. The walking wounded.

Pain knifed her again. Deeper, sharp as a scalpel; she understood its message now – what it was taking from her. Anger would follow the blood, an anguish of rage. She knew she had to let the anger come, at its own cruel pace, like a birth.

In the morning she recalled it first as a dream, but the blood was there again as proof.

She followed the funeral downhill towards the chortens, walking behind the widow in the dawn. High above her, on Taweche, a single speck, motionless, directly below the summit. She left the funeral at the cairns near Dhugla and walked steadily towards Pheriche. Behind her, in a sudden plume the grey smoke of cremation rose into the air.

A TALE OF
SPENDTHRIFT INNOCENCE

I'll begin with a bang and save the whympering for later.

We cowered near the violent summit of the Dru, Tom Curtis and I, trying to bury ourselves alive on a high mountain ledge. The midnight wind was acrid with the sulphur of a storm. Hail pelleted against the anoraks wrapped around our sleeping bags. Lightning flailed and the slender mountain jolted like a whipping-post.

Shall I introduce Tom first, or the Dru? Tom, I think. The Dru has been there forty million years and knows how to wait. Tom was twenty-one then and not expecting to get much older. After five alpine seasons, including climbs like the Walker Spur, the Frêney Pillar and the North Face of the Eiger, he was probably the best of the young British alpinists.

Stocky and bespectacled, with a tangle of fine, fair curls, he had plenty of other ambitions. He wanted to find and liberate the joke trapped in everything; he wanted to expose the exploitation of the Third World; and he wanted a permanent sun-tan for his social image. Earlier in the week, relaxing in Grindelwald, Tom surveyed himself with a happy gush of satisfaction: 'Brown legs, North Face of the Eiger ... I've had a bloody good holiday!'

The ledge was agonizingly inadequate. Two bodies in a single grave. Before the storm struck we spread the sodden ropes under us. We slid our feet into the rucksacks and pulled them up – up to the knees in my case. I insulted Tom's stature, insinuating he could pull his up as far as the shoulders. Our axes hummed like Chinese fiddles in the electric air. Wet hail built up in mounds upon our huddled forms. It slid down between us and melted into our bags. Cold encroached with the insidious certitude of disease. The intense wait for incineration was a slow death in itself. We couldn't challenge the lightning, but we must defeat the horror.

'It's not enough, you know,' Tom pronounced, hiccups of effort in his voice, 'to boycott Nestlé because they supply baby-formula to Third World maternity wards. Do you know how much tea-pickers earn so that you can drink tea for next to nothing in Ireland?'

The wind stalled. A sense of violent revelation. The air chilled and tightened. The axes hummed their unearthly requiem.

'It's coming again!' I warned. 'Keep talking, Tom. How much do they earn?'

'The tin industry is even worse.' Tom's voice vibrated with conviction and electricity. 'In Bolivia – '

A roaring hiss. A flash hit the summit. The explosion blocked our ears with pain. Electricity seared down the cracks. A hundred and fifty feet below the summit the charge hit our niche, the gap in the sparkplug. It picked us up like puppets, heads, legs, arms jerking and twitching. Fuses buzzed in the nerve-circuit. 'Next time,' I thought, dazed with survival, 'it must be next time. We can't get away with this.'

Tom was on the outside of the ledge and getting the worst of everything. He was still kicking and twitching well after my strings had been dropped. I thought he was overdoing it to get more space.

'Jesus Christ,' I swore and prayed simultaneously. My voice wobbled, as if worked by elastic bands, 'Are you okay, Tom?'.

'I think so,' he quavered. 'Do people survive this kind of thing?'

'Electric shocks are good for you,' I assured him bracingly. 'They tone up the nervous system.'

The Executioner peered down into the death chamber at his two victims strapped to the electric chair of the Dru. He ground his teeth with chagrin, looked surreptitiously around. There were no lawyers at 10,000 feet to demand a technical reprieve.

'Go again!' he thundered. The air was a cold, dead skin. Nerves stretched in the body, like barbed wire, the scurrying mind caged in the skull, trying to bail out through the window slits. As the tension tightened again toward crescendo, my hair stood entirely on end.

Tom was cursing out of a mixture of hysteria and hilarity, blaming the statue for the inferno. Some of the Alpine peaks have a little storm-scarred Virgin on the summit to aggravate the pagan elements. He swore the thing was attracting the lightning and conducting it onto us. His language had the crackle of blasphemy in the tense air. I felt the primitive pull of old superstitions in my blood.

'Not now, Tom! Not now. Don't talk like that just now,' I advised.

Long years of indoctrination had left scars on me that reappeared when extremity pinched the skin. Nothing too embarrassing, no rosaries or anything like that, just ... a Catholic sense of voodoo.

I cast around for an explanation of my unease for Tom, who was actually brought up in the same sorcery, though nothing in England approaches the claustrophobia of the Irish version.

'It's – it's Bad Magic,' I offered lamely.

The Dru itself is a gigantic lightning rod anyway, and a massive statue in its own right.

Hundreds of miles from the Alps there is a particular little town in the south of France: clay-red roofs, medieval walls and tiled towers, olive trees on the stony hillsides, cicadas in the dry light. Overlooking that town is an ancient statue of a saint. It was built of bricks and stones and then plastered over crudely to create a column of a body with a rudimentary head on top. It has weathered to the textures of its rough components – broken bricks gaping out of the belly, fleshy strips of plaster stuck to the shoulders and the sides, the face entirely eaten away. It is a terrifying statue for its cruel depiction of corruption and decay.

The Dru has that kind of shape and compulsive presence but its meaning is radically opposite. Overlooking Chamonix, it is the archetypal column: a monolith, an obelisk, a round-tower, a cathedral spire, depending on the angle of view, comprising all the symbols of human aspiration. Difficult to say whether it is phallicism or a sense of architecture that attracts, but the great column of the Dru has been a seminal source of mountaineering progress.

The rock is granite, but the colour and texture vary with the aspect. The North Face is cold and austere, riffed, cracked and grooved. The rock contrasts darkly with the eye of the Niche, a hooded icefield in the centre of the face. The West Face, with its southerly pillar named for Walter Bonatti, who spent six days and nights, solo, on its first ascent, is a sheer, smooth wall from base to summit, made all the more elegant by the rougher rock on both sides.

The first time I saw the Dru, from the squalor of a climbers' campsite, I thought it achieved an impossible perfection of form, and something like the magic of myth. The Sword in the Stone. Only a king could rip the sabre out of the rock. Hadn't Bonatti done it? He proved that like every jutting handle in history it was not a sword at all, but a challenge to the imagination.

I was impressionable that year and determined to be impressed. An hour earlier, alighting from the train at dawn, I had been transfixed by the serration of granite peaks sawing the sky above the town. That high horizon, I learned gradually, could act like the jawbone of some insatiable carnivore, but for the time being I was all elation and spendthrift innocence. I watched the Aiguille du Midi engrave its precision on the sky with the point of a needle. Later that day I discovered from a cheap postcard that the exquisite peak of the Midi has a concrete pillar built on top as part of the téléphérique station. I felt embarrassed, caught out in a Three-Card-Trick on the first visit to town.

But the Dru didn't deal in illusions. If an imaginary architect had to design the ideal mountain, the result would be some kind of Dru: inspiring in appearance, accessible, though not without effort, with classic climbs on a number of faces and the potential to challenge new generations. Finally, it should be possible to escape from the mountain in bad weather, though not so easily as to diminish the commitment required.

Few mountains qualify under all these conditions, though they may be none the worse for that. Some boast an excess of one quality, which can be a virtue in itself. The Eiger, for example, offers a poor exchange-rate between life and death, but it pays a higher dividend on success. The Matterhorn – to stick with the public mountains – is all aesthetics from afar, and whoever makes the mistake of probing its instability will only succeed in kicking holes in that perfection. Mont Blanc, I suspect, is more than one mountain. The great faces of its Frêney, Brouillard, and Brenva aspects simply happen to share a broad summit. I calculate with a little geometry that if Mont Blanc were twenty thousand feet high instead of fifteen, all the good routes could finish directly on a pinpoint. There'd be problems of course: those easy routes via the Grands Mulets and the Dôme du Gouter might overhang in their upper sections!

It must be obvious by now that I'm reluctant to rescue those twitching wretches from the summit of the Dru. Curtis will be all right, of course: he was born to survive. But shouldn't I do the decent thing by my alter ego, zoom in on the Dru, typewriter clattering like a chopper, and pluck that lanky insomniac off the ledge? *Deus ex machina.*

But this is an irresistible chance to conduct an experiment, an advance on those infamous cruelty tests when people were instructed to give massive electric shocks to other individuals, with medical assurance that it was for the victims' own good. The torturers were the subject of the real experiment, since the patients were only miming pain: there was no current. The object was to see how much pain people would inflict, under instruction, against all the evidence of agony.

Now, can I bring myself to extend the storm, step up the voltage, intensify the whip-flash, and make a true hell of that bivouac halfway between earth and heaven?

Back at the experiment the wires are heating up nicely, sparks spitting, and I must admit there is a strange temptation to step up the pressure on those unfortunate characters on the ledge. An obscure desire to *make something happen*. It is, of course, a futile urge to shock one of them into some glorious statement, a timeless speech from the dock, a fist brandished in the face of fate. Something, in short, I didn't have the courage to shout when I had my chance up there to challenge death. But after all, survival is more important than heroics and, finally after two hours of torture, I had yielded up no secrets other than a feeble sense of irreligion and the politics of the left. The storm had appointments with other souls. It packed its black bag of truncheons, wires, and batteries and moved on to the next cell.

They will sleep till dawn, exhausted by trauma and the second bivouac. And there is time to abseil down the dangling puppet-strings, back to the real beginning.

The weather was perfect for the North Face. A cynic would have smelled an ambush. The mountain sweated under the strident cosmetics of the sun. It was like a thawed-out film star back in fashion. Long days of heat treatment caressed the rock, massaging the ice out of the deep wrinkles. Scores of people came courting. Half Belfast was up there. They found the face in a carefree mood, autographing guidebooks, having its grapes peeled.

A clean translucent dawn greeted us – that suggestion of a polished glass sky – when we left Snell's Field, stumbling heavy-loaded toward Argentière. The sulky statue brooding on the skyline didn't look in the least like a mountain anyone was about to climb. Along the road I fought that trudging lethargy, as if trapped on a milk train passing sleeping villas, dewy orchards, and shuttered bars. The real morning streamed past me in its urgent air – light, colour, excitement speeding by on another track. I felt the illusion of sliding into reverse. Tom was leaving me behind too, with the reproachful air of one who has never quite learned to be angry. I tilted forward on my toes and kicked a gaping hole in my lassitude.

The climb began at the base of a broad gully, three hundred feet high. A long stripe of fresh snow bedded the groove, rockribs showing through. A lip of ice barred entry. It faded out on a brief rock bulge. Tom hacked a few moves upward, dispensed with the axe, and pulled up on rock, crampons scraping and hooking. Water flowed as the fresh snow melted. The moves were unexpectedly hard. I locked my hand between ice and rock and groped uneasily for a hold.

A flurry of small stones introduced company. Three bedraggled climbers had bivouacked overnight on a ledge system to make an early start and were outraged by nocturnal snow. They were going down, they informed us in shivering French, and formed a low opinion of our judgment when we continued. But we, after all, had spent both a dry night and a cable-car fare. As other groups of refugees plunged down past us, it was obvious that a general exodus was underway. We were pleased with the thinning out of the queue.

There was no longer any impression of the inaccessible magnificence of the Dru. It was simply another mountain-shaped cliff. After partnership on the Walker Spur, the Fréney Pillar, and the Eiger, our procedures were automatic: brief immersion in a lead, and then while Tom climbed I contemplated savagery and civilization as proposed by the wild aiguilles and the teeming valley below.

The roofs of Chamonix glowed with miniaturized perfection in the depths of the daily world. The sinuous river and the gleaming motorway flowed together through the long, tight valley. I swung a size eleven boot out over the void and casually obscured a vast area of civilization. I experimented thoughtfully, stamping out the town of Chamonix, and then, with a quick jab of the heel, I stubbed out Snell's Field.

Paying out the rope to Tom, who was involved with a steep and intimate crack, I wished I was down there, sitting in a warm bar in front of *un grand cafe au lait*, dunking the flaky subtlety of a croissant, with the climb wrapped up in a neat cassette of memory, playing away quietly behind the eyes and ears.

Half-an-hour later, I was balanced in a steep, wet groove, the minutes leaping off the face like rats, wishing I had an extension ladder. I was supported by one boot braced with an air of strained credibility against a rib of wet rock. The flared groove contained a malevolent core of old ice. It left just enough space for a fist and a boot. I scrounged and grudged painfully up the groove, my back lodged against one gurgling wall and a sodden knee genuflecting piously against the other. At the top I hauled onto a flooded ledge, soaked, scraped, and enraged.

Ladders were on my mind because the situation recalled a filthy day spent painting gutters on a Dublin school. Water and dirt had turned the paint to greasy sludge. You can save time on a long ladder by bouncing it at the top so that it jerks along the wall and gives a wider reach, while the bottom remains in the same position. Tilt too far and the ladder will slip, of course, but if there is a gutter or a window sill to hang on to, you can lean to a ridiculous extent. I had reached the angle of absurdity, clinging to the gutter and painting away, when the wind whipped the ladder out from under me. As it went, I grabbed the lip of the gutter and hand-traversed along it until I got my knees on a windowsill. Water poured down my sleeves and trickled inquisitively into my armpits, while the window was opened out against me from within by an entertained audience.

I stood dripping on the stance above the icicle and the wind skinned me like a knife-thrower's target. The weather was going downhill. Chamonix exuded a desperate nostalgia as mist erased it like a lapse of fond memory.

I shouldn't shift focus again, since mountain and story are already littered with stranded Doppelgängers, spitting images awaiting deliverance from ledges, windowsills, and waterfalls. As I write this in an old cottage in County Wicklow, I'm no better off than any of them. It's pouring rain outside, and the roof is sieving it mournfully into buckets in the kitchen. The vast, cranky fireplace has its priorities obstinately reversed: the heat goes up the chimney and the smoke comes into the living-room. At intervals I have to stand at the back door for air and relief, sprayed by rain and wreathed in smoke. There is no comfort here at all for the man on the mountain, shrouded in mist and spat upon by the elements.

There was an airlock in the plumbing too and earwigs living in the taps. I coupled an aqualung to the sink and gave the system a blast at two thousand pounds per square inch. It cleared the blockage, and the earwigs, but now there's an inch of rusty water on the bathroom floor. Yes, and the rent is due. I wish I were back on the mountain. It might take my mind off things. Meanwhile, the fellow shivering on the ledge wishes he were back here! People are never satisfied.

Mont Blanc and the higher aiguilles were still clear of the weather and Tom was fully in favour of going on. That, I pointed out severely, was a suitable sentiment for an effervescent youth who had climbed the icicle with a rope from above. But I was less optimistic. The effects of last night's storm would be worse the higher we climbed. And how could we trust a forecast that had already betrayed us once? With all the hard climbing still above there was no guarantee of the summit that day. Still, I wanted to go on too – Tom's great ability and enthusiasm, and the deviousness I had developed with age, fitted us for this route in almost any condition.

Onward then! We turned heroic eyes once more upon the heights and blinked blindly into the mist.

We were not alone.

A pair of voices, one faint, the other frantic, had been yodelling above us for some time. Burrowing vertically between fog and rock, I arrived below a blocky wall just as a large rump and rucksack disappeared overhead. French climbers dress to a high standard of elegance, but this rump was clad in a rough boiler suit. The rucksack bulged prodigiously and was saddled like a hiker's backpack with a roll of canary-yellow Karrimat. The scene had the mock-serious quality of a cartoon: hapless hitchhiker takes a wrong turn in the fog, the road gets steeper and steeper, until he is hanging by a finger from an overhang, still thumbing hopefully. I pursued him and he lurched upward, blunt boots scrabbling, voice hissing desperately for a tight rope.

'*Avale! Avale! Merde! AVAAALE!*'

The slack rope jerked suddenly – a lasso coming tight on a bullock – and he was hauled bucking and kicking over the horizon. I was intrigued, as by a circus act when a bucket-footed clown wobbles on a tight rope, but the pitch ahead demanded full concentration. Its massive ice-bedded flakes stuck out at eccentric angles. Some of the bigger blocks made minor overhangs. A hundred feet higher I reached a flat ledge, hooked my fingers over the rim of the cartoon frame, and squeezed into the picture beside the portly boiler suit. I saw his slimline partner silhouetted above us, entirely unburdened by any sack at all. The mystery cleared The dungaree-man was carrying the lot: two sets of bivy-gear, double raingear, all the food. And since the leader was wearing a light pair of rock shoes, his heavy boots, crampons, and ice axe must also be in the bag.

The man in the boiler suit welcomed company with a broad, red-faced beam.

'*Est-ce que vous avez fait bivouac sur les terrasses la-bas?*' I enquired amiably.

A flash of teeth. 'We haf bifouack on ze terrass las' night,' he informed me.

My sympathy hardened instantly to resentment. If there is one linguistic conceit I cannot stand, it is that continental habit of speaking English to foreigners no matter what the foreigner wants to speak. In resorts like Chamonix and Zermatt the shops employ staff who can speak Anglo-American, and they are so anxious to prove their competence in threadbare slang that they will speak nothing else no matter how earnest your French or German may be. The hitchhiker was one of these. 'Where you are from?' he articulated proudly.

'Irlande,' I gritted. *'Je suis Irlandais!'* with a pronounced accent on the 'Irl' since nine people out of ten hear Hollande instead. If they grasp the Irish angle they differentiate between North and South, Catholic or Protestant, often accompanied by gunfire mime. We are characterized internationally by the twin terrors of violence and religion.

'Ah! I haf' been many time in Amstairdame.'

'Est-ce qu'il y avait beaucoup de neige pendant la nuit?' I interrupted the autobiography.

'Zere was much snow,' he assured me with satisfaction, as if that was in order and the place wouldn't have been the same without it. I busied myself bringing Tom up, and soon the Anglo-garrulous Jacques was winched creaking and panting off the ledge like a fat pantomime-fairy with yellow, rubber wings.

'We'll have to pass them,' I warned Tom as he prepared to lead through. 'I'll be damned if I'm going to listen to pidgin English from here to the top.' A lot of British climbers would have taken this as a reflection on their own conversation, but Tom let it go.

The rock was continuously sheer and difficult now, a grainy grey-green granite with clean corners and cracks, and there was no chance of passing the pair ahead. Jacques and I worked out a stubborn compromise: he practised his foul English, and I responded in what I hope was slightly less atrocious French. Tom led our rope with panache up the severely exposed Lambert Crack, a thin slit in a solid wall, hounding Jacques' heels, and I stepped up the pressure on the next pitch. Unfortunately, Jacques' partner wasn't always responsive to his panted needs - *'Avale,* imbecile! *AVALE!'* – and at times a dribble of slack rope gathered on his paunch while he hung by his fingertips and hissed for tension.

Finally, we seized our chance to pass when the route branched in the uncertain mist. I jumped into one of those evil grooves that appear to have been built upside down, and emerged somewhere along the lower edge of the Niche. Visibility was down to twenty feet and the thick snow cover blended with the mist to rob the eye of focus. Progress in the haunted half-light was arrested by huge warts and carbuncles of rock, rheumy with ice. We were lost. A voice mewed piteously out in the mist. He wasn't talking English now, I thought spitefully. Tom was brilliant on this kind of terrain. Being lost suited him: he could pick the hardest way ahead and pretend it was the only way to go. The guidebook had nothing to offer. I shoved it down my jumper and sent Tom out into the unknown with the air of Columbus throwing pigeons at the New World. He ducked beneath an overhanging bulge and was gone. I was left with the frail rope, the sling that bound me to a flake, and the shapes that came and went in the pale fog. The mountain was no more substantial than a pillar of cloud and snow scoured by the wind. Hunched within myself, I brooded. The human body has reflexes common to all creatures, and a mountaineer on a windswept stance bears a marked resemblance to a hen on a windy day: clucking disconsolately, the head withdrawn, elbows clamped against the ribs like scrawny wings, alternate legs doubled up under the body. Every now and then the querulous head extends a squawking inquiry into the outside world.

Eventually Tom called and I thawed into movement. I'd love to have left an egg on the foothold in a salute to the surreal. Instead, I lost the guidebook. Ducking under the bulge, I saw it swoop into obscurity, covers spread like wings. It was lucky we had maintained diplomatic relations with the French! Guidebooks, I realized, were above language barriers. I listened ardently for Jacques' voice in the mist. Beyond the ice, at the base of the pillar, lay a sloping terrace, broad enough for a few uncomfortable bodies. The wind screeched into a higher register and a spatter of hail raked the ledge. The weather was hardening, breaking up into pellets of its own solidity. The day's climbing was over, and we settled into an amicable ambush for the French.

'Allo! Can you 'elp me, please?'

Thus, we had been warned in Catholic myth, the voices of damned souls cry for release from Hell, and must be kicked in the teeth by the righteous.

'Ici,' we yelled, 'Ici! A droite!'

Jacques stumped out of the mist like a refugee from purgatory and cramponed across the ice.

'Ou est le sac, Jacques?' I quipped, wondering if the pack had joined our guidebook at the foot of the Dru, and if it had, was their book in it?

' 'Enri 'as ze sac now.' Jacques beamed with the satisfaction of justice done. He squatted on the tiny portion of ledge we had allowed for their occupation and anchored himself with extraordinary thoroughness. No danger of him being pulled off his perch.

' 'Enri 'as no – ' He pointed at his feet in explanation.

'No crampons?' We were surprised at such an oversight.

'No boots,' Jacques corrected calmly.

'No boots!' We gaped at each other in amazement. No boots on the North Face of the Dru, on a second bivouac, before a second storm?

' 'E 'ave only 'ees – '

'Rock-boots,' we filled in automatically, still stunned. No crampons, no boots. How was he going to tackle the icy cracks and chimneys above? Worse still, how would he descend the crevasse-ridden Charpoua Glacier on the other side? Were we being cast as guardian angels when we were looking for guides ourselves? The blind leading the blind – we were going to need a description in Braille.

As Jacques began to take in the rope, bawling instructions at Henri, an impossible suspicion struck me. Jacques was advising Henri to climb down first and traverse lower across the rock. That could only mean . . .

'Est-ce qu'il a un piolet?' I asked faintly.

' 'E 'ave no axe,' Jacques sighed, as if he too was beginning to find Henri's nakedness a little trying. Invisible offstage, Henri swore that he'd be damned if he would descend any of the frightful rubbish he had just climbed. He insisted he could traverse the ice in his rock boots. Jacques was adamant that he couldn't do anything of the sort without ice tools. He promised Henri that when he fell off his body would swoop in a great bruising arc across the Niche and smash at high speed into the side of the pillar a hundred feet below us.

I knew this scene from somewhere else. The dialogue and the characters were absurdly familiar: any moment now the mist would sweep aside like a cinema curtain and something wildly incongruous would come trundling up the ice – not a hen or a hitchhiker but . . . *a grand piano*!

That was it, Laurel and Hardy mullocking the piano up the thousand steps all over again. There was something simultaneously disastrous and invincible about this pair – the rubber-bones of roughhouse comedy. I felt that if Henri took his hundred-foot swing and pancaked onto a rock he would simply raise his little bowler hat of a helmet, measure the lump on his head, stalk up the rope, and punch Jacques on the nose, who would promptly somersault a hundred feet down the North Face only to spring back like a Jacques-in-the-box, and . . . .

I settled down to enjoy myself, and then Tom spoiled it all. He put on his crampons, took both our axes, and disappeared into the mist to rescue Henri.

Henri and Jacques, it transpired, had embarked on the North Face of the Dru under the impression that it was a straightforward rock climb. They knew nothing of the complex descent. Henri was a good rockclimber and Jacques wasn't bad on ice, so here they were. They had light sleeping bags, already soaked from the previous night. They had no stove and little food, but they gave off a fine sense of tolerance for their shortcomings. The final touch of distinction came with a pair of old fashioned cycling capes that buttoned around the neck and covered the sleeping bags in condensation. We gave them tea and studied their route description. It was a French pamphlet notable for the number of synonyms it offered for the word fissure. Everyone knows the North Face of the Dru is composed of slits, slots, fissures, cracks, grooves, chimneys and off-widths, but this pamphlet was a full page from a thesaurus.

It snowed intermittently through the long night, but the weather cleared before dawn. Shining snow amplified the lucid brilliance of the light. The Vallot Hut, a gleaming trinket, winked on the shoulder of Mont Blanc. Chamonix had sunk to an immeasurable depth below the huge headland of the mountain. Lightly hazed in blue mist, the tiny, clustered town – pale pebbles and mica flashes of light – was no more than stony shingle at the bottom of a deep pool. It had sunk beneath us while we tunnelled up into the cloud, and now it was submerged in a slow, fluid light. The current of the hours flowed into the high end of the valley, meandered through towns and tents, and washed wasted time and silted light down and out into the lowlands.

The first téléphérique cabin spidered down from the Midi: alpinists descending from the Vallée Blanche. If they considered the iced confection of the Dru, they quietly congratulated themselves on gliding down to hot coffees, warm tents, and dry clothes.

I felt the resentment of the bound against the free. There was an ice pitch ahead to avoid a snow-plastered pillar. We must bring Laurel and Hardy with us, not only for humanitarian reasons, but to share their guidebook. I chopped and kicked up the ice, warming the blood with a flurry of action, and suddenly, in that vast purity of shining altitude, the resentment burst into a flare of exultation. Breakfast sugar in the bloodstream, of course, but it had a spiritual thrust far above biochemistry. I could have rung hosannas and echoes from the great belfry of the Niche. Belayed, I hauled in the innocent climbing rope, summoning the faithful to a celebration. As a small altar-boy, it was my job to ring an old church bell with a rope that hung down the gable into the Gothic porch.

A few brazen clangs were sufficient, but one splendid morning I got carried away by the mighty clamour I was arousing and the way the rope hauled me high into the echoing air with every ring and then hurled me back to earth again. I could no more stop than I could resist the temptation to pull a fairground swing-boat high enough to flip it full circle, human contents stuck to the upended seats like that mystery of upside-down water in a whirling, arms-length bucket. The valve for a fit of jubilation is a song at full volume, and I cracked the crystal air with Ewan McColl's great anthem of hard labour, *Kilroy Was Here*.

'Who was here when they handed out the heavy jobs?

Jobs with the hammer, the pick and shovel.'

I substituted crampons for the shovel under the circumstances. Tom came groping up the rough, easy-angled ice.

'Who was here in the furrowed field stooped over?

Pain shapes a question in bone and muscle.'

He had the French rope in tow, and I brought them up while Tom jumped into the golden cracks overhead. Crafty Jacques held onto the route description for an exercise in translation. Every time I asked, he translated laboriously with the hangdog hesitancy of a pupil who hasn't learned his vocabulary but is determined to bluff it out.

'Take ze fissure ... ze craque? on ze right ... no, ze left, I tink ....'

'*%£@! Donnez *£% moi!' I snarled at last, and grabbed the page.

Snow, ice, and error slowed progress to a crawl. There was a tedium to the terrain now, best left undescribed, or catalogued in weary syllables: long, dull, slow, wet, cold, steep.

A hole, often exaggerated as a tunnel, led through a thin ridge a couple of hundred feet below the summit. Crawling through the little hatch, I emerged on the Quartz Ledges, on the other side of the mountain. Tom's shoulders and rucksack jammed. For a moment his curly, grinning head protruded, outlined in the northern light, and he seemed to wear the rim of the hole like the frame of a baroque portrait.

In a little niche on the Quartz Ledges lay a couple of characters, sound asleep, smouldering with sulphurous dreams. We kicked them back to the start of the story and settled down in their places under a sky pregnant with apocalypse.

'*LES HAUTES ALPES: spectacle en Son et Lumière.*' The performance began at dark, with muted pyrotechnics in the distance, spotlights warming up, flickering across the walls and ramparts of this Acropolis among mountain ranges. Tympanic voices rumbled the ritual responses among the ruined temples of the aiguilles. Lightning outlined quivering horizons. The storm drew in its acolytes toward the great central altar, and the focus concentrated on Mont Blanc, the very Parthenon itself, the ice-marbled temple of the Alps. A subtle crown of lightning glowed behind the peak.

The scene was prepared for some unearthly set-piece now, a tableau vivant to generate the temple goddess, Athena, who sprang by parthenogenesis from the cleft skull of Zeus. But within the burning chamber of the storm an infernal metamorphosis occurred. The spotlights, arc-lights, footlights, and floodlights forked around the laboratory, and, instead of Athena, the mountain gave birth to a fire-and-ice Medusa, with lightning snake-locks to turn observers, if not to stone, at least to ash.

'By the way, congratulations!' interrupted Tom.

'Congratulations? For what?'

He broke into an excited sports commentary: 'Mr. Dermot O'Murphy, first "Oirishman" to climb the six north faces!'

Ah, yes, I thought, shivering in my bag: *This is Your Life!* And isn't it wonderful?

The magnificent menace of the *Son et Lumière* spilled over the edge of the stage – the occupying Turks stored ammunition on the Acropolis, and in 1645 lightning struck the powder. Then they placed their guns in the shattered walls. Massive eruptions ripped through the orchestra pit, drums and cellos burst like balloons. Flash-fires raged in the front seats. The audience fled up the aisles, out the exits, into the téléphériques. Modern theatre is okay, but who wants audience participation in a Greek tragedy? Who wants to go home with his eyes poked out? The flames were racing through the balconies now and licking up into the Gods.

The sports commentator came on again: 'The award was conferred posthumously on O'Murphy.'

At daylight we began the descent. Jacques and Henri, further along the ledges, were having a lie-in, so we left them there in their cycling capes and bowler helmets. Another fine mess. The abseils went smoothly, stitches of rope unravelling, and soon we were on the knife-edge of the Flammes de Pierre. The blazing sun stripped the sheets of snow off the rocks like an angry host whisks off the bed-linen of an unwelcome guest. We left the hungry ice behind, shuffled down weary paths, and then scrabbled across the endless gravel to the Mer de Glace. I loathed the mountains and every atom in them. After every hundred yards of jarring descent I collapsed on a rock, cursing the gratuitous idiocy of mountaineering and the pangs of hunger, thirst, and pain.

Tom pinned down a mirage and filled a mug. Life held nothing more exquisite than the icy treble of water in the throat against the pounding bass of the blood.

And still the Mer de Glace to ford, threading a path across the ice in a maddening labyrinth of crevasses. Then up and up, up the far side to Montenvers, boots dragging, sweat dripping, and the last train missed.

Hunger drove us at a run toward the empty station. On the platform, above the sweeping ice, in spite of the disapproving Dru and the outraged Jorasses, we plunged headfirst into the garbage bins. Buried to the waist, Tom rooted out six tins of pâte, four cartons of yogurt, and a hardboiled egg. The egg was unshelled and delicately dusted with Gauloise ash. Thoughtfully picking orange peel out of a salvaged cheese roll, I gazed around me at the savage splendour.

Satisfaction resurged as pain subsided. I savoured again the old pieties: on top of the world ... purity and peace ... at one with nature ... bird's-eye view ... lords of creation ... because it is there ... trackless wastes ... untrodden summits.

I wiped the cigarette ash off the finest egg that was ever laid and bit into it pensively. That humpy hulk of a mountain over there behind the Dru, the huge Aiguille Verte, we hadn't climbed that yet. What about the Nant Blanc Face, then over the top, and down that huge snow-gully – see it there raking down from the summit: the Whymper Couloir – to finish the season with a bang?

THE SINGER

A moment of simple magic. 7.01 on a winter's evening, the News over, fifty thousand – maybe a hundred thousand hands reached to switch the kitchen radio off. On a common impulse they turned the volume up instead. Such a simple thing –
All over Ireland they stood transfixed – newspaper, breadknife, dishcloth in hand. Rich and hard, a song. A woman's voice, unaccompanied. No harpstrings plucked in the heart.

> *Do bhainis gealach is do bhainis grían díom,*
> *'S is ró-mhór m'eagla gur bhainis Día dhíom.*

Ancient precisions shaped the lament. There was also the shiver of a new animation. Words that had grieved for centuries received an independent strength. The old anguish was still there, but this voice would not die of rejection. The song rose towards conclusion, improvised the crest, then tumbled in defiant spray. It did not spill easily into silence. The aftermath was rich with echoes, as if the voice had moved away and was singing powerfully through the chink of another wavelength into another hundred thousand homes. '*Dónal Óg*, sung there by Síle Connery ....' A quiver in the presenter's voice, the pride of a minor programme aware for once of a massive audience. Normally silenced at the signature-tune, tonight they ambushed the public with that voice.

'... recorded almost twelve years ago. Tonight Síle Connery is in the studio again ....'
For many people the mention of that beginning was a private shock, a spring without a summer; twelve years since they first heard that promise, and the scramble for songbooks, sleeve-notes, dictionaries, anything to unlock the voice, began.
Her face on the first record-sleeve was nobly serious with square-cut, even features. Calm, confident strength. Massed hair constrained behind her head. Dark eyes outstared the presumption of the camera. A stern, old-fashioned image. In Mary Keating's *Irishwomen in History* the expression is there in turn-of-the-century pictures; resolute women in drawing-room attire who raised families, commanded garrisons, played revolutionary roles, stepping in and out of convention at will.
When Síle began a series of major concerts the response overflowed.

She wore outrageous cloaks and robes and she commanded the stage, captained it with an air of piracy that drew allusions to Queen Maeve and Granuaile. The dignified critic of a great newspaper experienced an *aisling*. He wrote of his vision, in which he had seen a young woman in the concert hall, 'and she had the walk of ... etc.'

Caitleenism shimmered between the lines, a twilight phosphorescence. But Síle had no *spéirbhean* pretensions. Her roots were deep in the solid past where an unspoiled music was preserved, music – she insisted – that was closer to potatoes and turf than to harps, chalices or swords.

She took the old songs and projected them vigorously up to date. Her voice was far tougher than celtic romance, and too incisive for a folksy evasion of the present. She sang *Curachai na Trá Báine* and *Líam O Raghallaigh* with a force that made them speak not only for the old riders to the sea but the modern tragedies as well – the trawlers, the fires, the bomb victims, all the small lives mangled in small print. She took *Anach Cúan*, Raftery's obituary for youth, and made it clear that it challenged God, then and now, for the desolation of untimely death. She had the instinct for meaning that is akin to prophecy, and the audiences understood – as they always understand the sense of poetry, even if the words are obscure. A second reviewer of that original concert borrowed his opinion from another poet, without the compliment of quotation-marks. He said ... she sang beyond the genius of the sea. In all her phrases stirred the grinding water and the gasping wind – but it was she, and not the sea, he heard.

'... Tonight Síle Connery is in the studio again, after an absence of many years, to speak perhaps of *filíocht agus tost*,' poetry and silence. She is here to introduce a collection of work, *Thar Cuimse*, by Seán MacGabhann, to be published this week by Single File Press. It was compiled and edited by Síle herself in memory of the poet. She has also written an introduction describing his life and work and sources of inspiration.'

He began to question her with awkward intensity. She was not there for culture alone. He would have that story told.

Her stripped voice was a further shock; as if an actress had broken down on-stage and become an ordinary woman, trying to explain her presence there. 'I ... I wanted to show how much Seán had achieved in a short life, how much promise was wiped out. None of this work was ever published before. He seldom had time for a final version. There was always another poem or a song pressing for attention ....'

There was a tightness in the disused voice, a sense of strained control that might be more a perception of the listener than an actual quality of her speech – but it threatened imminent exposure – the pain of interview, her need to accuse. Too late now to switch off. 'And then ... he was so busy with my career. And looking after Cormac too. Seán practically reared him, you know, because I was away a lot in those early years. He came with me as often as he could, but that wasn't possible abroad. But I always felt he was in the background somewhere, looking after me ... you know, managing things. He used to write to promoters over and over, laying down the conditions – transport, accommodation – all the little details that made touring bearable ....'

Vulnerability was making her garrulous; listening, it seemed best not to move for fear of dislodging something.

'He tried to arrange for flowers to be sent wherever I was staying. Roses always arrived after an important concert; you can imagine that wasn't easily arranged – three red roses every time. He phoned a man in England once, not even a close friend, and got him to drive twenty miles with flowers from his own garden in the middle of the night. Tulips that time. The poor man couldn't tell the difference in the dark – '

The story faltered; the memories were rehearsed, but they didn't match her emotions at the microphone –

'. . . I suppose – I don't know if I was mortified or exalted; it's impossible to live up to someone else's ideal.'

'Did you find it difficult to approach this book, Síle? It comes across as a labour of love; how much labour was in it?'

'You know, for ages I couldn't approach the poems at all. If I touched them they were like sand in my fingers. Prayers to an unbeliever.... But they survived that. There's a passion in them that speaks through the darkness; despair couldn't quench it –

Romhatsa rachfad
Ag marcaíocht im' chroí
Thar machairi na h-oíche ....'

She trailed off, saying the rest silently.

'Let's remind ourselves of Seán MacGabhann's unmistakeable style now. This is Síle's original recording of his *Scáil na Gréine.'* And again that voice, old as tradition, pure as lieder, vibrant as jazz, eclipsed the kitchen radios and drowned the listeners in the mysterious distance between the singer and the song.

Early in her career her repertoire had begun to include this startling material. Someone was writing new songs in Irish for her. Most were love songs, others dealt with poverty and power. She sang them unaccompanied. The art was in the intricacy, as if she was singing a strand of illumination from *The Book of Kells*. The same melody-line in the next verse would stand stark – the notes single as stars, or perhaps the ghost of a constellation irrepressibly hinted behind a pair of syllables.

A controversial song put new lyrics to *Amhrán na bhFíann*, the National Anthem, and subverted the militant tune. After the celtic robes there was an attempt to give her a sepia image and sound. She recorded with a rock-band instead. RTE posed a currach behind her; she wouldn't go on the set till it was removed. There was speculation about her roots; she must be more ethnic than the teacher from the midlands she claimed to be. The midlands – Country & Western territory – rankled with the experts. Her style was officially defined by culture-lines on a Gaeltacht-map connecting her influences. Where the song-lines crossed was a kind of musical grid-reference. Somewhere near Carna, with an echo of Helvic Head. It might as well have marked a record-shop because her sources had emigrated or died long before. She spent years studying old recordings, singing note for micro-note over and over with *Darach Ó Catháin, Seôsamh Ó hÉanai, Caitlín Maude, Seán 'ac Dhonncha*, while her voice was classically expanded as well.

At first she had relished the romance of rumour. But as soon as she was established she dissolved the myths stiffening around her. She wouldn't sing the songs of aggressive history certain audiences wanted. Rejecting that tradition she hit nationalism in its softest part – where it kept its hostile identity for breeding. It did her no immediate harm. But an undercurrent swelled, unseen.

The effect was more dramatic, less enduring, when she clashed with another institution on a TV chat-show. She was asked about the new songs.

'Seán writes them for me. Seán MacGabhann!' Her face was full of humour and youth. 'That's what makes them genuine. He knows what he's talking about. And so do I!'

She was forever laughing then, a brilliant sparkle, white teeth, shining eyes.

'It's the poetry of shared emotion. Very satisfying for us, working together – '

'I'm sure it must be, Síle! Not many husbands and wives – '

She needn't have said anything, needn't have campaigned. 'Oh no, he's not my husband! He's my partner. We live in sin!' Seán was a lot of other things as well, she explained brightly; manager, poet, songwriter, father of their child. But he wasn't actually anybody's husband. He'd been married when he was a student and it had broken up, but of course he couldn't get a divorce and remarry in Ireland. She shrugged her shoulders, not quite laughing now. Anyway, she continued, they were absolutely devoted to each other but they weren't interested in marriage – well and good for those who were, but she hoped love could be its own guarantee.

'Ask me again in twenty years' time!' The romantic innocence of it made her laugh with delight.

On the radio *Scáil na Gréine* faded like a sunset. Again there was an afterglow, echo of a force-field.

'Síle, what are your particular memories of Seán MhcGabhann – as a poet? I mean, are there ... are there things that distinguish the poet from the ordinary man perhaps, qualities that might ... elevate us all?'

The answer was slow in coming, the silence a bitter confrontation with memory.

'It's dreadful, I know – but it's the falling away that stays in my mind most. When sensitivity lapsed and the poet crashed to the human level. It's not really a flaw in the man, no one is perfect; it's the curse of poisoned memory. At the worst of times, in nightmares, that's the meaning of his death – becoming an ordinary man. But I'm beginning to hope again ... these poems, and the songs – and Cormac too, especially Cormac, he's getting to be a miniature of his father now – they'll salvage some kind of grace from under that shadow.'

'Síle, you've said repeatedly that you won't – that you can't – sing again. Are you saying now that there may come a time when ... grief must give way to the future?'

Was he edging closer, or had he balked at his script?

A long pause. In the background a producer nervously prepared a record.

'People keep asking me. I'm grateful for their interest – but I wonder if any of the survivors ever sang *Anach Cúan*; wasn't it always someone else who sang? Isn't that why they had poets and keening-women?'

Time was running out, nothing had been said ....

'How did it happen, Síle? That night – '

The silence trembled. A different resonance. She was in the grip of an audience, an audience that was stronger than her. She must perform. Description fell like rain on stone. But it was everyone's history – and everyone must suffer it.

Afterwards, the silence was full of shadows. A silence drifting from the radios like darkness. Everyone saw them – the child's face at the window, the woman alone on the wet road, kneeling by the body. Trying to make him speak. It was here. Not Chile or El Salvador. It was here.

'You know – I believe I could forgive the most terrible things . . . people can't help what they do sometimes. But they showed me something in Seán at the last moment . . . something I had never seen in him before. He threw himself away for nothing, threw everything away for the right to go where he wanted that night – as if it mattered. We could have turned around and gone home. He'd be alive today. He thought he was defending us, but we didn't count at all. They made him behave like one of themselves. He shared the madness, the rage for violence. It was like a mask they made him wear. . . . And I have to remember him through that. Everytime I think of his eyes I have to look through that . . . that death-mask, and try to find him behind it. And sometimes he isn't there.

How can I sing?'

Five more years passed before Síle Connery sang again. She remained alive on record. Her reputation held because she had no successor. Imitators, yes, but their inadequacy underlined her strength. Her voice alone was self-supporting, orchestrated by its own diversity – from the earthiness of a tinker's tone to the excess of operatic timbre. She had become a recluse. It was reported widely that she drank too much, that she could no longer afford silence.

There was no publicity for her first performance. She wanted to come back quietly. Rumour ran riot. She was expected to appear in a celebrity-concert to open a new theatre. Tickets vanished overnight, confirming the rumour. On the evening of the concert there was still no hint of her name.

Disappointed fans sieged the foyer. Ticket-holders had the dated look of people near their source again. They gave a string of entertainers faint attention, peering around them into the wings. The genial compère betrayed nothing, except perhaps his awareness that the occasion had its own momentum and needed nothing from him.

The intermission came. Contradictions buzzed from the bar. No unfilled spot in the programme. Hard enough to cram in all the hackneyed names, unless they came on in groups . . . reports of a black car at the stage-door, a tall woman in black lace and silk mantilla.

When the curtains opened an old comedian was sacrificed. He endured the brick-wall echo for five minutes, then stalked off. The compère salvaged some applause. He stepped forward to the footlights then and made a quiet announcement. So quiet that many missed her name .... A clamour of confusion, instantly hushed. She was already moving out of the wings as the lights went down. A pale presence in the shadow of her dress. The audience held its breath against the cold shock of the meeting, each person alone in a crowd face to face with loss. At the dull border of the footlights the collision of past and future occurred with silent cruelty, the crushing of visions, splinters of memory driven into the heart. She seemed to see nothing, her eyes empty, staring at the curtain of darkness beyond the lights, the audience behind it drifting past her. Would it hurt less to pass by in silence? Impossible to know who was more unnerved by the encounter. Her face was hollow under the high cheekbones, her eyes sunk in shadows, the skull claiming the skin. She might indeed keep going, leave them a second time staring after her, this time with no hope of return.

The compère intervened. He carried out a plain chair held in mild parody of a harp, stroking the wooden strings of the back-rest. He placed it centre-stage and dusted the seat with a flourish. A relaxed, charming man. Síle smiled in response. A stiff smile, expanding slowly with its own relief. The angles of her shoulders and elbows eased; the audience was slowly released from tension – forgiven.

Applause grew in the dark theatre. It began everywhere simultaneously, not the formality of welcome but the hard sound of emotion hammered out. It swelled to the volume where applause can only be amplified by cheering and stamping, but it passed that pitch and continued to grow without any utterance, a tumult of respect. Seated on the chair she lowered her head to weather the storm. The loose, black silk seemed to stream backwards in the crescendo.

When she looked up again she was ready to sing. Bone-thin hands settled on her knees, shoulders straightened, dark hair fell back. The curve of her throat drew all the light on the stage as the first familiar words emerged;

Dhá mbeinn trí léig ar an bhfarraige . . .

Verse by verse the ghosts of memory came alive to gather an old friend back to their island, a homecoming and a wake. Loneliness, not in death, but in distance. *'Amhrán Muighinnise.'*

Síle's voice had grown simple, functional like the kitchen chair she sat on. The song itself was everything, the singing no more than its projection. There was a hard edge to the sound, unclouded by flesh or emotion. It came ringing from the bones of the head.

She sang in her chair on the empty stage under a spire of pale light that narrowed in the darkness overhead. Shadows bruised her face. Her voice rose and fell. Slowly the song transformed the stage. She was an old singer by a dying fire. Embers glowed in the ashes as the lamplight waned. The walls and the low roof closed in. She wore a shawl of shadows. The old song filled the air around her and rose through the warped rafters into the thatch. It could not be contained. It was a prayer going on a journey through the night.

The song built up above the ancient singer, slowly the darkness arched and then it yielded to become the inside of a vast spire, a bell-tower high and hollow built tier upon tier of bulwarks and beams, the wood of Cill Chais and the dark centuries, masts and spars of sunken ships, shaft of pike and sleán, battering-ram and gallows-pole, and the smoke-black rafters of ruin. And the song kept singing itself until that darkness yielded and a spire of words and notes rose up and up into a free space beyond, where it shimmered and gleamed like a branch of stars, and drifted slowly back to earth.

JOHN PAUL II

After eight pedestrian years in the Civil Service John Paul bought a car. His colleagues had given up all attempts to dislodge him. Demotion, promotion, and the diagonal heave of secondment had failed. The new car was hailed as the final solution. A man who had serious accidents with umbrellas and toilet-seats would not survive a car.

Over the years John Paul had become the ultimate bureaucrat. But he was far from faceless. He brought a pointed nose, pinched lips, and prominent eyeballs to the forefront of the public service. Framed in a Social Welfare hatch, eyes averted from the penitential queue, he had at last achieved the confessional role.

The New Car – that was what they called it though it was six years, three owners, and 80,000 miles old. It fructified the barren romance between the hook-shaped hillsman and his obese companion.

John Paul made no secret of the fact that he was not a free man. His aged mother had first claim on his attention.

He was the kind of Irishman who would always pawn his soul to a greater cause and reserve his body to himself with the virginity of caution. Not just another bachelor but a lay celibate.

Maria continued to console herself with calories while keeping a pudgy eye alert for a better partner. It was not John Paul *per se* she wanted, but an actual, practising man.

John Paul's mother was growing younger every day just to spite Maria. She dyed her hair blue and tried make-up. Maria conceded the lipstick at least was useful; it marked where the old bat's mouth was the odd time it was closed. John Paul said that problem never occurred with Maria's mouth. The offended orifice flapped at him in speechless fury.

The New Car took a decade off the old lady. Out in the street she vetted it like a head of livestock. She felt the fetlock muscles in the mudguards, checked the rust-bubbles for warble-fly, and rapped a knuckle on the bonnet for an echo of catarrh.

Satisfied, she commanded John Paul to demonstrate his control of the vehicle. Maria recommended a white stick instead of L-plates. John Paul said she had no right to talk about eyesight – the way her cheeks were jammed against her eyebrows it was a wonder she could see out at all.

He waved his arm at the wide world and offered his widowed

mother a Sunday drive. They retired to her kitchen to consider the prospect. John Paul proposed a tour of the Phoenix Park, or maybe a round of Dollymount Strand. His eyeballs glistened as he conveyed the exotic splendours of the options.

He wanted to leave time to drive past the bus-stop as the Walkers' Club returned from the weekly despoliation of the Wicklow hills. That would be the sweetest moment. He must dump Maria for his image. He wondered where he might lay hands on a blonde at short notice.

His mother smiled dreamily as she planned her outing. Affability was a danger-sign. Her satisfaction spread to the lower orders. The cat in her lap leered and flexed his claws at John Paul. An old budgie in a rusted cage honed its beak for action. His mother announced her verdict.

'I'd like to Climb a Mountain!'

John Paul's mouth shrivelled with shock.

Pangur, the cat, stretched with poisonous pleasure. An old rug behind the door growled and got to its feet. Shuffling and sneezing Bran began his preparations for a long, long walk.

John Paul gasped his resistance. If he was seen walking with his mother he was ruined. Real mountaineers didn't even *have* mothers!

The old voice became charged with irresistible threat;

'I want to climb a mountain. Before I Die!'

John Paul was a sucker for blackmail. His mother had two handles on him. One was re-marriage. The other was death. He couldn't bear the thought of her marrying again. Nothing to do with filial concern. Simply that the shame would kill him.

Although death wasn't nearly as serious as marriage there was a problem there too. Who would look after him?

Worst of all, his mother was related to the Church. In times of stress she threatened to leave her money to it. Not that John Paul wasn't devoted to the church too. He was – as long as it stuck to being a church and didn't want to be a bank!

He was trapped. Condemned to appeasement. Remembering the agony of propelling veterans of the W.C. up a gentle hill he shuddered at the thought of a geriatric on a mountain.

At her best his mother resembled a precarious scaffolding of coat hangers supporting hand-knits, tweed skirts, and wool stockings in an upright position. Unknown to her son, a lifetime of such clothing had kept her as tensile as a mast under full sail.

'Any ... any particular mountain?' he croaked.

'A big one!' Everest was encompassed in her gesture. John Paul began to bargain.

'The Sugar Loaf?' He was starting at sea-level.

'How dare you? Your father and I walked up that hillock on our honeymoon.' She dismissed both the mountain and the occasion with contempt.

John Paul skidded south into the Wicklow hills.

'Tonelagee?' He doubled his offer.

'Never heard of it!' A ruder lady might have spat into the grate.

She rooted in her memory. 'What's that big one? Begins with Lug....'

John Paul's teeth crunched. The training at the Welfare barricades came to his aid. He pounced on a loophole.

'Ah, LugDUFF!...' It was a flat buttock of a hill near Glendalough. If Maria pushed and he pulled ....

'No! No! Not Lugduff.' Her voice had the rasp of rusty steel.

John Paul fired his last shot.

'Glendalug?' he whispered.

She rose in her chair and his concave chest collapsed.

'Lugnaquilla.' he conceded in despair.

'Lug-na-coille,' she caressed the name dreamily.

John Paul weighed up the chances of getting a ski-lift at short notice.

He dipped deep into his store of natural cunning. Reserves were low; only a faint fraud formed in his mind. They would have to drive to some simple pimple on the landscape and implement a massive deception.

Maria would have to be bribed. No real problem there. Double-burger and french-fries in a fancy chip-shop on Grafton Street. With a side-salad of course! One leaf of Kleenex lettuce on the edge of a carnivorous orgy and Maria thought she was a vegetarian.

'A very nice salad!' she would sigh greasily, mopping meat, veg., tomato sauce, chocolate mousse and cream off her plate-shaped face.

In return there would be no difficulty persuading her to make mountains out of molehills.

'A little white lie to bring pleasure to an old lady. . . .' His heart swelled with sentiment, and the chance of success.

His mother was rambling to herself again.

' . . . a lovely film on telly last week – *The Warrior of Wicklow and the Stronghold of Glenmalure* – he was an ancestor of mine!' she claimed possessively, as if the privilege did not extend to her son.

'With Lugnaquilla at his back he held the Saxon at bay.'

She waved an invisible sword at her S-shaped son and warned him not to let a Saxon cock cry out upon an Irish rock.

'. . . a very historic film. They showed the way up the mountain too. First the Fisherman's Track, then the Carroway Seed river. And Percy's Table, whoever he was. And they showed the cairn on the summit, the highest point in the province.

I remember it all clearly. Do you hear me? Clearly!'

Bran, Pangur, and the anonymous bird all remembered it clearly too. And each in his own way began to sharpen up for an expedition.

The New Car reached Glenmalure at midday on Sunday. It lurched slowly through the valley, shuddering with internal conflict, and came to a halt at the foot of Lugnaquilla.

The windows were closed to prevent escape. A curious technicoloured vapour issued from all the vents. John Paul fumbled for the door-handle and opened the window by mistake. At the whiff of the outside world Bran bounded from the back seat. Only the dripping snout squeezed through the opening and his hind legs thudded into the dazed cat in Maria's grip. The hook-nailed front paws drummed deep into John Paul's lap.

The cat responded like war-pipes kicked in the bag, and John Paul harmonised on an equally injured accordion. The crazed dog hurled himself around and around the front seats. Every time John Paul opened his eyes to grope in anguish for the door-handle he was confronted by one or the other dribbling end of the animal.

Pangur had succumbed to agoraphobia the moment they left the city but he was temporarily cured, arched and spitting on Maria's head while she screamed in a piercing falsetto that would have to be turned off at the mains.

From outside came the peremptory rap of a walking stick on the tarmac. The old lady had alighted and was eager to be off.

And it was indeed a promising afternoon, full of those deceptions of light and weather that seduce the unwary in Glenmalure. Steep ground rose sharply on both sides of the road, an emphatic V for valley. The rough 'Fisherman's Track' zig-zagged upward through bracken, gorse and boulders.

But the swathe of blue sky overhead was no guarantee of the mountain weather, and the nearby horizon gave not the slightest indication of the rambling heights spread out behind it.

Dishevelled and overwrought the little group assembled behind the car.

John Paul was wearing his best breeches. They were made of a lumpy grey tweed that looked as if it had been scraped off the inside of a porridge pot. The waist rode high on his chest and the seat hung low at the rear. Plenty of room for expansion and storage. He was bent double by his encounter with Bran, but it was only a slight accentuation of his normal posture.

His mother was encased in Aran jumper, Donegal tweed skirt, and hand-tooled brogues. It was more a mobile habitat than a form of dress.

And Maria ... well, it seemed Pangur had pinned himself in terror to her thighs every time the car swerved and now the claw-marks in her jeans were expanding under pressure of flesh. There was an awesome prospect of sawn-off shorts if exertion tore along the dotted lines.

John Paul dragged two weighty rucksacks from the car. His mother had packed the picnic with an unusually heavy hand. Normally she did not favour feeding Maria and had coined a maxim to the effect that bread and water cured more than crime. He was about to close the boot when she shouldered him aside and lifted out the ancient shopping bag that accompanied her everywhere. She hooked it over her arm and went to survey the cat.

Pangur was quivering and sweating under the front seat. His tail and front paws were clamped across his eyes to block out the terrible suction of the open spaces.

Raised among terraced houses and sunken gardens he had led an almost subterranean existence. Now, too late in life, he realised the world was a steep and bulging place and he was about to be shrugged off its surface.

'We'll have to leave him there.' the old lady conceded sadly.

It was impossible to blackmail a cat. She had dreamed of uniting the whole clan on top of Lugnaquilla. Already Father Pat and Sister Mary had refused by telephone. And now the cat was backing out.

John Paul had other ideas for his New Car. Pangur was notoriously incontinent! Nothing smelt worse in a car than catshit. Except maybe sour milk ....

Which reminded him with fury that the ... the Animal had already spilt the saucer of milk his mother had hidden for it under the seat.

When John Paul stopped sharply a hundred yards from home, mistaking the brake for the clutch, the milk shot forward into his boots.

But at least he had won a major victory persuading her to leave the stunted parrot at home. John Paul was convinced that the flakiness of his own scalp was an allergy to budgie-mange.

He had convinced her that they should spare the gentle creature the proximity of the cat in the confinement of the car. He loathed the infested clump of feathers and was therefore surprised by her acquiescence. Normally his mother adhered to the principle that unpleasantness was good for the soul – of man and beast alike.

But he had a sudden vision now of Pangur devouring the bird, and Bran in turn engulfing Pangur and expiring of food-poison, and he regretted interfering with the law of the jungle.

He lifted the shivering animal out of his car by the scruff of the neck, pinching it viciously as he did so.

'He might be lonely on his own!' he pleaded tenderly. 'We'll bring the poor old thing with us. Maria can carry him!'

His mother stumped across the old bridge with the proud tread of a pilgrim. They struck up along the grassy track. Maria dropped behind as Pangur presented his arguments for retreat.

It was an excellent opportunity for Maria to assert authority. As a teacher she was trained to subdue small creatures, and Pangur was going to buckle down. He was for the hill and that was that!

Bran had recovered from his travel-sickness and shambled lustily after the sheep. Fresh air had confused his elderly instincts and he was keen to practise the mating-notions he dimly remembered.

John Paul's mother was unhappy with the rate of progress. She poked at a half-buried boulder with her stick. Without warning she insulted the New Car; 'Not much use if it can't get up this!'

John Paul was not the first Irishman to realise he hated his mother, but in his conservative piety it hit him hard. He had brought his first car home for her approval – and got the thumbs down for his pride and joy.

On the final zag of the short track he saw revenge at hand. The path went underwater. Not under normal decent water either, such as citizens expect in Wicklow, but under a slurry of midge-infested, bubbling bog-spill.

The slimy seepage would surely turn his mother back. That, and the mass of appalling mountain lumbering into view.

Maria and her stunned burden were catching up. John Paul shrugged off his heavy sack and stood to await developments.

His mother misunderstood his mulish pose.

She stepped behind him and threw her arms around his shoulders. With a brisk hop she clenched her knees about him, piggyback.

– Hup! she commanded impatiently.

John Paul reeled into the swamp. Brown tobacco-juice oozed into his boots. It mingled with the milk and made a sticky syrup between his toes.

The shopping bag dangled from his mother's wrist in front of John Paul's face.

His long nose dipped in. A savage tweak between the nostrils shot his head back to collide with his mother's skull. Her grip tightened across his throat choking off his rage.

From the depths of the bag a scaly eye fixed him balefully. The sharp little beak opened and closed like scissors, a silent threat that signalled;

– Shut yer gob, misery-guts, or I'll go for yer throat. From the inside!

John Paul splashed wearily on. He landed his mother on dry ground and waded back piteously for his sack. Had Maria in turn demanded a piggyback he would have complied in silence and allowed her to pile-drive him into the mountain.

He was – temporarily – a broken man.

John Paul's mother saw no need to conceal her stowaway now.

The budgie came out for air and jaunted side-saddle on the ridge of her knitted hat. He hid his droppings in its woollen folds and hurled abuse at all the redneck birds of the mountain.

The appearance of his ritual enemy cured Pangur of the horrors.

He stalked the woolly hat through the long grass and up the grinding slopes. Hatred reassured him. He was searching all the while for the overhanging bluff from which he would fall upon his prey, as crafty Gaels of old had fallen upon cocky Saxons in the valley of Glenmalure.

Up they marched and up again, hour upon hour, step after step, and one by one. They followed the Carrowaystick stream past the mirror-fragment of Kelly's Lough. It was murderously tufted terrain all the way, tougher than the broad ridges on either side, but John Paul was determined to break his mother's spirit. The further up they went the longer the return. He fretted for his car at the mercy of tractors and thieves.

Cloud was filling the wide afternoon but the head of the valley remained clear. At last they glimpsed the serpentine curve of the summit ridge.

John Paul's mother paused to look back at the lowlands, her staff raised in true apostolic style. Acres of bleached swamp-grass stretched beck to the rim of the valley of the zigzags. Dense forestry smothered the opposite slopes in suffocating green, and then the lesser hills of Wicklow rolled on into the distance to break in little waves against the faint seashore.

The old lady would not entertain a proper rest. She vowed not to halt until she had paced the rim of the universe. She was in her element, storming ramparts, singing ballads, beating down the vegetation. Her bright eyes burned with conquest as she reached the edge of the summit plateau.

Rising cloud cut away the lowlands and isolated the hulking mountain.

But the summit was still clear, and the climbing over. All that remained was a cursory ramble along the plateau to the cairn. The path curved around the rim of a cloud-filled, cliff-edged coombe adding a thrill of exposure to the position.

'The East Prisons' John Paul grunted in response to his mother's geographical query. He was too exhausted to invent a source for the name.

The almost-crags of the Prisons below made it a real mountain at last, the old lady decided triumphantly. She had been sorely disappointed by the lack of excitement on the approach; she would have enjoyed a rope-move or two; and had no doubt of her ability to master crampons.

She announced an exultant vocation for this kind of thing, and John Paul's heart dropped finally into the catchment area of his breeches. Maria silently resolved to ditch him and better herself. He was a walking Jonah! She did not pursue the identity of the whale.

As they approached, a tendril of mist flicked up over the plateau and obscured the black hieroglyph of the cairn.

John Paul knew how serious the long summit of Lugnaquilla could be in bad weather. The plateau was broad and banana-shaped, and navigating in mist required intelligence and precision.

It also required a map and compass.

It was hilariously common for people to stumble down the wrong side and face a disgruntled eight-mile trek around the roads below. John Paul knew all about that. He had done it himself. Several times! It was lucky he was here today to guide his womenfolk!

And there were worse possibilities than detours. The yawning Prisons awaited the unwary. Goose-pimples crowded between his acne-scars as he imagined the heaps of skeletons down there, the wind whistling through vacant ribcages.

If he shared nothing else with the mountaineering fraternity John Paul had a climber's fascination with death. It outlined the mountains with a tasty black rim, just as sunset and snow etched them in gold and silver.

The one he was on, however, was no longer outlined at all. It was completely shrouded in mist.

They pressed forward anxiously in search of the cairn. The black mound of stones, with the Ordnance Survey pillar on top, loomed suddenly.

Two rucksacks hit the ground with weighty thuds and John Paul and Maria slumped wearily to rest.

Pangur sized up the trigonometry of the situation. When the woolly hat approached the cairn he would launch a flying ambush from the triangulation-point. But the old lady walked around and around peering in puzzlement.

'What's the pillar for?' On TV it had the far-off dignity of a church-spire; close-up it looked more like a gate-post.

John Paul considered it from a horizontal position. He would never admit ignorance. Truth was a matter of assertive tone.

'Oh that? – it's an ancient gravestone.' he offered 'Fiach MacHugh might be buried under there. There ought to be a statue on the pillar. And a plaque!' he added with civic zeal.

'Someone's taken them to melt down for scrap.' his mother complained. She had very little faith in public morals.

'Can we eat now?' Maria interrupted. She ripped open her rucksack and rooted voraciously within.

A battered tin bowl emerged. Maria blinked and hurled it aside. Bran lined up behind it. It was his dish. He watched the rucksack with anticipation.

Maria scrabbled again. A blue plastic dish flew through the air. And Pangur joined the queue.

Maria's eyes began to water, as if her saliva had run amok and surfaced in the wrong place. She dug out six large tins.

Three of them had kittens on the labels and contained – chopped chicken, fish, and liver. The other three featured pups, and offered beef, rabbit and lamb.

John Paul's mother lined the tins up in front of the slobbering animals. 'They like to make their own choice.' she explained.

They both chose fish, and Bran had to be fobbed off with liver.

Maria was overcome by weakness. She began to lower herself to the ground. The empty rucksack collapsed beneath her and she tumbled silently onto her back.

John Paul fumbled with his pack. He gripped something hard, cold, heavy, wrapped in his new anorak. Grunting from both ends he lifted it out.

The last time he had seen this particular rock it lay at the end of his mother's garden between the vegetables and the flowers.

It was a hunk of quartz, rough and dull like diseased marble, the seed of an ambitious rockery that had never grown.

His mother took it from him, strode across and heaped it reverently on the cairn.

'Just a little offering,' she explained. 'We all have to do our bit.'

She stood back to admire the addition.

'If everyone brought up a rock we could make this the highest mountain in the country!'

John Paul said nothing; hunger had consumed his voice.

His mother dug a square of chocolate from her bag and tucked it in the folds of her hat for the bird to nibble. He lifted his tail and covered the offering in a blob of disdain.

'Time to go!' the old lady announced briskly. 'When you've finished your lunch!'

Pangur and Bran had already finished theirs. Bloated and belching they staggered around the empty bowls bumping into each other.

A sudden panic stabbed John Paul. There was no map and compass in his sack! His mother had removed them to pack the rock.

Phew! Lucky he had a natural nose for navigation. He squinted into the fog. They had approached from that direction, ... no, from over there .... Ah! now he remembered. It wasn't that way at all ... it was *that* way ....

Wasn't it?

An hour later John Paul's party peered over the cliffs into a seething cauldron of mist.

It was – his mother suggested – the Third time she had examined the so-called East Prisons today. Further, she suspected her dizziness was due to circular motion around the summit.

John Paul assured her she was mistaken. These were the West Prisons she was looking at. A short cut, he explained.

He veered off diagonally and soon they teetered on the edge again.

The North Prisons this time, John Paul announced confidently, as if the feature confirmed his route.

'Do not – . . .' his mother warned him dangerously, 'Do not DARE produce South Prisons!' Having seen one prison she had seen them all.

'Get . . . Me . . . Down!!' The spaces between the words were crammed with echoes of disinheritance.

A curious phenomenon occurred.

The shroud of mist melted slightly, and a man stood on the grass before them. He was dressed for speed, in light, bright clothing, and shoes with whimsical wings on the heels. Elegance and strength were combined in his tall, straight figure. A kindly mouth softened his serious face. His dark hair was thick and curly, bejewelled with sparkling drops of dew.

He looked sadly at John Paul.

'Lost?' he queried, and added softly '. . . again!'

'What . . . what d'you mean?' John Paul blustered in rage.

His mother disowned him instantly.

'I'm lost!' she said. 'Don't mind him!'

Maria was gazing at the apparition with such moonish adoration that it was obvious she was lost too – if only for words.

'Don't interfere in family matters!' John Paul hissed.

He was completely ignored.

'I'll see what I can do.' the figure graciously promised the ladies.

He bowed and melted back into the mist.

'*Who* was *that*?' the old lady demanded in awe. 'Thor?'

John Paul gritted his teeth and snarled in sullen fury;

'Dermot bloody Somers. Calls himself a mountaineer. He thinks he's God almighty!'

From the look on Maria's face she thought so too.

The voice that had addressed them a moment ago seemed to grow out of the air again. There was no sign of anyone in the fog now, but the voice filled the plateau with a subtle thunder. In the valleys below it would be heard as the echo of a summer storm.

– Send out a Dove, the voice boomed. – Send out a Dove.

John Paul's mother understood perfectly. Columbus had received the same message in his hour of need.

She plucked the budgie from her hat and tossed him into the air.

'Ite missa est!' she improvised hastily, in the right spirit.

'Deo Gratias!' Maria responded piously.

'Deus ex bloody machina!' John Paul growled.

Unfortunately the bird had not been briefed for its mission. Instead of soaring towards the Promised Land it flew in crazy circles excreting like a machine-gun.

A 'tch! of impatient lightning flicked across the plateau. The cloud parted and a streamlined shape hurtled into view.

A black paraclete! The bird of the gods. The real thing; all arrowing beak, sleek neck, and coal black, backswept wingspan. The great beak opened smoothly in mid-swoop, and the ex-budgie disappeared.

The guide glided ahead of the party. It did not shine or gleam but absorbed the evening light into its dark core so that it was the black heart of a flying shadow.

Pursuit was delayed by Pangur. His worst suspicions of an unstable universe had been confirmed. He bellied along the ground, clinging to the world with every claw and biting into the grass-roots for increased adhesion.

– To die, Pangur thought, was bad enough. But to be knocked off the earth by a giant blackbird . . . !

After ten stumbling minutes the silver gleam of Kelly's Lough broke through the mist below.

They were safe!

As it turned to glide away the visitation took a sudden fit of retching and spat in disgust. Ptuii!! a feathered bundle shot from its beak and fluttered furiously to the ground.

John Paul's mother genuflected graciously in the direction of the summit. Maria kissed her fingertips and waved them wildly upwards.

The benefactor's voice boomed courteously from the clouds;

'No problem, ladies' it assured. 'Anytime . . . .'

'Bloody know-all!' frothed John Paul, shaking his fist. 'Think you're God almighty, don't you!'

KUMARI'S HOUSE

Terry Macken saw the world below him break into Himalayan waves. It had taken him most of his adult life to realise that the earth is truly flat, but he understood now with a nervous sense of homecoming that he had held onto a secret hope for Nepal. Here, at last was his promised land, where life might be lived in improbable directions – curves, echoes, ricochets. It was Monday morning and the early flight from Delhi was approaching Kathmandu.

He didn't know if he expected to find Carla, or if the excitement he felt was just a blaze in his memory. Down there, between the highest mountains and deepest valleys in the world, in Kathmandu or by the lake in Pokhara, lay the answers to questions he had never quite abandoned – love, euphoria, freedom . . . could the dream still live? Was there a haven where hope survived on organic dope and Hermann Hesse, while its outriders explored the wilderness of the mind? Airborne, out of time and gravity, Terry weighed his existence. He was a journalist, sent out to observe an expedition – rope and muscle, boots and steel – but, in a corner of his heart made poignant by increasing age, he was dreaming of a wandering tribe and its lost queen.

Monday afternoon he sat on the temple steps and focused through a film of sweat on Hanuman Palace. Old roofs and galleries, carved timber. The wood was cracked with age, but the peacocks, gods, devils, she-devils, human figures coupling and tripling in a maze of exotic geometry retained the energy of a passionate craft. Nearby, the modern heart of Kathmandu beat with a frantic rhythm in the pop-electronic shops and the pulse of traffic in the surrounding streets. In the whole mêlée of vulgarity and art, in the roar of traffic and the slap of sandals on stone, he chased the logic of his arrival here twenty years too late.

The movement had burned out of course, as hectic spirit does. He knew that – but the knowledge clashed with the revived romance in his heart, a powerful ache composed, at its best, from the adolescent dream of a better world, and at its weakest, from adult desire and loss. All that loss was embodied in Carla. She was twenty-two years distant. Twenty-two years. How could that huge span coincide with a twelve-hour trajectory from London? There was some hope of meeting the love of a life once in a lifetime; it had happened already. That it should happen twice was beyond the unlikely. That it could be the same person the second time . . . came out the far side of the impossible and . . . in a circular world veered back towards the possible? When he imagined her in his arms again, corn hair bleached by a sixties summer, the skin of her sea-limbs sun-smooth, grains of sand like gold-dust on her cheek, his breath seized, his heart hammered in the silence. Returning to the past was like diving through blue water down to where shadows quivered and patches of icy light rippled on vacant sand. When he let go it was hard to surface and breathe again, the tide had run in so deep.

His affair with Carla represented, not experience, but something missed. If he had loved her when he should but didn't know how, he would have a different imagination now, with adult dreams and mature emotions. It reminded him of something compelling, and obscure – art films on sunny afternoons, full of powerful images, confused narrative. And simplicity missed; beaches, grassy riverbanks, green hillsides where the mind goes quiet in its shelter and life speaks mouth to mouth.

In the confusion he had missed the passion of his life – skimming its surface, always on the wrong shore, seeing it only in the flesh when it was emotional, not grasping it in the flesh when it was physical. Carla had been sudden, different, overwhelming; the same age, but only in years. He had kept one eye open, ready to back away into ordinary air, as if he could come and go when he pleased, confident of his effect. It seemed incredible afterwards not to have known how much he was in love, how little independence he had. In those heady days he simply thought that was the way life felt at twenty, the intoxicating taste of existence.

It took a while to realise he was in actual pain – and not long to anaesthetise it. That period was a blur of temporary attachments. Then, as life settled into the seventies and he found his niche writing lazily for Sunday supplements he hardly thought of her at all for days on end – but there was a way of waking, sadly puzzled, in the middle of the night, the wrong body by his side, a mistake that never left him.

In the heavy heat he patrolled Durbar Square, round and around the palace, as if he had an appointment there and dared not leave in case someone turned up hours late and breathlessly important. Urchins selling trinkets bobbed about him. Tourists cast a second, curious, glance. Even in his rumpled, distracted state Terry reminded them of someone from public life. His fine, sculptured head had a sense of intelligent weight without physical heaviness. He was tall, unstooped, and his clear skin was ageing kindly. The nose was strong and tilted to an angle of humour and curiosity. Recently he found a tendency towards nasal hair, and he was inclined to peer into mirrors. He laughed at himself, knowing he shared this uneasy vanity with forty year-olds whose hair was thinning, making them reluctant to walk downstairs in front of younger women. Terry didn't have that problem. His black hair was still dense and glossy over an unstressed forehead. At an earlier age the blue of his wide eyes startled and charmed. The colour was still there, but it burned transiently in deepened sockets beset by drifts of inattention – the gaze of a tired romantic.

A week before Terry left his London home James Boland rang from Dublin.

'I hear you're off to Nepal, Terry – Kathmandu?'

'I'll have a few days there. Mostly the mountains.'

'Everest?' Jimmy's interest quickened.

'Not Everest. I can't remember what it's called ... maybe it is Everest.'

With old friends Terry made a virtue of vagueness, to show he was still easy. Boland had sold out; gone from Jimmy to James, advertising to insurance, jeans to suits.

A pause – 'Did you know Carla might be out there Terry – ?'

'Jimmy ... I can't talk now – there's someone here and I'm away the rest of the week on a story. Send me the details. I'll talk to you when I get back from Nepal – maybe before I go .... '

Afterwards he stared in shock at the one piece of work-in-progress on his idle desk, and was further shocked by the force of his evasion.

And now he was at the mouth of Freak Street; it was there, waiting, in the middle of his forty-second year, an address to be approached obliquely, to minimise disappointment. On the other hand ... perhaps he'd be relieved not to find her? Maybe he wouldn't care? That could be the worst discovery; that a vacant memory had sabotaged his life.

He wasn't ready yet ....

The story of Kumari, in his guidebook, drew him into her shady, inner courtyard, to escape the pressure and the heat. Kumari, the "Living Goddess", deferred to by all, even the King. A group of young girls endure a ritual of fear by men in animal-masks; the girl who is least frightened becomes Kumari, enclosed in the old house in Durbar Square. She may be glimpsed occasionally at a window. At puberty she returns to normal life and a successor is chosen ....

Stories like this were the meat and metaphor of the magazine-trade. Giving himself a job, Terry ducked into the house through a low wooden doorway. The three-storey building enclosed its miniature courtyard on all four sides. Ornate windows, unglazed, looked in on the sunlit space. Voices drifted down into the deserted courtyard. He saw no one. Terry felt himself an intruder in a private house – male, Western, a tourist. He heard a light shuffle and turned to see a Nepali woman behind him. She wore a clean, faded sari and carried a baby in a sling-cloth on her back. It slept, its tiny head covered in the lightest of hair, faint as pencil-shading.

'Kumari?' She pointed at a high, gallery window. You wish to see Kumari. Her smile was tired and pleasant. In sign-language and a few necessary words she outlined a simple procedure. Place ten rupees on that plinth in the centre of this courtyard and Kumari, the Living Goddess, will appear at that ceremonial window above. 'Kumari will come.' Ten rupees, a few pence. Beguiled by her delicate face, Terry placed his money.

'No pitcher!' She shook a warning finger at the camera, then called with unexpected authority to the latticed window. As if the money had triggered a mechanism, a little girl stepped from a doorway, took the note briskly and disappeared. 'Not Kumari – '

She called again.

Terry was intrigued. There was no reason to think she was anything more than a passer-by who had followed him in from the street.

A girl's face appeared in the shadow of a room, exquisite features, soft, brown skin. Interrupted in a phone-call she held a white, plastic receiver in her hand. 'Not Kumari – .'

Kumari was at her lunch, and would oblige a little later if Terry cared to remain or to return. This information from his guide came in the same smiling sign-language. On impulse Terry gave her a small clump of rupees. She accepted, neither as a tip nor as alms but as a simple transfer of ownership. He had not expected to see Kumari; he might even have been disappointed to have seen her, the extraordinary made ordinary for ten rupees.

He crossed towards the pagoda-temples again, agonizing over Carla. She walked beside him as she often did. In contrast to the Nepali women gliding by, Carla's style had been vigorous. Energy enlivened the space around her and dramatised everything within range.

Her cropped hair glowed with the cool, blonde light of a Scandinavian sunrise. Dubliners on their grey streets were jolted by the contrast between that colour and the brown Mediterranean skin drawn tight on delicate bones. Her wideset grey eyes observed life with intense expectation. When she entered a room, or a conversation, light came on, the volume turned up, as if she trailed a party behind her. Anything absurd seemed doubly, entertainingly so. The dowdy veneers used by Irish life to bluff the twentieth century were exposed in their comic pathos.

She saw education and politics as quaintly repressive. Carla was looking for inner revolution, expansion of the imagination into some intense universe far beyond routine. No one, not even herself, suspected that she was an envoy of a worldwide movement trying to achieve meaning through excess.

Terry didn't need meaning; for him, the present was perfect – a summer without end. He didn't have to work at anything; charm, intelligence, style, came easy. He took imagination for granted, the ability to conjure images and fire them with colour. But, to create *himself*, to be the things he dreamed, to live the ideas he strewed around like confetti – he differed from Carla on the need for that. Perhaps he was right, and Carla unconsciously knew it; there was a temporary perfection in the achievement of such ease, and she had no choice but to absorb him, as he was, for as long as his idyll lasted.

Still unprepared for Freak Street – just a hundred metres away, beyond the pavement market – Terry circled the palace again, puzzled when the Nepali design gave way to a British facade in a country that was never colonised. Hanuman, the Monkey-god, a statue draped in red, its shapeless bulk comfortably grotesque, disturbed him with its image from a deep dream. Beside it, a guarded door led into the palace. He peered inside, so involved with the past that he could have seen her coming lightly towards him, oriental sandals slapping the wooden cobbles under Trinity College arch, acknowledging with a grin the pique of student-protest.

No older than the placard-bearers, Jimmy Boland amongst them with a teenage beard, Carla had grown up in Europe, lived in several capitals, daughter of an Irish embassy official and an Italian mother. This was exquisitely cosmopolitan to students in Ireland, where the morality of a summer in London was still in question, and a bishop's dispensation had been needed for Terry to attend Protestant Trinity College. Carla had been everywhere; Morocco, Greek islands, Istanbul, Afghanistan.

October, 1965; a week late for second-year lectures, she hadn't returned from a summer in Nepal. At the Front Gate Terry loitered in undergraduate ease watching placards prepare to free the world. All week he had been erasing her sadly from his mind. It was obvious that Carla, with all her options would not spend a second year in a back-alley of Europe. Through the old, ornate railings, he saw a busy, blonde head approach from Nassau Street. Like an astronomer watching a comet blaze into a familiar sky, his heart turned over; the world would never be the same again.

The shock of an embrace promoted him from student-acquaintance to a dizzy status. He was illuminated for the first time by an adult sense of grace, and he might have caught a flash of the real meaning of university then, but there was nothing else in that laughing, third-level schoolyard to fix it in his mind. The year before, Carla had been too remote to approach directly. Her mature-culture style was austere and challenging. Taking Philosophy and Languages, she had a crisp approach to tutorial debate, an impatient reach beyond meaning. She wrote challenging articles for college-magazines. Terry, still inventing his intellect, gleefully pursued argument. But her cool, appraising eyes melted now in affection, revealing a pressure of normality behind the foreign confidence.

Receiving it all his life, on school buses, at parties, on the street, Terry was used to that melting look. He wasn't proud; he assumed it happened to everyone. He returned it in proportion to interest, and went on from there. He had no trouble giving himself – but he was never sure who, profoundly, the recipient was. A coy, adolescent sameness had prevailed. Carla was obviously different – adult, individual. Apart from appearance and manner, he didn't understand exactly how. There was a promise of adventure there. He imagined sex, love, travel, knowledge, excitement – but he couldn't anticipate the daring, darker romance of her mind. Instinctively, he ignored it, and responded to what he understood – the sexual tension between them.

He was led upstairs to Carla's rooms to hear exotic stories and to sample contraband. Nineteen years old, in Dublin, 1965, he smoked dope for the first time, and he smoked it in a hand-carved, ceremonial chillum. Because he'd never had to work at seduction Terry was unaware of anything unusual happening – he couldn't have described an event – but as Carla sat opposite him in a sweet flood of light and music, her eyes, lips, skin, her fluent body became the shape of his desire. Her presence melted and flowed towards him – bringing only what he wanted, leaving behind that foreign character, that inconvenient self-awareness seated invisibly apart, rueful eyes balancing his charm against his determined innocence. For a year and a half, unknown to him and never understood when she explained, Carla struggled to re-unite herself. Throughout that time, Terry's ideas and language dazzled on the brink of fulfilment, requiring some simple, undiscoverable mode to lift them into passion.

In sex, after the wild preliminary rushes, he sensed dissatisfaction, never his own. He understood it as a command to try harder to project himself. Himself? He tried harder, and sometimes his body felt like a projectile that was difficult to reclaim. They made love dramatically. It was something to be seized on the run and reeled away from in a delirium of sensation – during lunchbreak, a skipped lecture, after a party, instead of sleep. They were forever racing out of intimate rooms, late for some other encounter Terry had arranged in a hectic attempt to match what he felt to be the pace of Carla's life.

At first she was intricately inventive, contriving experiences he recognised within himself, but would never have achieved without prompting. Later, he was shocked to feel her cling silently, frowning up at his worried questions. He couldn't acknowledge youthful hurt in an adult. Although she was only twenty he didn't see the girl in her; from the start he responded to an older woman, invulnerable, complete. She could vanish into languages and foreign memories and leave him stranded in confusion. He concentrated on her sensory presence, and he never caught her own image of herself at all.

Drugs were sacramental then; promises of supercharged awareness. Terry knew he didn't need it. He was already wild with sensation. When he tried LSD with Carla he experienced a brief pirouette of ecstasy, then the thin shell of the world cracked. Terror sliced in through a brittle sky and scraped at his skull. He heard a thin scream, a fear of death sharp as a blade, operating from within his brain on fault-lines in the bone. Just before he shattered, Carla floated in and tranquillised the nightmare. He saw white pebbles in her palm, light in her hair and skin, a merciful light, warm and distant, like sun on high snow. Afterwards, he knew that the skull, with its quivering cargo of self, is like an egg bumping through a glacier. Later still, he traced his caution to that brief exposure to terror.

Drugs were different for Carla. Mescalin and LSD almost proved her questing intuitions. Scheduled one weekend a month, she treated them as serious experiments. Terry was nervously on hand, smoking dope as a gesture, primed to tranquillise if necessary, but it never was. Hallucinogens projected her towards an expanding universe where all that was needed to survive was the courage to go further, until the ego burned away like a shadow.

When she came down, exhausted, she spent a day or two gasping at the grimy surface of the city, its interiors excavated from river mud. She protested against this life on the dark side of colour, on the shadow side of light, on the numb side of feeling, in the gaps between the rhythm, on the inside looking in. She couldn't define the alternative; all she received was enigma, metaphors in sound and light, film without visual codes. She struggled to explain ... but she knew above all that it had nothing to do with definition, nothing to do with meaning; it, whatever it was, could only be reached when the intellect dissolved and the self was erased. Something held her powerfully back – the chemicals maybe, trailing their formulae in sinister subtitles across her vision, or, maybe it was emotion.

The cooling fever of her gaze settled on Terry; she smiled a sad, captive smile, a trapped angel sinking back down into Dublin.

Terry understood she was searching for 'enlightenment', not yet trivialised. He argued for self-discovery through relationship. He liked the humane sound of the idea, but there was self-preservation in it too. At some urgent level of awareness he knew he could lose Carla. She was training for total detachment.

Increasingly she expressed herself in self-absorbed images. She was walking into her life as if it were a wide mirror that showed exactly what she already knew in minutely familiar detail. The mirror was always just ahead, blocking the view, insisting on repetition. The vital life lay beyond the monotonous reflection. How to find a way through, without shattering it?

For reasons he was never sure of apart from what he saw as her unpredictability, they suffered several brief sunderings, then came forcibly together again. There was a different need in her afterwards, and he was almost afraid she might have considered other partners; not knowing how to deal with humiliation, he dismissed it as paranoia, and went on using the relationship not as a window into her existence, but as a smug mirror of himself.

Carla began to trip occasionally with a small group of older, ascetic hippies, most of them foreign, stranded in the shadows of Dublin, a city which they mistook for an island in time. The men wore long, scattered hair and prophetic beards. Their emaciated women had the raptness of medieval mystics. They lived on brown rice and hashish in muffled rooms where sitar music and incense hung in the stale, insidious air. With long, unfocused pauses they murmured abstract banalities. Carla's voice rang like an impatient bell among them. Terry felt they were no threat. They looked after her during her strides into the unknown, they knew the poisonous from the pure, and some of the antidotes to terror. His own glittering scepticism they treated with surprising tolerance, and he could never decide how much of their wrinkled eccentricity was wisdom.

Very little of this outside life was apparent in college. There, Terry and Carla were treated as models of radical romance, a showcase for the new, international culture coming to Ireland at last – liberation and style exquisitely sharpened with sexual tension. They weren't part of student upheaval either, because it was as predicable as anything on the syllabus; but as a principal in the style-faction Terry of course knew the political activists. Jimmy Boland was hardly an agitator; he was an organiser and tactician. He could make things move, get people to meetings, much as he might have run a debating-society in a conventional time.

Jimmy was fascinated by Carla; as her direct opposite he was probably closer to understanding her than Terry was. Entirely practical himself he admired the hungry, spiritual energy that gave tone to her physical existence. He approved her mature aloofness from the student issues he was involved in. He claimed detachment himself from the adolescent mêlée, except as an exercise in practical politics. Yet, despite Terry's taunts, cynicism could not be proven against Jimmy; he argued that it was honesty instead. Curly-headed, square-faced, blue-eyed in a wholesome way, he had the blunt fitness of a football-player and he cheerfully envied Terry the grace that made Carla possible. Coming from the same school they were necessarily friends, but Jimmy had managed to assert superiority over Terry that began in boyhood and would continue into adult life. It took the form of a humorously firm dismissal of style in favour of value and effect. He goaded Terry into absurd flights of fantasy, while Jimmy argued material substance. They enjoyed these extremes and the mutual tolerance that permitted them.

Lounging on a bean-bag in Carla's rooms as solidly as he would occupy a bourgeois sofa or a seat in a church, Jimmy in broadly filled denim flares, took his toke on a joint and continued, unruffled, to reason. When he went too far Carla might puncture his logic from some mystical eminence, but she never belittled him. Sometimes, when their exchanges as opposites seemed almost scripted, Terry thought Jimmy was as necessary to them as an avuncular spy to a revolutionary clique.

But Jimmy's business with Carla was more complex than that. He never gave up the effort to win her, to possess in some personal way her attention and interest. He did it openly, even as part of his friendship with Terry, and in a way he was successful, because – at some level – Carla was always enmeshed in Jimmy's complex strategies, arguing, altering, conceding, as if Jimmy was the model of an plausible society against which she had to prove her resistance. Terry never resented Jimmy's persistent presence; in a sense he collaborated, as if – unaware of rivalry – he needed a witness to this extraordinary romance.

But they had a deeper bond, perceived by Carla. Her foreign background – the difference in her which refused to be over-ridden –

provoked a provincial sameness in them, directed against her. Faced with this European independence, which was the first wave of feminism they had met, they united in Irish masculinity and resistance. Carla worked patiently to expose it. It involved things as basic as teaching Terry to make love as an equal. In the style of the time she had an innocent concept of Civilised Man, as if he had already been excavated in the rich layers of the future, brilliant, benign and beautiful, and sent back by archaeologists-in-reverse to recreate the present.

She had another displacement too; a romance with a country that didn't exist – the primitive land of early Yeats. Brought up in Rome and London, with an Irish parent, she had a strong sense of her Celtic origins. She saw Ireland in a mythical light, made of mountains, rebels, rhetorical excess. That vision gave way painfully to the dereliction of Dublin, the rotting river, chemical sunsets, the churches full of old women.

Years later, at bitter moments, Terry understood how innocent Carla had been. The need for heroes and mysticism was part of the blind quest of a whole generation for a spirituality to counter the decay of its time.

As part of that innocence Terry had been cast in an impossible role; to become a hero, Renaissance Man reborn. He couldn't possibly rise to it. Afterwards, there were layers of pain in his understanding; he had neither been loved for himself, nor could he alter himself to her expectations. He was doubly trapped. At those exposed moments a threadbare sense of self would stretch unbearably between these contradictions, rendered the more transparent by the way he had believed in himself through her.

He had had the attributes, but not the sharpness to put them all together and convince. He was attractive, expressive, athletic, creative, good-humoured, linguistic – in the Irish time-warp he knew two dead languages – he lived on a once enchanted isle in a post-romantic culture; despite all that, Carla was a victim of a fantasy which no one could fulfil. His ultimate fault was the failure to overpower her fantasy, kill the dragon, and win her back down to earth, to know her and himself as they really were.

She was trapped in the unreal, born into it abroad; he wasn't – he chose his image from vanity. And yet, in the heat of his life, in that inflamed time, how could he have known what was superficial? He learned to avoid these lucid moments. But the buoyancy had left him, and he sank slowly into his situation. Carla moved on.

Six months later she returned without warning for someone's wedding. In the same casual way she had often disappeared into Europe for a weekend; now Dublin was the periphery of her attention. Terry knew she was there to see if she had made a mistake. Carla was thorough and would always check her conclusions. He had had no warning and the day was a disaster. He was with another girl, who made that very clear to Carla.

Fired by a mixture of hurt and anger, he was perversely protective of his girlfriend. It was as if he owed some noble duty to an emotional child, and the insufferable folly of this pose froze him into its trap. In desperation, feeling life slip away again, he tried to break through, but twitches of hysteria behind forced him to withdraw. Carla observed coolly.

On this fraught occasion her manner was a flawless blend of intelligence and humour, without a hint of stress. She was the focus of the event, and yet, lending it her presence she didn't attempt to upstage it in any way. She wouldn't let the past intrude on someone else's party. He had to leave. He caught a sardonic gleam in her eye, and knew what she thought; if you want them beautiful and stupid, take the consequences.

Nevertheless, he understood he would see her alone the next day, that she would at least wait for that. She had given no explanation when she left the first time, although he had known vaguely that her waning presence was a constant warning. He understood how much he was in love now because he didn't want an apology – all he wanted was a second chance. He would never know if he'd been given one; when he phoned in the morning she was already gone. He took a taxi, too late, to the airport and ran to the departure-gate. A first, self-conscious thought was that he had arrived in a graveyard after the funeral. Then it struck him, staring in panic around the deserted lobby, that the funeral was indeed over and he was the one left behind.

There was a parting gift – wrapped in brown paper, marked with his full name, as if she had to distinguish between various Terrys. It was a bottle of pale liqueur containing flakes of pure gold. Geltwasser. It could have meant anything. But for the first time in his life, he was frightened by someone. He had a nightmare in which a gold ring dissolved slowly in acid. He broke the seal on the bottle, almost expecting that sharp, corrosive smell. The liqueur was richly, profoundly healthy and alcoholic. He could hardly bring himself to taste it. He savoured its existence sadly, a message from a different life.

He found himself obsessively looking back, reading her essays – there were no letters – recalling conversations, listening to her friends. Carla had been their catalyst, a messenger from outside. She had opened their eyes to a different way of being, a determined freedom that had to be its own reward. She challenged everything and made no concessions.

She was recalled, with the exaggerated relish of the time, as mould-breaker, seeker, iconoclast. But in an age of postures, none of the others had the courage to sustain that style. They had imitated it, warming their hands at her dangerous glow. He was the one who had been brought close enough to see how much it burned. He hadn't helped or understood. He'd had a kind of observer-status in an emergency zone where his neutrality was eventually found to be a lack of passion.

One night at a party, when Terry was too drunk to notice, someone passed the liqueur around like cheap gin, in tea-cups.

'The gold – ' Terry raged, 'didn't you see the gold – ' They thought it was sediment, and rinsed it down the sink. He found a dull speck in the muck in the U-trap, but it wasn't worth keeping.

Jimmy Boland had been involved in that drunken riot, Terry remembered bitterly. That would have been his style; break the bank while you were at it, but keep a separate account of your own for tomorrow. He remembered that bottle of gold-water as a kind of inspiration he had lost. He could have savoured it slowly for years, and it had all been spilled in one night.

Jimmy Boland followed Carla. After a year in advertising he set off on a world-tour; London, Spain, Morocco, Istanbul, Afghanistan, Kathmandu, Pakistan. While others stretched themselves beyond their limits to slouch in long-haired sloth to the Greek islands, where they fried in the sun wondering nervously where all the sex and dope were, Jimmy marched around the world, too energetic to be a hippy. He sent back intensely observed letters, written like notes towards a travel-book. Terry sensed a sub-plot. He tested the language obsessively, tapping its surfaces, sounding its hollow spots, a censor hunting subversion. Everywhere, between the lines, in place-names and itineraries, he found echoes of Carla.

Jimmy didn't find her, and Terry was never sure afterwards whether he was actually searching, or simply imitating her travels with the very typical intention of surpassing her image.

In the gathering years, when she was only heard of in those faint echoes that have lost their origin in sound but travel on in time, Carla had become a myth to her contemporaries. She was living in the Orient, and dealing in illegal substances; she was living in the Orient, had given up illegal substances, and was a Buddhist nun; she had lived in the Orient and was dead. The myth put her at a safe distance. Times had changed, they had grown away from style and ideals; they did not want a measure of themselves now.

Terry noticed certain signs. As a group of graduates, they seemed to stay in touch, and intermarry, as if they had a special kind of loyalty. Was it to each other – to their shared capitulation – or was it to a symbol of distinction they remembered? None of the women ever disparaged Carla's memory, no matter how much their security was undermined. Their men had all idealised her in some way – from the sexual to the philosophical, with obvious overlaps – and the women liked to borrow some of her dangerous quality, like a perfume to wear when it suited them.

Jimmy Boland, when he came home, compressed his adventures into a thoroughly useful guidebook for students. He went back to work in advertising and quickly became successful. He was able to fuse contrasting styles, linking rock-music and banking, for example; if it did nothing for music, Jimmy said, that was a small minus compared to the way it sexualised saving.

He enjoyed business. It was like a safari, travelling light through the boardrooms of capital, the last wilderness. More than anyone, he kept up the social connections of the past and he cherished collective memories in a clubbish way that seemed to substitute sentiment for reality and set Terry's teeth on edge at the implications that they had all been one, big family sowing wild oats.

Even when he was successfully married, with two substantial children, Jimmy still reminisced fondly. Terry thought the more deeply compromised Jimmy became, the more he needed that bare foot in the sixties. He retained his careful, not unpleasant cunning, by which he balanced all his options, moral and practical. He was proud to have emerged whole, having enjoyed the excesses of the sixties, and to be capable now of enjoying the harsh, profitable world of the eighties. Could Carla have managed that, he teased?

She wasn't on the same planet, Terry thought angrily. Now that the pretension had died down, he remembered her with a poignant understanding. She had experimented systematically with experience. Pursuing consciousness she had coolly tested the resilience of the imagination. She had maintained direction and control. She had absorbed trauma and shock, and kept her bearings in a nightmare. The Irish couldn't do this, she reasoned, because of their burden of neurosis and repression.

He tried once to explain this to Jimmy who had always brushed drugs uneasily aside. In a rare burst of anger, Jimmy put another view. Carla had said she wanted a partner who could kick back beyond the blind alleys of the present to her Celtic roots, and beyond that again to the origins and the future of the psyche. It was just a silly notion, like Karma and all the rest. But a coincidence had occurred. Those undergraduate poems Terry wrote with their pagan echoes? None of that stuff came from Terry's comfortable, Catholic soul, but how was Carla to know that? She didn't realise he was part of a fashion, clearly visible in the illustration of record-sleeves and concert-posters. Carla believed in Terry for a while because she needed something different to believe in. Anything at all . . . .

Terry jumped to his feet. He glowered into Jimmy's plump face from which the anger had receded; 'Carla was a maker and a seeker of magic with her mind and senses. At any cost. She would give you all the magic you wanted, if you knew what you really wanted, but she would give nothing short of that.'

It was a confused obituary. For both of them. Terry had formalised his grief, as tales of deaths in Istanbul and Kathmandu came travelling back.

Passing Kumari's House for the third time he knew he couldn't delay any longer. Time was melting away in the greasy afternoon heat. He suffered a dizzying burst of panic; twenty years seemed to have drifted by as disconnectedly as the last two hours. He had to seize the moment, before it was gone in a sluice of years. He drew out Jimmy's last-minute message with sweating fingers, and checked the Freak Street address again.

The fax had arrived in London three hours before he was due to leave. He had waited all week for Jimmy to phone the information through, determined not to embarrass himself further by asking. On the final night he cracked and began to ring. There was a persistent, somehow deliberate absence, and Terry finally left a tense message on the answering-machine; 'Jimmy! Ring immediately. Leaving tomorrow afternoon.' He resented that 'immediately', as if an admission had been dragged out of him. Jimmy was wielding the power of his superior knowledge. At that level of self-interest he was not a pleasant man. Perhaps that was part of his success. Still no call next morning, none by midday, and no answer at Jimmy's home number. At his office, a secretarial voice said Mr. Boland was out, and promised to pass a message when he returned.

Hurling together the toothbrush arrangements he should have made the previous day Terry foamed with fury. Without Carla's address the trip had no purpose. He had researched the mountain, and done some interviews. He found them predictable; climbers obsessed with the meaning of their event as only they would see it. He was committed to writing about the nobility of senseless, self-inflicted suffering.

He stared into the shaving-mirror . . . and saw what he was doing.

Decay crouched in his shadowed eyes and in the dark cavern of his mouth. Behind the pale skin and hollow eyes hovered the ghost of a boy who had not survived the sixties. Consciously, he conjured Carla, with Eden-eyes and silken skin. The glass warned him she would have aged, but he jerked away from shadows. Sunshine, the past, reprieve, were a flight away. Time stalled, heartbeats piled against it, waves against a wall, building to a damburst. He was breathless, a fever in his eyes. The ghost within him came alive.

He ran downstairs to ring again. Just then, Jimmy's fax came in; the scrawl of a disturbed decision.

Nilgiri Hotel, Freak Street, Kathmandu. Good luck!

There was no Nilgiri Hotel. He had prowled up and down the dismal street several times in a jostling crowd of tourists, locals, porters. Freak Street had none of the illicit glamour it must have had in the decades that made it famous. It was tired and seedy, reclaimed by its own people, and the anti-climax in the faces of visitors betrayed their resentment of the ordinary.

'Change money. I give good rate.' The dealers were convinced he wanted business. 'You wan' buy good dope?'

He tried the nameless extension of the street, and all the mouldering alleys to the sides. Sounds and smells of cramped existence struck his senses, and yet he found no trace of aggression, and little real dirt. Nilgiri meant nothing at the transient stalls selling cotton trousers to the passing trade. In tiny craftshops silversmiths hunched over brooches, bangles, rings and pendants of wearying intricacy. It would be unforgivable to squeeze his affluent bulk into those workshops, to trigger hope, and then simply ask directions.

Part of him was relieved not to find the hotel. There could be no happiness in this drab street – the magic he remembered could not live here. On another level, foreboding gnawed his heart. He was afraid of what he might find if he did not escape quickly to the western hotels in Thamel. Freak Street was one of those impersonal zones, cracks in the surface of a city, where the edges of different worlds grind carelessly together. An ancient porter, barefoot, with a crumpled, leathery face shuffled by, bent under a stack of cardboard cartons. Slung from his traditional headband, it was a cargo of European cheeseballs. Toyota taxis skidded past, horns blaring, raising dust, full of tourists, businessmen, serenely pretty women in bright saris. The porter weaved from side to side without lifting his glance.

Terry collapsed wearily at a street-cafe. Umbrella-shaded tables stood on a terrace overhung by scorched bushes and old brick walls. A grinning waiter brought muddy milk-coffee. He wanted to talk, to improve his international idiom. He'd never heard of the Nilgiri, but he knew plenty of hotels in Kathmandu that Terry might be looking for instead. His smile and patter were too insistent.

Terry examined the patrons. There was something dispirited about them all. They didn't have the well-fed blandness of the tourists in Thamel. He had seen this same look on refugees. Some of these sallow wanderers would argue that this was the real Kathmandu, man – but he thought they'd rather stay upmarket if they could, and visit the real thing from time to time like everyone else. Two Englishmen in their early thirties argued some obscure event in slurred accents. They had pale, bony faces, greasy hair, and their eyes glistened vacantly. With an anxious shiver Terry turned away.

At another table a sad scene unfolded. A tall, stoop-shouldered woman of about forty sat and smoked, playing idly with her spoon. In her listless eyes and sun-bleached, greying hair was the drifted look of the involuntarily rootless. She knew Amsterdam, Delhi, New York, London, but she had nothing at all to say. A much younger man, with receding hair, ponytail, waistcoat and cloth satchel, worked on her in a self-pitying tone. His letters, his cheque, hadn't arrived. In her sad, nodding solitude she invited his opportunist whine. Eventually, she would pay a little for the tedious flattery of his presence.

'Excuse, sir.' the waiter was at his elbow. 'Nilgiri, sir, we know it, sir.'

An old man approached from within, and bowed with the traditional salute, palms lightly joined in front of his face. He had the established air of an owner, in a culture where property is part of the personality. He spoke courteous English.

'That name is finished, sir. Nilgiri has no name now.'

Terry's heart thumped with foreboding. 'The hotel – is it still there? I'm looking for someone at that address.'

Calm eyes examined him shrewdly. The gaze lasted seconds only, but Terry felt his motives acutely sifted. Distress, he knew, was foremost on his face. Beckoning sombrely, the old man limped into the street. Bumping and floundering, Terry followed.

'The Nilgiri? It doesn't look like a *hotel*.' The dilapidated house was dark and shuttered, weeds growing out of the rotting brickwork.

'I wouldn't recommend it, sir.' Again Terry was subjected to that measured gaze, the old man raised an arm lightly, and with the other hand made a half-formed hypodermic gesture towards the elbow. He bowed again, and turned away. Terry swayed like a broken statue in the traffic, taxis swerving angrily around him.

There was no front door. A brick-lined hallway with a pitted dirt-floor tunnelled into darkness. At the end, Terry found two closed doors. Low voices murmured to the left. As his knuckles hit the heavy timber he knew he had turned irreversibly aside.

Sudden silence within, shuffling feet, the door opened a wary inch. In the gloom Terry saw a withered child surveying him. He stumbled back, then realised it was a wrinkled old woman bent at waist-height.

'Nilgiri Hotel?' Already the door was closing on his question. Anger flared. His fist thudded on the door. He barked again, then shouted Carla's name. A bolt rattled, the door was solid. Feet scuttled, alarm spread throughout the house.

Blunt as a police-raid, Terry threw his shoulder at the other door. He pitched through into a yard. A straggle of balconies reared overhead. Gaunt faces stared down. In a ghastly, sun-blurred glimpse he saw her, high among the latticed slats; photo of a crime, scream on a rooftop.

Thudding footsteps in the hall. Into the yard. Thick-set, muscled menace. Terry ducked aside, skidded in the dirt, a fist caught him in the ribs, slammed against a wall. Bone hammered on brick, eyes reeled up the balconies. Empty. He slid down the wall, skull rattling on rough edges. A bare leg braced itself to kick. Terry rolled, seized a brick, slammed it on the other foot. Grunt and stumble, the kick glanced cruelly off his shoulder. His own voice baying, he rolled to his feet and reached the door. The jamb caught his shoulder, he spun around. His attacker lunged on broken toes –

In the tunnel Terry saw her, outlined against the street. It could be anyone, it would be her. She flickered onto Freak Street in a long, light robe. Her unmistakeable stride. He grabbed her shoulder, spun her roughly. Frail as a Nepali girl. Eyes and mouth unknown, dark with fear. Photo of a crime. Grey skin clenched drum-tight on bone.

She spat Nepali between gasps for air, fluttering in his grip.

'Carla! Carla – it's me. Terry!' The struggle increased. Determined to exist he named himself in full; 'Terry Macken. Dublin. Remember me! Remember me!!' He shook her against the blaring traffic.

'I don't care – Let me GO!' He almost released her, then fiercely clenched again. 'What do you want? What do you want?'

'Nothing. I want nothing. – To talk to you. Talk to you! Carla! Look at me! You know me. I want to help – ' He freed his grip.

'Help?!' She rubbed her shoulder with spider-fingers. 'Ok, talk then, damn you. Talk!' Inexplicably, something redeeming struck her. Tendons slackened in her face, her wild stare calmed, expression jerked her thin-lipped mouth. Shock-waves coursed through her body, but she had control.

'Where do you want to talk? In the middle of the fucking street?'

They sat in the far corner of the cafe. The terrace was deserted. No sign of the old man; doubtless observing from somewhere. The waiter was slow to approach, his smile erased. She called him sharply. 'Must be a special occasion – ' She lit a trembling cigarette, ' – I'm not allowed in here.'

'Why – ?'

She shrugged. 'They don't like junkies.'

It hammered into his heart, the pain of the syringe, but it drew no blood; he already knew. Her eyes tracked restlessly around like damaged sensors, flicked across him without interest, dirty fingers rapped the table in obsessive rhythm.

Questions ticked behind his lips; what happened; how long have you been – ; how much longer? Pared to the bone, nerves twitching in transparent skin, she was grotesquely beautiful.

'You do remember, Carla – '

'Remember what? You nearly broke my shoulder – ' She bared her arm to look for bruises. He flinched in horror. 'Of course I remember. I'm not senile. Dublin, Trinity College. You. Jimmy Boland – ' Co-existent in her memory.

Desolate anger shook him, a single, sour gust as memory collapsed upon itself. Simultaneously, a strategy formed in his brain. There was nothing to reclaim here. This stripped, haggard face was impossibly remote from anything he had ever cherished. He experienced the cold clarity that appears in the presence of death and carves a path through emotional loss, while the mourner weeps at his own hardness. He had to help her; he had to deal decently with this death – and come out of it whole himself. Appalled, he felt his own body flare with vulgar strength. At the same time, he wept bewildered tears.

'How is Jimmy?' She could have been sipping coffee in Bewleys of Grafton Street, except for the poverty and decay. He could not add to the horror of her life. That was his strategy; to protect her dignity, spare her the comparison with comfort and success. He knew he could not tell Jimmy what had happened either; Jimmy would grieve, but he would manage to make Carla's fate an affirmation of his own lifestyle.

'He's okay. Getting old – ' But she had forgotten the question. 'Why are you here, Terry?' Irritable suspicion edged her voice.

'I'm a – ' He was going to say 'writer', but remembered you couldn't bluff Carla. 'I'm going to Annapurna to cover a mountaineering expedition for a newspaper.'

'The Sanctuary? We used to go there before it was ruined. Haven't they done enough damage yet? They are so careless and greedy. We see expeditions here all the time. They make a supermarket of Kathmandu. I hope you will make that clear. In your newspaper.' She might have lost everything else, but she hadn't lost that tone. Crusading in the sixties, it was harrowed and querulous now. It had all been said a million times. But it forced him into defence, as if she still owned moral superiority. Neither of them had that; yet he felt a rush to justify. Then pity again when he looked at her. 'You're still fighting battles,' he offered. 'Does it get any easier?'

He flinched as she almost accused him of patronising her. The walls of her existence were so thin he could see inside. She thought better of it.

'It does. It becomes a habit. I don't care about winning. It's not the point.'

'Why – do you do this to yourself?'

'Ask your climbers.' A harsh laugh became a coughing-fit. 'That's their territory, isn't it? Mountaineering as a metaphor. What do they find up there in the snow? They don't bring anything back either, as far as I can see – not even their rubbish.'

As she struggled to breathe, paper lungs tearing, Terry felt the astonishing proximity of death. He caught a flash of what the climbers found; life like a flame in the wind; the nearness of extinction. An illusion of control. They tested their limits time and again, reaching for exaltation, but it was a disease that devoured them, one by one.

Carla had begun to shake. It was an insistent vibration, as if a small engine, overstrained, was working loose. This was how she would go; the bones would rattle apart in the dry skin, and the tiny engine would spin dizzily out. What then?

She wanted to leave, but – she needed something. Cruelty sparked in him, two wires touching, love and revenge.

'How long have you lived in Nepal?' he delayed.

'Forever. They threw us out years ago, but we keep coming back. We go to India in the monsoon – ' She set her frail jaw, and the rapid words absorbed the vibration. ' – we're illegal now since they changed the laws. We have to be careful at the border. That's why I ran from the house. We thought it was Immigration.'

Terry heard the sad wingbeat of a marginal life – barred from her country, barred from the cafes, barely at home in her body. And yet that 'we' suggested a migrant flock, made him feel unaccountably lonely, a refugee in his own life. This was the tribe he dreamed about. Lost, but sacred in their wandering.

'How did you find me?' She resented it. 'Jimmy, I suppose. I told him never to give my address.'

'How the hell did he know it?'

'He tracked me down. No – I tracked him down. I was in bad trouble. Jimmy always stayed in touch through friends – and he wrote, *poste-restante*, every Christmas. We always picked the letters up, but we seldom answered. He knew there was someone there when they didn't come back. That was an answer in itself. Jimmy is loyal. My – Jeff – my husband, was in prison. You don't get out unless someone pays. Jimmy paid. He got an embassy onto it. Jeff would be there still. He would have died .

' – He helped me too, cheques and food-parcels. I felt guilty in the end. I had to stop him. Why should he support us? I sent word we'd moved to India and wouldn't be back. How did he find the Nilgiri – ?' She slumped back into a tense vacancy, her face hollow as a painted skull.

'Carla, – '

She rose from the table on shivering limbs, took his bundle of notes and disappeared into the street.

'I'll bring more – ' but she was gone, a whisper of wings.

He sat still a while. Rush-hour filled the street. Past and future merged within him. It was quiet in there. A shaft reached down into the darkness of his life. Time dripped, like blood, at long, slow intervals, and echoed later in the liquid depths. He heard himself grow old. When he left the cafe, he walked up Freak Street towards Durbar Square. Crowds shrilled and swarmed. He turned into Kumari's House.

The shadowed courtyard was enclosed in hidden space. He found a last banknote in his pocket and placed it on the plinth. It had no meaning in the dark, until a breeze fluttered it like a candle-flame.

There was a faint glow from a light within. A wistful silhouette leaned at the window.

A voice called and she melted away. Much later, she reappeared. In a blaze of desire he jerked the camera from its pouch and pointed.

The flash exposed a withered housekeeper, shocked eyes framed in straggling hair.

BLIND DATE

'You need a woman! I keep telling you – '

Henry leaned forward and winked his rural wink in a Dublin drinking-factory. ' – not a wife, mind. I'm not talking about a wife. Or a mother – A woman!'

Michael recoiled from the lewd eyelid. All over the place men were winking privately. A conspiracy of nods, a nodding-club. He wasn't a member.

In the late Sunday lounge Henry looked the full family-man. Early fifties, plump face, thin reddish hair, comfortably stout, tweed suit, signet ring, good gold watch. Out of place among the suburban lower-paid and the unemployed, their cheap suits and washed-out wives. The vulgar tie lying on his chest struck a wrong note – not a cancellation though – even if it was vulgar it was also silk. It contradicted the expression of the suit, shirt and shoes, and illuminated the meaty features from below with a sensuous, self-indulgent look.

Michael stared at the older man. It was true that he needed . . . something. Somebody. At least Henry was no longer trying to sell him the rubber woman secondhand. Still, like everyone else in the lounge, Michael felt his blood moan with a relentless dissatisfaction. At the next table two young wives with faces so nakedly bare that the bones might break through the skin took matching gulps of vodka to appease their blood. They grimaced, patted their hollow chests, screwed up their eyes and reached for smouldering cigarettes. Armed, they turned on their round-skulled, moustached men and blew smoke at them like quenched fire-dancers.

Michael switched stricken eyes back to Henry. Too late to do anything, duck into the toilets, dash for the door. Two . . . two ladies came heaving through the haze, squeezing between stand-up drinkers, bending around the seated, approaching with organised intent, and Henry waved a welcome while the other hand reeled in a lounge-boy. The tie came excitedly alive, fat lips smacked, he winked with every fold in his flesh.

'Stuck beside the "Ladies" Henry, knew where to look, didn't I? This is my friend, Bernie. She's from Belfast.' The voice lowed happily above Michael's head, and her heavy hand caressed the dandruff-trap of his collar. He turned slowly to the women, his vision congested as always by a sense of his own appearance. At a distance, to a passing glance, Michael had the gallant, dashing look – sculptured features, manly chin, modelled hair – of an upmarket tailor's dummy.

So oddly cleancut was the image that the passing glance returned – and found the flaky skin, chewed lips and twitching eyes. Close up, his hair had a homemade appearance, as if each black fibre had been glued on individually with random spaces in between. It was, he knew, the kind of head found in drapery displays alongside kneelength woollen underwear.

The large, doughy woman, metallic blonde, mouth and eyes wide open, tilted him back for inspection. His dry lips stuck to his smiling teeth; he was afraid the strain would split the skin and fill his smile with blood. She smiled with ridiculous, unwarranted warmth.

'Sit down here, Eileen girl, what'll you have?' Henry had her by the plump cardigan somewhere along the upper arm, hauling her generous rump across his body to sit beside him. 'No, no – I'll get this one – ' Michael was desperate to justify his presence. He'd got the last one too.

'Right, right, O.K. Let Bernie in there near you. What'll you have, Bernie? Michael's buying. You're in good company now. Michael, this is the famous Eileen I'm always telling you about –

' – Jim! Hey, Jim! Two large vodka-and-whites, another bottle of stout is it Michael? – give him a large bottle, Jim, he's going to need it – and I'll have a pint and a large Jameson – and hey, Hey Jim! Twenty Major – '

Michael peered at the blind date hunched on a stool beside him and his eyelids locked with fright. Six inches taller than himself and broad in the shoulders. A hank of black hair hung down either side of her head hiding her face except for the inner halves of two cold eyes, a bony nose, and a pout of lipstick smeared around a thin mouth. There was a sinister swipe at romance in the lipstick and the hair – danger dressed for a dance.

All around him Michael saw bone-brained, bullet-headed men sucking pints and loosening up their partners. Later on the earth would move – from sheer weight of numbers, if nothing else. He took a stuttering sip of stout. It tasted like nettle-soup. Guinness and smoke were as elemental to this crowd as water and air. Eileen sat opposite, her middle-aged skin so plumply pink it looked inflated. There was so much of her he couldn't take it all in. Henry could. His busy hands palpated the fluffy cardigan and tight slacks, checking she was all there. When he found nothing missing he concentrated on one large knee, massaging it as fondly as if it were his own. Vegetarian by nature, Michael shrank.

'Hiya, Bernie,' he hiccupped.

'Hi.' The corner of her eye glittered at him, a glass splinter. He recoiled. Eileen sensed stalemate and leaned across.

'Where are you from, Michael?'

'Sligo.' He tried to make it witty, 'Where are you from yourself?'

'Wait'll I see now, who do I know in Sligo? D'you know your man Willy at all?'

'Willy?' His heart sank. 'Willy who, Eileen?'

'Will-he-or-won't-he, Bernie! Willy Yeats, who d'you think?' Laughter rattled inside her padded frame.

Henry nodded in pleasure at the mention of poetry –

'I will arse and gonad, go to Innishfree .... '

'Or Ben – ', she broke in, 'd'you know Ben, Michael? Ben – what's his name?'

Michael knew they always had you in the end, answer or not –

'Ben Bulben, that's it! D'you know him? He's a friend of Willy's?'

She took pity on his embarrassment. 'I'm from Roscommon myself' by way of apology.

Michael considered 'Even the crows carry lunches when they cross Roscommon.' Too dangerous.

'Bernie's worse,' Eileen went on, 'May God in his mercy look down on Belfast .... '

Bernie ignored her. 'What d'you work at?', she attacked Michael.

'I'm – an accountant.' No one ever asked further. Accountancy killed questions.

'. . . and this yoke here,' Eileen knuckled Henry in a bicep, 'no one knows where he's from. The original man from nowhere. What's the big secret, Henry?'

'Oh-ho, now that'd be telling!'

Strange that Eileen didn't know either. Country people knew everything about each other, and revelled in it. Michael had nothing on Henry, just spots of local colour – the flushed pursuit of large women, and ties like panting tongues. There was probably nothing to him behind the shallow mystery he cultivated as an identity.

'What do you do yourself?' Michael tried Bernie again.

'Unemployed.' An accusation.

'What did you do before – '

'Knitting.'

'What – what kind?'

'Balaclavas. Paramilitary balaclavas.' The syllables rattled like hailstones on tin.

'Did you – did you sell them?'

'Bags of them.'

'Over the counter?'

'Fella called to the door. Friday nights.'

'A terrorist.' My God, what was he like?' It was the longest conversation he'd ever had with a woman.

'I wouldn't know. He wore a balaclava.'

'One of yours?'

'Damart'

'Don't believe a word out of her,' Eileen advised, 'she told the Labour she used to knit Tricolours. There was no demand for them with the Flags and Emblems Act.' She tossed her head in scorn. Bernie's veiled eyes glittered. Henry winked, juicy lips smacking, 'Drink up! We'll go after this one.'

Rows of bleak houses, neither a city nor a suburb, a maze of concrete streets pushed blindly into the country, amber lamplight thickening the dark. Michael paid for the taxi.

'Enjoy the party, girls!' The driver's snigger was full of innuendo.

Henry danced Eileen across the waste-ground, tripping on her heels, shrieking. Bernie slunk along behind, and Michael carried the drink. Elation and depression wracked him.

He was being fixed up tonight for services rendered – and for greater dues to be exacted.

The account began in a dancehall, and built up debt over two years. Michael had been hiding in the "Gents" the first night. Henry crouched bow-legged in front of a bit of mirror, combing water into his foxy hair.

'Some talent here tonight, boy. Must be the moon brings them out. I'm after scoring big, and it's feck-all use to me. The one bloody night I'm skint. Be a sin to waste it, all the work I put into warmin' her up.

Come here. I'll point her out and you take over. You'll score, no problem, don't worry about that. She's dyin' for it – the right man is all it wants, and the taxi-fare to lift her. Look over there, man, look – the big one in pink, says her name is Maisie – ' he leered happily at that, 'what more could you want? Go on over and get stuck in. Jesus! – ' he shook his head with noble regret, 'the one night I can't afford it! Come on anyway, I'll introduce you. Any name'll do; don't give your right one. Say I had to go in a hurry, the mother's dying or something. Don't say I was broke, money turns them on . . . . '

Michael shrank in hideous terror. 'No! No! I couldn't – don't – ' The sight of the warmed-up woman in pink clung him to the floor.

'Why not, man? You can't let a good thing go. You'd be doing her a favour. I've been sweetening her for hours. Can't help it, it's in the blood. I had to tear myself away, said I had to make a phone-call.'

The yearning patter was hypnotic, a tubby lecher with a red, razor-polished face. Out on the floor the woman wheeled in shortsighted, bewildered circles. '. . . the one night I can't afford it! You'll have to take her off my hands, or one of those gobshites'll be in . . .' nodding contemptuously at the rows of upstanding countrymen, most of whom held important, muscular jobs in the building-trade.

'You can't let it go! Maisie – ' He marvelled again, 'she's all yours. I saw you here before; you must have an eye for the talent.'

'Listen,' Michael was desperate, 'Listen! I'm here every Friday, but I have to go now. I'll lend you a tenner – you can give it back next week.'

Henry tore at the strap of his watch – 'Here, take this to cover the loan. It's worth a hundred any day – ' The strap was stubborn –

'Not at all, not at all, I'll trust you. You can do me a favour some time.'

Not next Friday, but the one after, Henry re-appeared. He said nothing about the tenner, but he told Michael in carnivorous and gynaecological detail about the encounter with Maisie, whose name had changed to Dolores in the meantime.

Somehow they were partners in the success, and the relationship prospered, Henry taking the active role, the sleeping partner – while Michael invested nervously.

Tonight – A small, ugly house, half pebble-dash, half brick, the middle unit in a row of five. Two of its neighbours defied the night with lighted windows. Henry's house was not only dark, but the upstairs windows were curtainless black squares.

The key wouldn't fit. Henry peered, 'Bastards! Swine! Stuffed with matches again!' He seized a brick from the garden, smashed it through the glass, reached in and kicked the door open. Silence deepened in the neighbouring houses.

A torch clicked, lit a bare hall and naked stairs.

'Is it a p-power-failure?' Michael whispered.

Bernie laughed, the first sign of appreciation all evening. 'Didn't pay his bill. I wouldn't either for a dump like this.'

Henry fussed with bogus hospitality, octopus-arms bundling them into the front room. A jagged draught whistled through the broken pane. Eileen knew her way around. She cracked a match at the mantelpiece, and a hissing gas-lamp threw her squat shadow on the wall.

Henry pressed Michael and Bernie together, 'Don't mind the state of the place, I'm doing it up slowly.' Eileen bustled proudly, busy as a housewife with unexpected guests. The room was freezing; one threadbare rug on bare boards; the curtains were old sheets, dubious stains exposed. But the squalid room was entirely dominated by a brand new suite of furniture, a sofa and two armchairs, bulging proportions upholstered in plum plush with a frilly, white trim at the seams.

'Put a match to that, Eileen!' Chopped-up scaffold planks stood by the hearth, and the grate was full of newspapers and splinters. 'Make yourselves at home now,' Henry pressed drink on his guests and caressed the rump of an armchair.

'What d'you think, Michael? Nice? Bought it last week at the front door. Hundred quid, cash on the nail. Gave him seventy-five and a promise.' He pushed the back of the armchair and it sprang into a stiff, nasty-looking bed. 'The sofa makes a double. You could sleep half a dozen here!'

'They wouldn't get much kip with you,' Eileen grumbled.

'Not bad, is it?' Henry smirked round the room, 'rent-free with the job.'

'What job?'

Henry tried superiority on Bernie; 'Protection of the vacant family-home, a vital community interest in this age of vandalism.'

'Security! You're keeping squatters out. Squatters has a right to live too, you know – '

'Not in this house they don't!'

Bernie's glance scorched his possessions, 'I don't suppose they'd want to.'

Eileen's grip stiffened on a bottle. With her straw hair and fighting stance she could be standing guard on a hooped tent and smoky fire.

Michael made peace. 'It's a great place, Henry. How long are you in this one? You've done a lot of work on it.'

The redness faded from Henry's glare. 'A few months. They're getting it hard to give them away now.'

'A fine house like this,' Michael ploughed on, 'You'd think they'd be queuing for it – '

'They don't know what's good for them. They want palaces with free transport and shops giving food away. Do *you* know – ' hands on her hips Eileen was proud of her social conscience, 'there's scores of good men like Henry minding the best of houses all round the place, and the Corporation can't *give* them away! And who's paying for it all? The taxpayer – '

'When did they start taxin' what you do?' Bernie kept one eye on the bottle, reaching for a weapon herself. For the sake of the furniture Henry disarmed them. 'Cut that out. We're here for a bit of fun. Who knows what'll happen yet – ' He took a juicy swig on a bottle. Michael, copying, got the lip-suction wrong, and sour liquid dribbled down his chin.

'I must be three months here, anyway – I'm up to H in the phone-book, page 300,' Henry worked it out, 'that's two pages a day is a hundred and fifty days, thirty days in a month give-or-take – God! that's five months – '

'You've a phone here?' Michael was impressed.

Eileen laughed, 'He uses the phone-book for toilet-paper. He reads it too. It puts him in the mind for his puzzles and quizzes.'

'How's the writing, Henry?'

Bogus self-deprecation, 'Not bad. I'm trying to break into radio. Words and riddles and that. I'll try a few on you while I have you here. You're an educated man.'

'Fair enough; might as well be useful.' Michael swayed on a choppy sea of drunkenness, unnerving lurches in his brain. Ideas tugged at their mooring, chunks of identity crumbled away.

'Poor Henry,' Eileen sighed, as he lumbered upstairs, 'he takes this stuff terrible serious.'

Henry sat opposite his audience, opened a copybook. He shot his cuffs, fondled his tie, grinned nervously at Michael.

'Good evening, listeners – ' The burning plank spat derisively.

'Good evening, Listeners! What are words but the raw material of communication, the threads we weave to clothe ideas? 'Curses, poems, weather-forecasts, jokes and prayers are all composed of words.'

Michael's brain and eyes glazed, but Eileen beamed approval, mouthing the mealy phrases. 'Words are the currency of the intellect, minted by philosophy and science, polished by poetry, spent by the common man.

'But let us, listeners, consider tonight, not the weighty works of Shakespeare or the Bible, but the lighter side of language in a new panel-game called – 'Word Play!!'

The dismal razzmatazz of his voice faded, leaving flecks of spittle on the velvet couch. Eileen clapped, brisk staccato in the silence.

A yawn bulged in Michael's throat. He clenched his teeth and glared fiercely at Henry until the yawn was about to burst a hole in the back of his neck. His jaws sprang open, a rush of gas brayed out. Tears squeezed down his cheeks. It was shocking – as if he had shouted at the Consecration. Henry crumpled. 'You don't like it . . . .'

'Of COURSE I like it, Henry! I *love* it. The c-currency of the intellect! I *love* it. Go on, go on!'

'Well – ' Henry hesitated in case there was more praise, 'I start 'em off with riddles. This one's a Shakespeare-play.' The special voice again, 'This fellow wouldn't open up to strangers; this fell-ow wood-ent – '

'Hamlet!' Eileen clamoured, 'is it Hamlet, Henry? Or Macbeth? King Lear? It's not Henry the Fourth anyway, nothing backward about Henry – ' He turned on her with the full contempt of the male intellectual, 'It's Shylock, you daft eejit. Shy-lock!'

'He's not a play! You said a play. Didn't he Michael?'

'Not a play!? not a PLAY?!? Isn't he the bloody Merchant of Venice, you daft – '

Insult reddened her, 'I'll get you, you bastard! Makin' a fool of myself for the likes of you!'

'Eileen has a p-point there, you know, Henry. You did say a play – '

'It's a trick-question,' Henry dismissed them irritably, 'we're not giving prizes away for nothing. Now the next round is a new idea. I'm still working on it. I say a sentence that ends in "he said" or "she said,' and you have to fill in the adverb that suits the sentence. For ten marks. And you lose ten marks if you don't get it,' he threatened, 'so you can keep your trap shut, Eileen, you wouldn't know an adverb if it kicked you up the arse.'

' "I'm in a hurry," he said – '

'Quickly?'

'Good man, Michael, you're on the ball. "I'm in a hurry" he said quickly. "I could eat a horse" he said – '

'Hungrily? – Greedily?'

'No. Hoarsely! "I could eat a horse." he said hoarsely. Tricky one that.'

' "I'm trying to lose weight," ' Eileen interrupted.

'Are you?' Henry answered absently, 'don't bother.'

' "I'm trying to lose *weight* !" ' she insisted obstinately.

'Michael faced her unsteadily. 'Thinly?' She shook her head.

'Stoutly? "I'm trying to lose weight," she said stoutly?'

'No. I'm trying to lose it and I can't.'

'Oh, I see. Infatuatedly?'

' "I'm trying to lose weight!" she said indefatigably!' Eileen said emphatically.

'Undo - What!?' Henry was staggered.

'In-de-fat-igABLE! Not able to lose it! D'you not get it? Eejit!'

'Here's one for you, Eileen – ' Michael glowed with excited alcohol. 'This is his wife to Henry the Eighth. That's a clue. "Your majesty is overweight," she said –

Will I tell you, will I tell you, you'll never guess? It's "unthinkingly." ... Cost her her head!'

'Why didn't you give me a chance? I nearly had it!'

'Here!' Henry broke in belligerently, 'whose programme is this anyway?'

'I have one! I have one!' Michael bounced on the couch, 'just one more. Please!' he begged. His head swirled with giddy intelligence, a cluster of bottles stood by his shoe.

'It's this late-night radio programme, see, and the D.J. reads a complaint from a young listener – "Dear D.J., why do you always play my favourite record after midnight?" he said – ' Wild-eyed he leered at Henry, Eileen and Bernie in swaying succession, then exploded 'Disconsolately!'

Henry stamped upstairs, in a huff. The stippled ceiling shook. 'You trumped him,' Eileen explained. 'He'll be himself in a few minutes.'

'Always makin' excuses,' Bernie sneered. 'You think he'll marry you for it. He'd better – no one else will!'

'Who asked you, you tramp?' Eileen's ear was cocked to the room above.

'P-pardon,' Michael hiccupped, 'are you two supposed to be friends?'

Eileen considered the question wearily, slumped in the chair, even older than he'd thought. 'We work together. We live together . . . . Protection, not friendship.

'Eileen doesn't have a pimp. She's too proud. Hoping someone'll make her an honest woman before it's too late.'

'That's my choice. You haven't one because they won't touch you!'

'There was a woman burned to death by a pimp not long ago – ' Bernie smiled a threat.

'Lord have mercy on us!' Eileen crossed herself.

The room whirled. Michael blanked out all sense and tilted towards sleep. A piercing squeal – 'Ha! Look at her. The tramp! Snuggling up. She has her eye on you . . . . '

He felt the coarse hair whip off his shoulder, and for a split second Bernie's red fingernails lingered inside his jacket pocket.

Her breath hissed against Eileen's vindictive squeals.

Cheap music accompanied Henry's descending tread.

"Two worlds apart;
I was the Joker,
You were Queen of Hearts."

He danced into the room, cheap tape-recorder cradled against his chest. 'Ladies and Gents! Take your partners Please, the next dance Please. An Old Time Waltz!'

He snapped the tape on and a pedal-guitar intro slurped through the crackle and hiss. Taped from a radio.

"The-e / stars / we-ere bright / la-ast night / in Galway,
When you wrapped me in your charms;
Tonight the bulb in your front hallway
Lights a new lover to your arms."

Henry drew Eileen upright. The two bodies flexed together like intimate muscles.

'On your feet, boy!' Michael tried to stand to order – an obedient reflex, rising for the Gospel, the National Anthem. His coat strangled his knees. A fierce lunge, he forgot to straighten his back and found himself pointing headfirst at the fire. His thoughts were still sitting down. A lurch, and they passed him by, his brain grabbing clumsily at Bernie's body, while he skated on rolling bottles.

The wig – how did he know that? – swung across her face, the sour lips . . . and a searing scar down the jawline, laced up with livid stitch-marks. It was covered instantly. He *had* to see it, verify. It was the sharpest truth in the world. It reduced everything to scar-tissue around it. He grabbed.

She slapped him. Darkness flooded his eyes. He slumped on something solid, head between his knees.

The chorus swung round again;

"Last night the stars shone . . . HEY-GET OFF – "

The room roared, chairs toppled, thudding feet, shouts – a Shot!

No one moved. Stock-still all four stared in white-faced shock. The psychotic music jingled on, ready to lash out again.

Henry bellowed with sudden laughter. 'I heard the little bastards at the door when I was taping it. The mike was against the radio. It picked up everything.

'Listen – ' He wound the tape back,

" . . . stars shone – HEY GET OFF

When you wrapped me in your – BANG!"

'Bangers in the letter-box! The little bastards!'

Michael moaned. Explanation meant nothing. Judgement had blared from the pulpit of his conscience.

'He's throwin' his guts up,' Bernie complained, 'can't hold his drink.'

'Off the sofa. Quick!'

Dumped on a stool, a bucket rattled at his ankles, head pumped up and down between his knees. His stomach erupted. Hot, harsh liquid spattered his hands and knees, splashed into the bucket. On and on. Knuckles on the back of his neck. He opened sticky eyes, stared into a coal-scuttle. Awed nausea at the quantity. 'Let me – let me up.' Trying not to taste his mouth. His eyelids were gummed together, acid running in his nose. Without taking her eyes off him Eileen opened her shiny handbag, held out tissues.

'Don't worry about it,' Henry reassured, 'a bad bottle. You're like a bilge-pump. Best ever I saw.'

'Bad bottle!' Bernie sniffed, 'no guts, more like!'

'No, I – ' Michael retched, 'I – ' disgusted with himself, 'I'm allergic to drink – '

'What!?!' Henry was shocked to the core. 'God, that's a good one. Allergic to DRINK!'

'Yes. I am!' Suffering gave him the right to anger. 'I've damn good reason for it. My mother – '

'Sssh' His mother – ' Eileen rebuked the laughter.

'My mother, Lord have mercy on her, drank like a . . . like a f - f - f - ' he couldn't afford the fluent rhythm of profanity, ' – Fish.' Their eyes slid away. Mothers were embarrassing – except to Bernie, who raised her bottle truculently to the dead woman.

'You don't *understand!* – ' Michael strained for sympathy, 'That's what has me this way – ' The enormity of pre-natal fate swamped him in tears. He gestured fiercely at himself, rejecting the bloodshot eyes, white face, limp hair, and the gangling body. He saw it with disgusted clarity and wanted to be rid of it. It wasn't his *fault*!

'Before I was even *born* I was p-pickled in alcohol. That's a fifty-fifty chance of deformity before you start. How's that for odds?'

'Get a grip, man!' Henry pleaded.

He would not be stopped. He had a searing vision of himself as victim. 'That's right, 50-50. Half the little hoors come out defective. Russian Roulette before you're born. Genital damage, unitary ... urinary damage, brain-damage; it's all on offer. And no choice!

'I didn't know anything about this for years,' he wailed, 'no idea at all. I knew there was something wrong somewhere, but not me and her, not us. She was supposed to protect me. That was how I saw it. We were alone, see, the pair of us, no f-f-f-f father. He was – gone away. Dead, disappeared – I didn't know.

'I thought the smell off her breath was perfume, the way mothers are meant to smell.'

'For Christ's sake,' Henry hissed, 'knock it off – '

Michael was oblivious. He was telling it to Eileen. She was locked moon-eyed into his story.

'She died when I was eight. The house was coming down around us, fists at the door all the time for rent and foodbills and all she'd pay for was bottles of medicine. I used to shout at them, "Go away! Me mammy is sick with you banging on the door every day." I'd threaten them with a cap-gun.

'I was her hero, she said, she'd take me with her when she went. I didn't know where we were going. I got hungrier every day – I couldn't wait for us to go wherever it was ....' His voice rose to a cracked wail. 'It wasn't her dying that crippled me – it was leaving me BEHIND.

'I wasn't at the funeral – I didn't know. I kept waiting, in my uncle's house, for her to come back and get me. I never even unpacked the little bag. I used to lie awake at night waiting, listening to the house creak with footsteps.

'One night the curtains moved in a draught and I ran to her screeching with joy. I broke the window with my skull.

'I held the curtains in my arms, like I used to dance with her empty dress, and the blood ran down my face – I thought I was crying blood. There was a smell of mildew and mothballs off the curtains. I knew everything in that moment. Everything was wrong – cold wind and rain outside, lies and broken promises, empty days and nights. Nobody comes back.

'I went to school in town, and the other kids caught on to me straightaway. I used to pee sideways, and I had to go about twenty times a day; except when it got blocked and I couldn't go at all. I'd turn blue in the face and swell up. They'd be poking me with pencils and rulers – '

He glared accusation at the bucket. 'I realised she hadn't l-loved me at all, she'd *ruined* me! I got the same smell off a few other people, I saw the bottles and I knew what it was – dirt and desertion.

'There I was, an orphan, running to the toilet every hour, and pissing round corners! And it was all *her fault!*

'Someone said she drove my father to an early grave worrying about her – and then I knew it was Him I missed all the time, and not her at all.'

Eileen stared open-mouthed, and he felt a powerful surge of elation. Getting his own back –

'Give us a break – ' Henry begged again, 'this is meant to be a party ....'

'And h-how would *you* like to be born deformed?' Michael's indignation was fierce and simple. Eileen switched to Henry for his answer.

'So what did you do?' he groaned, 'It's not like that still, is it? I mean – you're a grown man now, aren't you? Well, Aren't you ... dammit?!'

'I had an operation. But it still twists when it's cold – very painful, I assure you.' Michael was overcome with dignity.

Eileen leaned over. 'Show us it.'

'Show you – '

'The bend in it. I never saw a bend in one before, did you Bernie? Is it like this?' She cocked up a fat thumb and wiggled it experimentally at the knuckle.

'Go on!' Henry had a glint in his eye, 'show us! I dare you!' Maybe there was a party in this yet –

Michael's lower lip trembled. 'Jesus, cryin' now!' Bernie sneered.

'At least you had a feckin' mother,' Henry argued. 'I never had one at all!' He saw the weakness in this, ' – not that I ever knew anyway.'

Mouth and eyes full of quivering pity, Eileen swivelled, great arms branching towards him. 'Hush,' she soothed, 'hush, don't cry, don't cry. Sure, you have me .... Did she die when you were born, acushla, was that it? Musha, you poor divil, come *here* to me, alannah!'

Henry shoved her off. 'I don't know – and I couldn't care less!' He took a furious, compulsive breath and, to his own amazement, plunged in after Michael.

'I was like a lot of other poor fellas, dumped in a church doorway, or handed over to the nuns by some misfortunate skivvy washing pots in a convent – '

He struggled to get a grip on himself. 'They have it easy now,' he raged, 'Any young one gets in trouble can skip off to London, not a word said.' Henry hád put a few on the boat himself. 'I was put out for adoption. No one took me. I was always a bit sickly as a child – you wouldn't think it now – and we used to get terrible sores from feeding calves. The nuns had to go behind the priest's back and bring in the seventh son of a seventh son to cure it. They were catching it themselves. I'd say it was the food did me in too.

'You can't beat mother's milk for nourishment. Very scarce in a convent.

'Anyway, in the heel of the reel they had to get shut of me, and – ' he knew he'd gone too far to withdraw, ' – and I ended up in an Industrial School at the age of seven .... '

Eileen jerked under an invisible slap, 'Letterfrack?' A petrified whisper.

'LetterFRACK! Henry cracked it like a whip. He seemed satisfied in a grim way, as if confession had relieved him physically.

Eileen went soggy with woe. 'Jesus, Mary, and Joseph! I'm back to that. You're lying to me! Tell me you're lying –

'The first boy I was ever friendly with, I'll never forget him, we used to play Tig in the yard, he got sent to Letterfrack for stealing. He was only an innocent little divil that meant no harm, ten years old and never mentioned again. As if he was dead! Like one of the lost souls, God help us! Purgatory, Limbo, and Letterfrack.'

'You never TOLD me,' she screeched at Henry, 'I thought – '

'She thought you had a rich family,' Bernie cackled. 'The black sheep, waiting to inherit!'

'Why would I tell you? It's hardly good news, is it? Look at you now! I don't even like to think of it myself. I never looked back until I passed through the place last summer on a mystery-bus tour. God knows what possessed me to go on that. Where could it lead only back to the past, or into the future? Letterfrack or Tallaght.

'My stomach was sick all the way out the road from Galway. I could taste the kip in the back of my throat. All it took was the rain on the bog to set it off again. I felt the rest of my life was a short holiday, and I was going back. I couldn't think of a single worthwhile thing I'd done in the whole forty years to save me. A few women – and where were they? I was on my own.' Henry's tone veered further into self-pity, 'Ah – I should have had children – ' and then into self-righteousness ' – by

God, they wouldn't have ended up in any bloody Borstal!
'When I got there I didn't even recognise the place. Full of Germans
and Americans buying jumpers and bits of Connemara marble. I had to
look for a roadsign to prove I was home. Never even saw the bloody
barracks, if it's still there. I stayed on the bus when everyone else got off.
Ten minutes was all it meant to them, a quick piss, but I gave ten years
there. Ten years!

'I had a pint afterwards in Clifden to settle my guts – all I could think
of was burnt porridge and mortal sin. Everyone else in the pub was
American. Like a different century. If I tried to tell them what it used to
be like they'd think I was raving mad. The young ones anyway. Some of
the older crowd might remember, no matter where they came from; all
the more reason why they wouldn't want to hear a word about it.'

'You should have told me!' Eileen warned bleakly, drawing herself
up. Her eyes were bitter holes in the pink make-up.

'Aye, you should have told her! You should have said you had
nothing instead of tellin' LIES. Yon wee woman wants respect and
security, and what have you got?' Bernie surveyed the room again,
added it up – 'Nothin'! Eileen thought you were coming into money
when the will is settled. I heard you as good as say it! Doesn't look like it
now, does it Eileen – unless they're payin' compensation for a hard
childhood; we'd all get a few bob then – '

'Shut your mouth,' Eileen snarled, 'I take a man at face-value, not
like you, you tramp, you're only interested in the size of his wallet – '

'Nowwwwww – ' soothed Henry.

'It's true!' Eileen turned to him tearfully, 'don't mind her lies. I never
gave a damn where you come from or what you have. As God's my
judge, all that talk of orphans put the heart across me. Ye're like two
children come back to haunt me –

'I had two myself, two boys – I should have told you that. I would
have told you . . . . Sure, we all had them then, we were young and
innocent, we didn't know any better. There was no contraception, and
the fellas wouldn't use it anyway; that'd be a sin. The babies went off for
adoption, the way calves are sold, and that was an end of it. After the
second I had the operation – ' She paused in fright, clutched her heavy
breasts ' – but I can feel them here still, both of them, I swear. That
feeling never leaves me! You're alright with me, Henry – I understand.'
She gave him a solemn squeeze, and thrust out her jaw, to let the world
know she had the moral victory.

Staring at her, Michael shuddered with hallucination. He saw her loose face gazing into sad, fly-speckled vacancy as she breast-fed Henry, his hairy body dressed in an old, cloth nappy and a rusty pin. They lay heaped together on an institutional bed, among rows and rows of babies in untended cots. Henry had a mother now ....

'I – want – a – child!'

'Jesus-wept' – Bernie leapt away from Michael. He pounded his fist at the palm of his hand, and missed.

'I Want A Child!' he bellowed again.

Eileen shook her head, sad jowls swinging. 'Don't look at me, son. I can't help you. Sure I had the Operation .... '

Michael threw a tantrum, drummed his heels on the floor, hammered his knees, 'I don't WANT any bloody Help! I want to have it MYSELF – '

Bernie hit him, hard and vicious, again and again, 'You – dirty – Pig!' Sober with pain, he fended her off.

'Wait a minute – ' Henry was thunderstruck, ' – what did he just say . . . ?'

'I – want – to – have – a – bloody baby!' Michael mouthed each word deliberately, Myself! I – want – to – give – birth! Reproduce myself. Make a better job of it this time.'

'H-how!?'

'That's no problem. The technology is all there – organ transplant, insemination .... '

Eileen bit her lip thoughtfully, 'It'd have to be a Caesarean,' she warned.

'But – but WHY?' Henry sounded as if Michael had proposed crucifixion.

'It's the only way to get total control, eliminate the gamble. Look at me and you, Henry – and thousands like us – abandoned, dumped, unwanted. But I know exactly what I want. The only cure for me is to reproduce myself. I know what I needed when I was someone else's baby, and I'm the only one who can guarantee to deliver that. If there's a mother involved as well, she'll hijack the child, or else abandon it. One or the other. And besides – ' he asked Henry bitterly, ' – where would I find a mother anyway? I couldn't even keep my own when I had one! Look at HER!' he pointed at Bernie with his wounded arm, 'Look at her! – beating me up after a few hours' acquaintance, what chance would I have against a mother? My own child's mother?' He thumped his stomach in a passionate *mea culpa* –

'When I have my own baby, I'll correct all the mistakes. Love, and

Truth, Protection, Security – I'll give him everything he needs before he even knows he needs it ... because I *know* what he needs!'

'Suppose it's a girl?' Eileen asked shrewdly.

'D'you think if they can organise my baby in the first place they can't fix something as simple as his sex?'

Henry blanched, 'How are you going to manage the – the plumbing and all that? You – you won't need the usual service, will you?' His party was really going haywire now.

'Not at all. I'll handle that end of it myself. A few eggs is all that's required for fertilisation, and the surgeons can supply that. They have their sources. No offence meant, going to a stranger,' he assured the ladies courteously, 'I'm sure you'll understand the need for anonymity – to avoid maternal claims in the future.' They stared at him goggle-eyed, and nodded slowly.

'The Church won't like this, you know,' Henry stroked his upper lip after a long silence.

'Not at first – but wait till they see the benefits! There's a lot in it for the Church. Self-perpetuation. Propagation of the priesthood without recourse to Eve – except for the ovum of course, and they'll get around that in time.' Michael jumped to his feet and strode around the room. His coat hung askew and his trousers were badly stained. He had the air of a major prophet.

'Listen – this is Messianic! It's the nearest you can get to Virgin-birth. The Church has a problem recruiting priests – this is the solution. Breed them from the stock they already have! Like royalty – a controlled line of succession, only twice as controlled in this case. No women: maybe the consecrated flesh might be hostile to the ovum at first, but they could get around that. Nuns might be acceptable ....'

Eileen sat in deep thought.

'If it works,' she told Bernie sadly, 'there won't *be* any nuns. There won't be any real women either. This is the breakthrough the bastards were looking for. They'll put enough eggs in the fridge to breed the whole future of mankind, and then we'll be redundant – for breeding anyway. I'm gone already.

'Maybe they'll still want the other thing ... or maybe they'll look after that themselves too. Worms are that way, aren't they? Then they'll do away with women altogether. Some tribes are at it since the world began, killing off babies to save on dowries. I'd say there was a lot of that down our way too – '

'It's a man's world, and no mistake,' Henry sighed complacently,

Bernie was on her high-heeled feet, crouching over him, viciously angular. She tore back her hair, thrust her face at him, crucifix at a vampire. He grunted in disgust, tried to look away.

'So you'd drive us out of business, would you? Leave us good for nothin' only layin' eggs, is that the way? See this – ' Slicing the full length of her cheek, eyelid to jawline, the scar was a stitched-up snarl. She stabbed it with a crimson fingernail; it spoke to Henry.

'That's a souvenir of a man like you. A fat slob with a purple face and hairs in his nose and ears. He used to stand behind me in the back desk and put his hands on my shoulders. I thought that was nice – I wasn't much to look at. I went round to his house for a grind in Irish – *Tiocfaidh ár lá!*, all that shite – and I put my arms round his neck, an innocent wee girl lookin' for romance. He took one look at me – 'Jesus, I couldn't face that' he said. 'Turn round, I'll have it the other way!' There was a breadknife on the table ... I stuck him with it. He did this to me then with the same knife, trying to cut my throat. His blood caused an infection and made it worse. They took half my face off – ' She rapped the scar and it rang cheap plastic, like a doll's face – 'He died of a heart-attack later, and I've no regrets. I done five years for that bastard, and I'll do it again.

'I have clients who like me like this. They want to be punished. I've plenty of practise at punishment – '

The crimson nails reached for Henry's throat '– so don't give me any shit about a man's world .... '

Eileen fell on her, screaming – 'Keep your murdering hands off him' Spitting and scratching, they rolled onto the floor. Henry, unsure of his strategy, alternated between kicking Bernie hard in the ribs, and pulling them apart. They were inseparable.

Michael backed towards the door.

'Well, goodnight all,' he whispered uncertainly, 'goodnight now. And – thanks, Henry. Thanks for the party. See you around!'

'Hold on!' Henry hissed. One last kick, and he tiptoed away from the struggle, 'Hold on, Michael, I'll come with you – '

CLIFF HANGER

Every warm Sunday crowds visit the car-park at Glendalough for the brooding scenery and monastic ruins. Tourists stroll the paths in leafy sunlight, separated from the landscape like an audience at a film. There is a sense of composed history and geology about the place. Imaginary monks and saints queue up at the ice-cream vans and Portaloos.

But the blind eye of the Upper Lake records time accurately – with the truth of a mirror. Time is in the still background, the mute skyline. Life flits across the glass, like an insect, without impinging on the deep reflection.

Not everybody stays within umbilical reach of the car-park. A mile beyond the lake, high above the narrow floor of the valley, there is a line of steep, grey cliffs. The granite glistens when the mica-flecks unite to reflect the sun. Every crack, every slab, every corner up there on the remote skyline has a name and grade, a detailed topography of holds. On any warm weekend climbers can be seen strung out below the rocky horizon like gaudy scraps of bunting.

One deep, blue Sunday a college club milled about at the foot of those cliffs, all sweating faces, strident mouths, parched throats from the gruelling slog up the boulder-scree.

There was a mess of ropes and climbing gear to be divided out among the novices. An air of hilarious incompetence prevailed, perplexed persons stepping into harnesses like bondage-straps, posing nervous questions about bowline knots and figure-eights, while a few of the expert – self-appointed – went about supervising the preparations, and especially paying intimate attention to the tying of girls' knots.

Mick Dowling had a special technique which involved brushing his knuckles across the victim's thighs and then in a low curve over the abdomen as he tied the rope.

Dowling certainly looked the part – burly, broad-shouldered, with a square-cut, rugged face, and an affectation of headbands and tight tracksuits. But if you took power-weight ratio into account he was considerably more meat than muscle, and would never make a dexterous climber. And if you knew a little about crags and mountains, it was obvious his experience didn't add up to much either; but shy, first-year students didn't know the Index from the Eiger and were wildly impressed when he showed snowy slides or waved to them from a rock-climb in Dalkey Quarry.

The only other third-year climber in the club was Vincent Barry, a silent youth with an inward air. He kept his distance from the club and its bantering intimacies.

Vincent was beginning to climb solo in the Quarry that year, lurching doggedly from one hold to the next on the impersonal granite that questioned nothing but his nerve. He was obsessed with the suspense and surprise of solo-climbing, the excitement of placing his body in an apparently implausible position and extracting it safely upwards, with what he hoped was polished skill. But there was very little elegance in his diffident persistence, slouching silently on long legs in baggy clothing. He was often pointed out to new members with a kind of derisory pride as the club's Odd Man Out, the exception that emphasised their happy unity.

What Vincent needed was a determined climbing-partner, someone to challenge him, the kind of relationship where he would fight his way up a hard climb, knowing that if he didn't do it his partner would.

There were several of those teams around and Vincent envied their confidence and commitment. They did new routes, free-climbed old aid-moves, chattered in pubs about handjams and overhangs, miming moves in the air with an extravagant semaphore.

Ideally he should have climbed with Mick Dowling for their mutual improvement, but their natures were antagonistic. Vincent had no interest in Mick's extrovert style which involved nonchalant repeats of climbs he already knew well, where the leader's protection was as good as a safety-net.

Today at Glendalough Vincent was preparing to take a couple of beginners up Quartz Gully, a fine climb of middling difficulty. They were strong and fit, and he saw no reason why they shouldn't be capable of the grade. He distrusted the tradition that kept beginners on easy climbs until they developed an awed resistance to difficulty. His nerves bristled when Mick approached with a superficial air of brotherly concern.

'What route are you bringing the lads up, Vinny? Have they done the easy slab yet?'

'I don't know whether they have or not. We're doing Quartz Gully.' Vincent's answer was sharp. He knew Mick was the sort who felt his own expert status was threatened by beginners who showed a lot of promise.

'Are you sure that's wise? Do you reckon they're up to Quartz?'

'They'll be fine,' Vincent snapped. His judgement was being undermined in front of the group. Mick shrugged easily and turned back to his own charge, capture-of-the-season, Janette Stirling, a striking, fair-haired girl who looked about seventeen until her cool voice and sharp, mature eyes cut deep into the observer's giddy pretension. She was twenty-two years old, had worked in Manchester for four years before coming back to College.

On a few evening meets in Dalkey Quarry with the club Janette showed a smooth command of technical rock, although she had no inclination to lead.

'I climbed a lot when I lived in Manchester,' she told her admirers in dismissal of her ability. 'We ... I ... used to go to the Peak District every weekend,' she added. Her listeners recognised romance behind that 'we' chopped off with a quick frown.

Vincent had been very excited by her self-contained poise as she followed his lead up the intimidating headwall of In Absentia but he could only nod and smile tightly in response to her thanks at the top. Then, as Mick appeared effusively on the path behind them, he turned away to coil the rope.

Mick had stood on the ground below while Vincent led the climb. He shouted up instructions to Janette about the moves and the holds, managing to demonstrate his familiarity with the route without having to risk leading it in front of her. Vincent raged silently as they walked back down the steps into the Quarry, Janette smiling affectionately at Mick who was sketching lavish moves in the air.

'I'll take you up a few good climbs in Glendalough ....' Mick's gloating voice had churned up through the intimate dusk.

Eventually all the novices at the crag were teamed up with leaders. Some had already gobbled all their supplies, condemning themselves recklessly to a day of drought. The majority were doing the short routes at the base of the buttress, a popular group exercise with scope for ribaldry.

It looked as if no one was ever going to ask, so Mick announced to a sudden hush that he was taking Janette up ... Prelude and Nightmare! He put a kind of ghoulish emphasis on Nightmare. Even those who had never heard of the famous climb winding its protracted line up the full height of the main face were struck with the dizzy romance of it.

Vincent thought grimly that this would be at least Mick's seventy-seventh ascent of the route; he should be able to climb it blindfolded, and it was all big holds anyway; for all its impressive steepness the climbing was mostly straightforward, and even the hardest section at the start of the Nightmare pitch was over-graded. There was a lot of nonsense talked about Nightmare, Vincent thought, but it started on a big, flat ledge, even if it was two hundred feet above the ground. And that steep crack somehow gave people a sense of peril. But modern protection was so good that the furthest you could fall at that point was about six feet. Fair enough, it was a different story in the old days, but people were still cultivating myths and legends just to invest the bit of ultra-safe rockclimbing they did with an aura of adventure.

He could imagine how Mick would milk the occasion for all it was worth, casually stamping his own image on the vertical landscape – '. . . that's Spillikin over there, the overhanging ridge. It's the hardest climb in Wicklow' – contriving the impression that he'd be off climbing routes like Spillikin himself if he wasn't nobly engaged in conducting Janette up routes he could climb with boxing-gloves on.

Vincent was seething with frustration as he eased his charges up their climb with a discreetly tight rope. He desperately wanted to try Sarcophagus, one of the great classics of the crag, unmatched for quality anywhere in the country they said, even on the cliffs of Fair Head. The line looked fierce. Boldly direct up the main face, and then into a clean, pure corner flaunting its architecture like an angle in a church-steeple. From below it seemed to lean in blind rejection of human aspiration, and yet there was a thin crack in the back of that corner, handholds and footholds on the walls, and there would even be traces of black rubber where hundreds of feet had tiptoed towards what Vincent thought must surely be immortality.

He would have to ask Mick to climb it with him. No one else could. Mick hadn't done Sarcophagus either, but he wasn't likely to try it today. He wouldn't risk failing before an audience.

A breathless choking in his throat muffled the hope that Janette might offer to follow him instead.

After a couple of hours he descended to the festive base. Anyone who had a lunch was enjoying it under the envious supervision of those who hadn't. Mick and Janette were the centre of attention. Vincent couldn't understand how anyone with a voice so measured, so self-contained, could allow herself to be the focus of that circus.

'I reckon we've set up a record for the club, Vinny,' Mick greeted him with grinning satisfaction. 'Prelude and Nightmare in forty-seven minutes flat. We were really moving, man!'

'Great stuff,' Vincent responded absently. 'Listen Mick . . .' he dropped earnestly on one knee beside the lolling figure. 'What about Sarcophagus? Since you're going so well . . . let's give it a lash after lunch?'

He paused urgently, but his face – unused to expression – looked wooden.

'Sorry Vincent. I'm going up with Janette to do Aisling.'

'I suppose you're going to time that as well,' Vincent jerked to his feet in disappointed fury.

'Well, now Vinny,' Mick was indulgent, 'you have to admit three-quarters of an hour isn't bad for Prelude and Nightmare. I can't see you doing better.'

He was teasing; it amused him to wind Vincent up.

'I'll halve it!' snarled Vincent blindly.

'That'll be some trick!' Mick laughed, sitting up. 'How will you manage that?'

'Don't be silly . . . .' Janette's scornful voice rang through the babble of exclamations as Vincent hurled away, stumbling ignominiously on the steep ground.

He rushed along the heathery base of the crag, sick with fury and fear as the challenge swelled from a defiant stab to a nauseous enormity churning in his stomach. His head tipped back and he stared up the wall reeling above him.

Where did it go – did he even know where it went? His eyes raked the blurring crag without recognition. Yells and running steps behind him, Mick's mates to the fore, the rest of them trailing.

His fevered vision raced down the boulder-field to the cool, enamelled lake and the distant track by the shore vanishing into the woods, away from this sickening mistake. He jerked his attention back to the brutal crag, and the track still hung in his eye with the diminishing dot of his own figure running along the edge of the lake.

Where was the start . . . ?

A ramp, wasn't it? He had climbed it two years before, on the safe end of a rope. The ramp, balancy, awkward, leading to a hard scrabbling pull up a steep slab. People sometimes hurtled twenty feet from those moves back down to the sloping ground . . . and off to hospital, his mind exaggerated absurdly.

He was standing under it now, the rock utterly inorganic, shining with slick heat. Looking up he saw ledges gashing the face from side to side, promising occasional sanctuary. But the baked, bulging rock between them . . . .

The anxious spectators – a lynch mob – he thought, were almost on his heels, but he felt entirely alone. Through the panting and irrelevant babble of voices he heard the hostile thud of his own heart. Each beat had the crisp overtone of a shell under stress, a kind of brittle tick.

There was a bird piercing the air with a shrill needle of song, another scraping its beak feverishly against a glass sky; and all around them, enclosing the voices, heartbeat, bird-sound, there was the waiting calm of a windy place on a still day.

His hands floated limply towards the rock, rubber fists in a nightmare fight. Before pulling into the first move he swiped in panic at the sole of each foot to dry off any grass-sap or cuckoo-spit that might subvert friction.

He hauled up on flaky holds, his fingers digging painfully into the rock, until his body was level with the tilted ramp. As he edged an agonized toe out onto its polished surface, his body tense, teeth clenched, fingers pinching the rock, he heard the first brazen shout.

'Ten seconds!' the voices yelled in clamorous unison.

The first beat of the blood-chant it seemed to him. His body stalled in mid-move. Heat rushed to his face and hands. Sweat beaded. Light flared on the rock, there was a buzzing in his brain. Bluebottles swarming on the Lord of the Flies.

Paralysed by the impression, he couldn't move, a skinny body hanging on awkward rock glaring its fear.

'Fifteen seconds, sixteen seconds, seventeen seconds . . . .'

Mick's loud voice penetrated his paranoia, an anxious entreaty.

'Come down out of that, Vinny, and don't be acting the eejit!'

He was moving again, traversing the diagonal ramp, toes shuffling on its outer edge, fingers clinging to the crease where it met the face, then a side-pull higher and he lurched out left onto a long foothold. He lay trembling against the short, steep wall that separated him from the ledges above. Stretching up to his full height he fumbled at the flat handholds, his fingers and forearms straining to lift the body that was making no more effort than a corpse to assist in its own elevation.

The thought of lifting his feet off the severe foothold and running his toes on friction up the exposed rock was unbearable. With his stomach curved in against he wall he strained helplessly, his fingers futile. Space gnawed at his ankles, and he shot a glance down at the narrow foothold for reassurance.

'One minute!' the chant brazened.

He had to lean out from the rock to get his feet up, but as his body arched the strain increased on his fingers. His toes kicked on to the gritty, holdless rock. On sweating finger-tips he pulled viciously, shuffling his feet up, shifting his weight on to implausible friction, and flung one hand high to a better hold, greasy skin welding itself to the coarse granite.

Heaving his body higher – while his imagination failed and hurtled horribly down the rock – he was pressing down now on the hand-holds in a mantelshelf move, right leg coming up inch by inch and scraping onto a foothold.

There was an audible release of tension below, a concerted sigh of relief which reached Vincent's strained perception as a menacing hiss.

'Two minutes thirty seconds,' piped a lone voice, callous with innocence.

The first hard moves were over and Vincent felt utterly drained. If he found that so hard, what chance had he higher up, on Nightmare? He was drained of tension as well. He knew he was safe: he was going to give up.

If he could have traversed off at that point he would, but the logical escape was a little higher, just before the start of Nightmare. He could scramble aside and descend a gully then.

Mechanically he ascended easy ledges towards the next problem. He was being funnelled upwards into a steep, inverted V in the cliff. He stood fifty feet above the ground, enclosed like a small statue in a rocky niche. His white shirt shone in the pocket of shadow. There was a piton in a mossy crack, the old-fashioned protection for the next move out left. He imagined the slender, nylon rope around his waist, clipped securely into that piton, and paid out from behind by a firmly anchored second.

He recalled a steep, blind move here, pivoting on a poor foothold with a hidden grip to swing around the edge of the niche. But there were handholds like gloves to reach after the first move. Get it over with! A moment of delicate balance, a fingery pull, and he had the good hold, fingers curled over the lip and then slotted as far as the knuckles.

A wall of clean rock hung steeply above him with a sense of friability where it had been scuffed bare of vegetation. It was split by a good, rough crack. Strenuous to start; he fixed his eye on a high handhold and launched himself vertically upwards, heart thudding, as the grudging holds multiplied.

A chorus of diminished voices announced the four-minute mark. They knew he would descend the gully.

He thought of athletes skimming over flat ground, a four-minute mile, five thousand two hundred and eighty feet. In four minutes he had dragged himself one hundred and fifty feet upwards, on his fingertips, to a narrow ledge with a gigantic flake of granite rearing behind it.

The absurdity of the comparison squeezed an hysterical giggle out of him. Four minutes and he was near the top of Prelude already. He could make the halfway mark in six or seven. At that rate he could finish the double-route in a quarter of an hour and make a total mockery of Mick. Why, a good climber – and he had no illusions about himself on that score - could probably solo Prelude and Nightmare in just a few minutes!

His brain swam as mental arithmetic took over from fear. Again he looked out and saw the sandy track by the lake-shore vanishing into the cool seclusion of the trees. This time he saw himself, not running away, but triumphant on the path. Victory bubbled in him. Another ten minutes could make him a hero. Not much of a hero, he understood. There were plenty of people who soloed incredibly hard climbs, and they didn't necessarily amount to much either. But heroism was all about who you needed to impress.

He didn't hear the five-minute call, if it was uttered at all, for he was working up the groove behind the huge flake. He reached the top of Prelude and its intersection with the escape route.

A pair of traditional stalwarts making their way up the gully stared in alarm at the pale spectre emerging from the top of Prelude, eyes set with belligerent intensity, face and hair slick with sweat.

'What's all the shouting about?' they demanded, with the nervousness of men who suspect that every crisis is bound to involve them. Wordlessly the apparition in baggy trousers and soaking shirt, shook its head and disappeared out rightwards to Nightmare Ledge.

Depending on a climber's confidence this flat platform in the middle of the steep wall is a small or a large ledge, combining an insecure or a safe stance with a fine or a frightening sense of exposure. Resolutely Vincent faced the crucial crack. His legs tightened and trembled as the short, fierce-looking problem reared over his ledge like a cleaver above a chopping-block. He realised in panic that he was viewing it like a novice.

An old piton protruded from the bottom of the crack and he grabbed it for security while he steadied his swimming vision. It seemed to twitch like a rusty nail and he jerked his hand away with a yelp of fear.

He forced himself to concentrate on the sequence of footholds at the side of the crack. He had seconded it once before and been carefully briefed. There was a hidden hold over the top, he recalled, but was it right or left ... or was that some other climb?

He dimly remembered a tense scrabble on the end of the rope before a small handhold swung him out onto a grappling traverse. He looked in horror down the plunging cliff to the boulder-field below. Experience dissolved in his brain, and rock became an insuperable barrier again. But there *were* holds, he berated himself frantically. Holds! He had climbed much harder rock than this with ease. On a rope! He tried to imagine it around his waist, reassuringly taut in case of need.

He saw himself instead, soft and wingless, trying to fly. His muscles slumped, helplessly.

A voice jeered from the horizontal past. 'Twelve minutes.' They were expecting him to slink sheepishly out of the gully.

Just another three minutes ... he prayed in a pleading whisper. Three more minutes ....

He clenched the side of the crack in a fierce grip, trembled his foot up onto a flat hold. It was still reversible.

Sweating fingertips grabbed a good edge inches higher. He stepped up again. Still reversible.

His body hung out from the crack, suspended from flimsy forearms. Fear locked his fingers like vise-grips on the holds. He tried to step down, dared not dislodge fingers or feet.

Irreversible!

The roaring air sucked at his spider-life. Teeth grated in his head, eyes screwed in agony as if the bone itself were clenching shut. Ankles shuttled and rattled. It was up ... or off!

He kicked a toe higher in the groove, wrenched on his arms, flung his fingers over the top of the crack ... a curved edge, rounded, smooth, slipping .... He clung, his body an unbearable sack of lead, lurched his feet up again. Hidden friction lifted ounces off his arms.

Unlocking numbness, his fingers fled out of sight, scurrying desperately for the hidden hold. No feeling, but something hooked, held, hung. Hanging, he thrashed his right foot out and levered his weight in agonized jerks. And the angle burst back, burst like the door of a car-crash slow-motion seconds before the fuel explodes. Threw him out onto the traverse.

He leaned in a groove above, gulping with dizzy nausea.

About to faint he fumbled for a handhold to anchor his body as waves of blackness ebbed and flowed. He was convulsed with the savagery of the struggle. Foul images seethed within him, over and over, his body hurtling out from the rock, wheeling and tumbling loose-limbed in the air, trailing a long, curling scarf of a scream. The bloody climax among the boulders repeated with the insistence of a jammed projector.

Behind the persuasive lie, seducing him slowly into a swoon, he felt the liquid throb of his blood-system. His body was a single pulse, a soft bag of blood jellying its way up the jagged granite.

He swayed out from the stance, pulled himself back in again, pressing his chest against the cold, grey rock, nausea loosening his stomach and knotting his throat.

A tiny, bantering voice grew in his imagination: Do you want a rope Vinny rope Vinny rope . . . .

Mean little playground tune.

He was mesmerised by the brutal texture of the mica-crusted rock sharpening and blurring in front of his eyes as his body swayed to the cyclic rhythm of the images falling and re-falling in his mind. Minutes passed precariously as he balanced on the patient granite. Every harsh breath was a victory for survival.

He underwent a bitter, little death of the heart, and a slow unsteady regeneration.

Heroism, he learned, wasn't worth the fuss.

His legs were splayed apart across the groove, stiff and wooden as stilts. Every quiver threatened to topple him. He moved up slowly, hating the cruel, inorganic rock.

Long afterwards, he descended to base. There was no one there.

He collected his gear and went down through the boulders towards the track without a backward glance.

Mick was bellowing instructions to Janette from Aisling Arête. From the top of the crag they saw him diminish on the lakeside path to an incidental dot.

Vincent vanished from the club. He denied himself any curiosity about climbing, and never heard that he had started a crazy trend of time-trials.

A week later a well-known climber soloed Prelude and Nightmare in four minutes.

THE FOX

Michael Hayes threw himself full length on the ground as the mist broke away from the hillside. He forced his body tight against the heather. He bunched one fist under a gaunt cheekbone to prop his head. The other hand clenched a short machine gun, supporting it above the mire.

His thin face, ginger hair and beard were daubed with clay. Dirt smeared his clothing. His body was part of the landscape, a smudge on the wintry hillside. His head moved, eyes raking the limits of vision where the mist was thinning his cover. Grey rock, stunted furze, heather, and the peat-black gash of a stream. A clump of reeds trembled against the sky. No sign of life. He was lying in a hollow and the rim blocked his view down the valley.

There were hundreds of soldiers in the hills, helicopters coming and going through six days and nights. They must have caught the others; they wouldn't last a day in this muck. Three guards shot dead after a car-chase. Seán smashed into a bridge in Glenmalure. Lugnaquilla sealed off with rings of guns. They knew they had Michael Hayes surrounded.

He lowered his face onto his hand and closed his eyes. Verses in his head.

'Reynard, sly Reynard lay low through the night.
They swore they would watch him until the daylight.
Next morning so early the hills did resound,
To the hooves of the horses and the cry of the hounds.'
A shudder ran through his body, wet denim plastered bitterly to his skin. After six days and nights the cold no longer reached his brain, senses disciplined to numbness. As long as it didn't freeze, or snow.

Waiting for the mist to lower again and let him continue crawling down the valley towards a road, houses, food. Not that he could surface within fifty miles of here. Every house baited like a trap, guns trained, dogs loose, but he must sustain the promise of heat and food within reach in order to go on surviving.

Swearing into the earth, concentrating his will, he demanded mist, darkness. It seeped across his mind behind the closed eyelids. His head nodded heavily, then jerked awake again with an electric jolt at the base of the skull. Fatal to doze. Images of the Bog-People, leather bodies dug up out of black turf, preserved over hundreds of years. To sleep now and resurrect in a glorious century, intact! Would the gun survive, or emerge as a rotten shadow beside him? He clenched the fierce muzzle for reassurance.

Michael Hayes bared his pointed teeth in a snarl of contempt. There were no resurrections, no second chances. A few miles away Art O'Neill died on a frozen hillside four hundred years before, stuck to the ground with frost; and all the years of imprisonment, the escape, the winter-flight through the Wicklow hills were a waste of history. Red Hugh survived that ordeal with frostbitten feet, and then threw the future away forever at Kinsale and Valladollid. Survival was the first law, and success the other one. Two hundred years ago, on the far side of this hill, Michael Dwyer stumbled out of a besieged cottage straight into the muskets of the soldiers to draw their fire, and let his companions escape. A hero or a fool? A corpse anyway.

'I am a bold undaunted fox
That always could outrun the dogs,
I made my home among the rocks,
Between the mountains and the bogs.'

He stiffened. Something on the hillside above. Movement flickering beyond the arc of vision. His finger slotted into the trigger-guard, his head swivelled an inch. Two big hares came bounding across the hillside a hundred feet away. He could almost feel the powerful hindlegs kicking the earth like heartbeats. But there was something wrong, a downhill grace, angularity . . . . They were deer! a pair of deer, and at least a thousand feet away. He could distinguish a faint web of antlers swaying above a small, fine head. The illusion frightened and warned him. If he could see antlers at that distance then he was far from invisible himself. Why were the deer running? Someone on the ridge? He drew in his head and lay motionless.

High above, binoculars were trained on Hayes. He lay crucified on the trembling cross-hairs of a rifle-sight. The soldiers shivered with the waiting tension. At first they had thought Hayes was dead. Then the glasses picked up the slow, evil swivelling of the head that had brushed by them in the mist on the rim of the Barravore Valley. They watched the weapon as if it had a will of its own dragging the body along behind it.

A scuffle of running feet, and the terror of responsibility lifted. A colonel and a special mission squad came running low from the blind side of the hill. He threw himself flat on the ground, crawled forward to the rocks. He studied the body five hundred feet below for a motionless minute, and then wriggled back to the radio.

'. . . Target static. Location 053 934 . . . . Forestry within reach.'

It was obvious that, short of a bullet in the head, Michael Hayes would reach the trees if he was flushed out of the hollow. If he got in there with a sub-machine gun men might die digging him out. If they flung a helicopter onto him now he would shoot it out to the death. And Hayes had to be taken alive. To stand trial. Those were absolute orders. A political imperative.

The radio drew a silent army into a closed circle around Barravore. A pair of ravens circled the valley, croaking raucously, refusing to settle.

The mist had melted away. A wash of pale sunlight seeped through the clouds and stained a distant hillside. Hayes lay among the reedy tufts of grass and heather, head moving an inch at a time. The gun was malignantly alive.

'I am a bold undaunted fox that ever yet outran the dogs . . . .'
Michael Hayes was not his name. He took it from a song and gave up his own. One of the hunting-ballads where the fox was a hero on the run leading the hounds of the law a wild chase all over the country.

'Connemara being remote, they thought 'twas there
I might resort;
As they were growing weary they thought they'd try Mayo.
In Swinford Town as I sat down I heard the dreadful
cry of hounds . . . .
. . . But still their search was all in vain for Farmer
Michael Hayes.'

Rotting on a hillside like a sheep carcase. Starvation had flushed him into the open this morning. Six days and nights in a sloping hole under a rock, lying twisted round a boulder, water flowing under his body and dripping down on him from the roof nine inches overhead. No use trying to escape at night, blundering into rivers, around in circles, until he hit a checkpoint or a tripwire. He moved out at dawn under cover of a thick mist, enough visibility to see ten or twenty feet ahead. Keep moving downhill, keep losing height. Follow a stream down and out. The mist betrayed him on the open hillside.

Blind hunger threatened to stampede him. They were waiting for him below, soup-kitchens steaming at the mouths of the valleys, wafting the aroma up into the hills. The army was poised to scrape him off a soup-wagon like a needle off a magnet. Rambling again; delirious. He opened his eyes and stared into the straggling vegetation inches away. Short, thin reeds, most of them snapped off at a yellow point, whether sheared by the wind or cropped by sheep. Clumps of withered grass, the roots almost washed out of the clay. As he stared at the grass his head moved slowly towards it driven by the blind volition of his belly.

Green-streaked mouths of famished corpses. Famine-victims eating grass. Textbook inspiration of hatred. They died spitting bile at their tormentors. He saw his victims lined up in a shadowy jury, red-streaked mouths open in the dark. And the three guards mowed down against the stone wall, dark bodies on the pale road, blood on the green grass. He knew there was no mercy in him. He nourished this savage freedom, knowing there was a world of his own kind.

He stared at the earth again. Green, spongy moss. The sharp tang of sorrel convulsed his memory. And the hint of honey in the clover tip. All the leaves and flowers the children nibbled. They had trained him in every aspect of guerilla war, self-defence, ideology, propaganda, but no one ever thought of a bit of Botany. The moss was mushy, dense, vividly green. He pulled a soft tuft and it glinted wetly at him. He was reminded, with the force of a blow to the stomach, of lime-filling in a chocolate sweet. The image was too rich for his wretched gut.

The chocolates he brought first time he called. So many of his gestures were second-rate. His emotions had needed a different world. He couldn't accept that it might be more appropriate to change the feelings than the world.

She opened the box greedily and picked the soft ones, Turkish Delight, Strawberry, Lime. His stomach churned with revulsion against the self-indulgent probing of the bitten fingernail, and then the tight teeth, nibbling at the lumps of sugar. Giggling, she held out half a sweet to him, the sick green of the filling shining slickly at him. He shook his head – he preferred the hard ones. Margaret remarked that men always preferred the hard ones.

She had black, curly hair and white skin; she wore tweed and thick-knit wool. She was ideologically right. But in his fantasies he harboured a quick-limbed dancer in skin-tight silk.

The chocolates were melting in his brain and convulsions racked his stomach. A hunger-strike would be paradise to this wet, hunted extinction. He thought how she would have cried dutifully, an inherited affliction, as he starved with the dignity of a patriotic saint, in newspaper headlines, breathing away his life for the dream of a new nation.

But even then he had known there would be no new world. The truths were money, religion, and blood.

Live, survive at all costs. The triumph of the body. Thinking of Margaret, her inherited belief in sacrifice, his teeth recoiled in a bitter grimace from the pale flesh and the chain of bones stretching back through generations of dutiful suffering. There was nothing in that past but oblivion and decay. Michael Hayes was going to live.

He gripped the gun with ferocious fingers, dirty, bloodless talons. A law unto itself, its own physics and morality. So hard that the fingers could have been wreaths of mist.

He remembered the kick of the machine, its contemptuous power like electricity, lightning, death, the external forces that flogged the world. The three men hurled backwards against the wall, limbs flung, heads loose, jaws dislocated, as if a whip had caught the puppet-strings.

The colonel watched over the body, without blinking. There were a hundred men in the valley already, and Hayes was still the only one visible. Fifty men had closed in from Cannow Mountain and the Table Track to the east. They were spread across the head of the valley. A troop was descending from the north through a deep gully at the end of the Barravore cliffs. Dozens more were filing up from below, concealed behind the dense streak of forestry that ran down into Glenmalure.

The ravens were giving it away. The colonel longed to raise a rifle at the noisy, black rags and nail them to a silent sky.

Hayes listened to the squawking radar overhead. The day was bright as interrogation now. He tensed his nerves in a steely mesh to keep him pinned to the ground. Perhaps it was he who was keeping the ravens up? Circling above his body like vultures. He twisted his neck to glance up and winced with disgust at the pellets of sheep-shit beside his cheek. If he could catch a sheep ... could he eat raw meat, warm and bleeding? He retched at the thought and his mind swam.

He pressed his wrist to his mouth and sucked hard, gnawing at the skin with chalk-dry teeth. A taste of turf, bogwater, his lips felt like cracked rubber.

You couldn't catch a sheep if you needed one. They were smart when it came to being stupid. Those stories of heroes surviving on fruit, berries, and wild meat – no man could live here without provisions.

Jack London told the truth, trying to kill the dog in the snow to warm his hands in its guts and save his own life. The dog kept his distance. The footballers eating each other in the snow. Catholic rugby-players. Plenty of meat on them. Communion and the Indivisible Body of Christ? It was dog eat dog up there, leave it at that.

Some of them got out alive.

Where was he going when he got out of here? None of the old reliables would hide him now. A dead policeman was like an anchor.

The dreamers would drive him out. No doubt there was a contract on him already. They would have to catch him first, and if he got out of this hole he could survive anything.

He wasn't trusted any more, they called him a "mercenary" because he staged a few jobs of his own. They'd come to that soon enough. Everybody came to it in his own way when the visions were threadbare. A man was supposed to retire quietly at that point and let another wave charge headfirst into history.

Maybe it was time to go home, take over the farm and settle down. Quit rambling the hills in all weathers . . . .

He knew a cleft in the ground in Sligo, a deep crevice in a rocky hill beyond Ben Bulben. Wiry mountain grass grew over the edges hiding the narrow slit from view. Sixty feet deep in the middle, and you could jump across the top of it. There was safety in the bottom of that. A little roof of poles and twigs covered with grass deep down, and lie under it as long as he liked. Forever.

Beside the mossy mound of old bones.

A day, five years ago, the sun blazing promises of a new world across the hillside, larks screaming revolution in the sky, Michael Hayes came hurtling down the mountain on a training exercise, blood pounding in his ears, pistons hammering in his chest, fitness flailing the spring air. Straight into a huddle of sheep behind a wall. They scattered in terror.

His own body seemed to hurtle through the air with the power of devastation, boots flinging mighty leaps off the springing turf soaring over rocks, bushes, and tumbling walls. He marked down a panic-stricken sheep fleeing wildly ahead of him, its lamb cast off in a frenzy of fear, and he pounded in pursuit. Bleating wildly the fat sheep hurtled ahead of him, zig-zagging across the slope. Twenty yards in front it seemed to miss a step, skidded frantically and plunged out of sight.

He dug his heels into the turf, lurched sideways and threw his weight back against his flight. The skid rattled his knees cruelly, his legs shot from under him, and he landed heavily on his shoulder and hip, every bone shuddering with the impact. He rolled over and over down the slope digging his fingers into the earth until the thin bones bent backwards and threatened to snap at the knuckles.

He came to a halt on the lip of the chasm, headfirst, staring into the rocky depths. The sheep lay tumbled in a heap of wool at the bottom, stirring slightly. He pushed himself dizzily to his feet and looked back up the steep slope. Far above, the lamb was coming, at a run.

The colonel tightened the circle again, pulled his men in closer. He suspected Hayes might be dying of exposure. He would prefer to carry out a bullet-ridden killer than an emaciated corpse cured by suffering.

There was a waiting arc of steel three hundred yards behind Hayes and pincer-jaws tightening from the front. He was at his most dangerous now. A trapped animal, nothing to lose.

That tent of skin and hair, lying in the muck on a frame of bones, with the space-age weapon beside it, was the shape of violence.

Death, when it came, would be a storm of destruction.

Michael Hayes felt invisible eyes drilling into his back.

The bubble of air trapped in the valley was tight with tension. He was pinned below a snow-slope – a ski twisted under him – the creaking mountainside about to avalanche. Huge cracks and crevices ripped across the tilted ice. He tried to roll, but he was frozen into the snow.

Lying in a river-bed below a dam, a concrete cliff holding a deluge back; the dam breaking up, slabs of concrete flung out into the air, whale-spouts of water in the sky; the river rising.

Move! He must move.

He understood at last why he was lying motionless on the side of the hill. Nothing to do with mist or camouflage. It was weakness, paralysis. He couldn't move.

He gathered the slack threads of his will, knotted them into a whip, and flogged himself up on his elbows. A blade of icy air sliced between his body and the ground. He had warmed up the patch where he lay, and the wind was plundering the warmth. He tottered dizzily to his feet, cradling the gun. Heavy as a jack-hammer.

The horizon reeled around him. He stumbled forward to the rim of the hollow ... and saw the trees.

The Fraughan Rock Glen! He cursed his blindness and his luck. A hundred yards further in the mist, and he would have been out now. The strength of rage flowed into his muscles. He began to run.

'KEEP HIM OUT OF THE TREES.'

Armed men poured from behind the forestry, rushed along the edge.

He was a dark blur of movement streaking along the ground.

One of the racing soldiers waved his rifle like a huge stick, shouting hysterically.

Hayes was going to get there first. The undergrowth of briars, and furze was fifty yards away. The soldiers twice as far. The machine-gun was flying over the rough ground as if the body it bore was weightless.

A soldier dropped to his knee, whipped the rifle to his shoulder, aimed between Hayes and the trees. The screaming shot stretched a line through space tight as barbed wire.

Hayes stammered his answer. Bodies jerked, and buckled to the ground. The manic rattle hammered against his ribs. He couldn't hold it straight.

The soldiers hurled themselves into the grass. A random streak of bullets raked the air.

There was a man still running, brandishing his rifle against the sky, screaming crazily. His mouth was wide open, his feet rose and fell in frantic strides. He was running away from terror in the very worst direction. He did not know how to stop.

The galloping boots and gaping mouth stampeded towards the gun, waded into the final trickle.

The scream died, the body toppled without a whisper.

The stuttering bullets stalled.

Tattered rags of silence hung across the glen, ripped by rows of jagged holes. From behind every single hole, from the dark side of that silence, a thin scream of violence poured into the still world.

Hayes lurched towards the forest and vanished among the trees.

The baying of the hounds was a howl for blood.

The valley shook as the flying horses thundered low over the ground, flailing the air. They landed in a huge circle around the wood, and the hills resounded to the amplified halloo of the huntsmen.

He slunk through the undergrowth, dragging his belly low against the earth, jaws open, trailing a dribble of white spit. He burrowed into a dense thicket, thorns ripping his skin. Turned within and listened. A frenzied yapping and snarling. The undergrowth burning with teeth and eyes.

A fresh clamour, howling and baying in front. He veered off to the left, but the trees thinned out.

He sloped back in, ears drawn tight against his skull, tail brushing the ground. He ran once round a small circle, and then stopped dead, facing his baying pursuers. He raised his snout in the air, and emitted a high-pitched howl of desecration. It cut through the trees and hung sharp and clear in the air above the hunt.

Trailing his scream, the fox ran straight towards the hounds.

STONE BOAT

The cliffs of Moher stand across the bay. At sea-level there is a legendary door. The woman and her lover arrive by boat. The key is in a fish's mouth caught without a hook. She sails the boat away, and the priest enters the rock. His footsteps die away in the caverns within.

The climbers brought excitement. There are always tourists on the island, but these were different. A new breed of bird, they came to colonise the cliffs.

I had known climbers in Dublin before I was sent over here. I tried it myself when I was younger, but I hadn't the head for heights. I was prised loose and lowered off. A pity. It seemed an ideal sport; intense enough to flare away the libido. I took to water instead, a solitary ocean-going swimmer. The salt and the cold cured desire.

On those urban days when storms arose I prowled the house and dreamed of sin, red rose on a white blouse. It drew me in. The east was harvest country. Fall was inevitable, blossom to the blade. Then the stony road to an island parish. What have they done to deserve us? Our clay-foot tramp on their Atlantic rock.

My work here is not consuming. People are superstitious, but they are also healthy and independent. I exercise a presence. My purpose is to swim the island completely round. A limestone pier dips in the tide below the village, a rusting ladder on either side. Down one, twenty miles around, up the other. It is my fate, my obsession.

I've done sections on summer days, cleaving the water on a running tide to fetch up exhausted at the White Strand, An Trá Bán. The currents and tides seem insuperable, and there is a long stretch under the western cliffs where the sea swells on the calmest day. There is no escape there for five miles.

From dreaming headlands I search the water, ebb and flow, rip-current and tide-race, seeking their equation. I may have to tread water at Poll na Scadán, Carraig Líath, Aill an Ghliomaigh, until the water runs my way. I want no cover, but sometimes a currach will follow without seeming; drifting near me on the trail of pots. Under peaked caps silent faces watch. I weave through the static on the trawler-radios; *'Seachain, tá'n sagairtín ar mhuir ....'*

The sea is my fate. It is another life. I must make the best of it. I choose it as I believe Saint Brendan chose, not a means to an end, but an element to launch the soul. Though I will never make an island of a fish's back and light a fire around its blowhole I am my own navigator. If it happens I will go down with my body. A doctor said I fall into the tide like a shot seal, that I have a death-wish and it springs from guilt. He may be shrewd, but he has no power. We alone have a cure – *Ego te absolvo* – but it is a poor illusion. It takes two to forgive.

Truth is arbitrary as a floating bottle, smashed in cliches on the shore. Hidden in sand it gutted me. Bloodied fragments flashed a truth: to still the flesh I need a sword, a symbol slashed across the spirit. I cut a drowned cross in the sand under the wave's edge with blood-rimmed glass. This is not psychosis. It is the heart making meaning instead of love. I was too close to the sea. It was all-pervasive, like war, pounding the beaches of my mind. I wallowed precariously, up to the chin in sway and temptation. I should not have been condemned to an island. But a desert, a forest, a mountain, a city, would have been the same.

Scorching a Latin breviary I walked along the beaches where the land dipped underwater with the weight of my presence. I was a sailor afloat on a table, racked with thirst. When I leaned towards the edge, it tipped me off among the sharks. On windy days, broadbacked in rusty black, I gusted along the shore, seagulls screaming overhead, as if something freshly killed was to be dumped.

When the climbers came the island lifted a little out of the sea. The first pair stayed a week, made miracles, and left. Like pilgrims they hardly spoke. I never heard their names. They climbed a lonely prow that sweeps up from the sea to prop the headland high into the sky. I swam that section for the first time then. Did they see a bull-seal lolling in the summer swell, a white collar under his grievous chin? I watched them, tiny figures on the overhanging rib, feet braced, tearing at the island with their arms. They would pull this pillar from under the rim, bring the island crashing down to pin me under, swallow me, as if I had fished that key too soon and entered the dreadful door. Abandon hope all ye who enter here. Watching, I revelled in wonder: could I climb out of the sea? Out of the grave? Out of hell? Like a jellyfish dreaming of hands, a current swept me three miles down the coast.

After the eagles the small birds came. And the scavengers. From novelty to nuisance overnight. They didn't see themselves like that. Even the bare-arsed illiterates among them felt superior to the culture of the island. It was hardly conscious; a condition of the colonial-nostalgia that rears them. All they saw were the very old and the very young. Everyone in between has abandoned the island, the country too. I do baptisms and funerals, no weddings.

They were a nine-day wonder themselves. Later, they were the circus that hasn't left. The glitter wore off and exposed the tawdry tricks. We learned how the ropes, the drills, and the bolts worked. We saw them fall off and swing, cursing, in a safety-net of preparation. There was not much magic. Tom Pháidín Tom, ninety-one, who had spent hazardous hours hanging on hemp gathering eggs across the vertical night-wastes of those cliffs attacked me as a raucous bunch passed his hovel,

'Bhíodar ag stracadh as Aill na n-Éan inniu gan meas acu ar ubh ná éan. Ní dhéanfaidís caoga blíain o shin é.'

There were courteous exceptions, awed as much by human tradition as by geology. Ropes on their shoulders they surveyed the island like a ruined cathedral. But without the language they cannot see the walls and roofs, the pillars and luminous windows of a past that towers above the present. All they see are the pink and yellow bungalows, the plastic blight feeding on ruined stone. But the old structure is still there, shapes of light and air, arches hanging in psychic space, built of word and memory on an island-plinth, spearing the sky with the Michaelian M.

After six years I am still tracing its blind shapes in the minds of old men, feeling for foundations in their everyday lives. I hear the high line of a rampart hidden in a verse, a gargoyle grinning in a sneer. I catch a fading glimpse of marble in an inward eye. It's an illusion. This is not their vision, this Italianate pomp I was born with and cannot shake off. I am not a pagan no matter how hard I aspire. Except at sea. Swimming the western shore under the cliffs I look up between walls of water and know the island and everything on it, heaped up against the end of the world, is the last great altar to the setting sun. We know nothing yet. We live still, the entire world, in the prehistory of ignorance.

One autumn day without a future I walked the remote headlands towards Dún Beag. Weeks of violent weather had blown the climbers off the island. They had never come this far anyway. In the half-circle of the ruined fort high above the sea I planted my feet in windswept grass and leaned into the gale. Nothing lived in that storm, not even a gull. I smelled the salt of sorrow. It preserves this dead flesh. Slowly my arms lifted in submission to the west. They rose until the hands touched above. In big, black boots I rocked on the very edge of the continent. Sea-water rocked within me, tilting the balance.

I felt a quiet presence behind, tugging my attention. Paper was offered, like the page a child will press upon you in a city street; 'Dear friend, Johnny is deaf and dumb ....'

The wind tore at the paper. The message was indecipherable, the language – even the letters – unknown. Exasperated, I turned it upside down, drivel, then over. From behind, the trace was clear; I knew those bulging, bellied letters. Copied from some tablet, some ancient gravestone. All the distortions of age and weather had been rendered as part of the text. I didn't understand it. It was older than the language I spoke. Turning, I recognised the short, fat climber . . . .

. . . short and fat, Johnny-Jump-Up, five foot five and thirteen stone. Bow legs, broad arse, no shoulders, neckless. Don't be fooled by appearance – in my mind I'm slim, suave, strong. I have the definitive style of my time. Imitators underline my perfection. I glide over ardent obstacles. My utterances are quoted –

But you won't have spoken to me. You are affected by external problems, pimples, boils, hairy ears, cross-eyes – no, no, mine, not yours! You think the sublime is only for the beautiful, and of course you are beautiful, aren't you? In your mind. When you lean back in some skintight position, perfection humming in your strength, and climb like archery on galloping horseback or whatever it is you do, you *are* beautiful. In your mind.

And so am I. You may have seen me at crepuscule, elasticating on unclimbed rock in my green jumpsuit like an adam's-apple straining for operatic pitch, or looking – that malicious girlie said – like a sack of frogs.

In the gold-and-purple throne-room of my heart I am no frog. Never Falstaff, but Prince Hal. Charming too, courteous, friendly, shy. For fear of rebuff I don't make first moves. When I fell off on your arrival, plumped among the boulders, I was not looking for the kiss of life, believe me – just stepping aside till you enquired 'Alright?'

'Fine, thanks. Fine!' I sang out. 'Abrasions only. Want to hold my rope? Hello! Hey! Hellooo?'

Participation was the wrong approach, but I wanted to belong. Then I saw your video and I resigned.

The first face spoke; 'For me it is the *move*. Hardness in a vacuum. Such difficulty that nothing else exists.' A grip of steel. His jaws steel-hard, ripping language into shreds.

The second wove seductive moves and words. Grace and elegance. Dancerly metaphysics. The body-language screamed IMAGE. And Image is about two things only; class and sex.

The third had nothing to say. He had been to an island. He showed a film within the film, to illustrate. Deserted corners, cracks, arêtes and overhangs. That was climbing. Rock. Not muscle, technique, image, point of view or scenery. The climbing, not the climber. Geology was its own commentary. The lines were pointed silently by a moving finger, the body pared to its extremity.

I left this barbarism, and fled to the west coast of an island off the western shore of an island way off the west coast of our island, where the cliffs prop the last arch of European sky above the rim of the western sea. I would achieve something colossal there, reeking of belief and transcendence, some outhung, suspended edge, prow of the great stone boat on which wise men fled to islands.

Exclusion made a thinker of me. Thought is outlawed in sport, confined to the asylum of the head. Philosophy is worse – banished to an inner island, without return. On a sloshing ferry I limped into exile. Shouldering through the ocean the tempest dropped, the island rose. I slipped ashore in Paradise, a wedge afloat upon the ocean. Not Napoleon, not Prospero, but, where the bee sucks there suck I. From frothing beaches the land climbed up and up and plunged so clean and sheer that a continent at least, perhaps a planet, has calved from this eternal shore.

But the athletes were already here, exponents of Image and the Move. I went to Aillanilla, forgotten corner of the island with its remnant of a fort overlooking blank, bleak cliffs undercut by time and the sea. Not for ordinary climbing; there is no place to start. I burrowed into the fort and lived on mushrooms, berries, eggs and dreams.

I'd seen the padre wandering land and sea. Like me he was alone. I envied the certainty of his solitude. A tall, powerful man, strong in the shoulders. Thatched with grey hair, his square face had stiffened before its time. The hooded eyes were not for looking into; they were the windows of an unhappy house but someone in there would never leave. Sometimes he wore the frocked cassock and biretta of a monsignor, and I knew how unromantic the toga would have been. Stripped to black bathing-togs he had white, unused skin without body-hair. I think he oiled it. He entered the sea with severe purpose, as if he'd stepped on land for a few hours and was finished with that. The Great Silkie. The seal-man.

> 'He came one night to her bedside
> And a grumbly guest I'm sure was he,
> Saying 'Here to thee's thy bairn's father
> And here for thee's thy nurse's fee.'

Sometimes he stumped to my fort and stared at the sea from under a stormy brow. He understood the island like a prisoner knows his prison. I wanted to ask him questions; I didn't dare. Was this Prospero?

Aillanilla, the poet's cliff. I guessed at the story. Only a poet would be lonely enough for this barren place, no access down to fishing, no ledges for birds' eggs. He might have thrown himself from the cliff, behaviour popular with poets. Or was he pushed, to shut his mouth? These people had taken poetry seriously. Song and story is threaded through the island, in and out of caves and coves, laced around rocks and ruins, the vegetation of history. Time itself is bound in sheaves of words.

The solution-pockets in the rock are footprints of the past. A race of giants marched across new ground to build at the far end of their world. Behind them history erupted and cast their footsteps in its flow. It erased their memory, but their forts and footprints remain. Down the millennia the west wind blows through empty holes where meaning was thatched to shut this oblivion out. Geology claimed the footprints, tourism claimed the forts.

The climbers hung out in the village hostel and the juke-box bars. They rattled like starlings in the damp, windy weather. Meanwhile, I abseiled towards the churning sea, and there, on a vast grey wall clean as a page, carved into the island, I discovered *language*.

. . . Wind and spray attacked his paper in my fist. No message would survive this weather. A rumour in a storm.

'Where?'

His stubby finger, warts on the knuckle, pointed at my feet. I stood beside a rope, thin as a stretched nerve, disappearing over the edge. I stared in angry confusion at the cable that had brought a message up from the sea.

I recognised the climbing-rope and understood how apt it was that I had stood there, arms renouncing revelation, and he had given me his message. We reeled into the shelter of the fort. Within the whorl of a clochan his domed tent clung to the ground like a shell.

The letters had been roughly traced onto the page. Each character was about two inches high, confused in outline, as if the surface distortion of the stone had been sketched in by a copyist who couldn't tell text from background. Irritably I smoothed the paper and turned it over. The tracing came through behind, without the added detail, and I recognised the g, the t, the d. It was gaelic script, quite ancient.

What was it doing down there? How much was there? What did it mean? Did it answer me? We communicated first in sign-language, silently, eyebrows raised, hands measuring, pointing, as if human breath were redundant, not only in that wind, but in that place where everything was cast in stone. Then, getting to know each other, we resorted to language. He began in a hesitant, rusty voice, unused to talking. I examined his unprepossessing surface for dishonesty or fraud. There was none. Only insecurity and unease. I sat sideways in confessional mode staring out to sea and his story flowed.

... That wall seemed perfect, a surface flawless as canvas. It couldn't be climbed. I wanted to paint the sea on it, paint a reflection as clear as a mirror. The sea would go right through its open window and flow out the other side of the world.

The first time I went down I lost myself in the blankness. The day was calm but the swell washed against the rock. I was looking vaguely for fingerholds, toeholds, a climber's line. There were no good holds, nothing to engage more than a fingerprint. Then, in the centre of the wall, right in the middle, I found the marks; a maze of signs, ten foot square.

I thought they were fossils at first, those worm-casts written into Moher-stone, like the carving on an old tomb. I began to understand. Hanging on the rope I knew the island was speaking to me. Whether it spoke in air or stone, thundered aloud or whispered from the corner of its mouth, I heard nothing, but I knew it spoke in some ancient tone, and there on the rock was the text, and it meant absolutely nothing.

And yet – I had seen it before, words in wild rock .... The drone of the ordinary dissolved my reverie; the murmuring sea, the whisper of a breeze, gulls crying, blood in the temples. I stared into the alien letters, remembered mantras and the creak as prayer-wheels turned the world. *OM mani padme hum OM mani padme hum OM . . . Om . . . om . . .*

It was old. The edges were blurred on the flint-hard rock. I had seen the carving and heard Buddhist mantras in countless expedition-films from Tibet and Nepal; cliffs, rocks, boulders, thousands upon thousands of exquisite stones, centuries old, heaped in hundred-yard walls throughout the Himalayas. Against the soles of my feet this tight little Christian island pulsed with an Asian heartbeat *OM . . . OM . . . OM . . . OM.*

Who was he, the anchorite who had dwelt here among the ruins of other mysteries, and left no trace in island-lore, no word in Robinson's pilgrimage? How long had this taken to carve? I chipped with the spike of a piton-hammer. After several blows the rock splintered incoherently. A flake lodged in my eye. I had barely scratched the surface. It might take months to shape my ragged name upon the rock.

His calm, copperplate characters hung there neater than print, as firm and right as the grain of the rock. Although I understood nothing I knew the nature of the mani-writing lay in that assurance. The monk found the language in the rock itself and brought it to the surface. For the believer faith lay at the heart of things. His task was to bring it forth. It would transform the surface, and the observer, by its presence.

But these islands were the preserve of Christian saints. Their brand was the crucifix and crown of thorns; yet, once upon a time, a man had come from somewhere impossible and left a different truth behind. How had he come? Above all, why choose the absolute obscurity of a sea-cliff? Was the impact of the text in its presence under sun and stars, and not in its meaning to others? Are we irrelevant? Or, – here I felt more profoundly afraid – was it left for an eye as wild and obscure as the missionary's own?

There might have been many monks wandering the medieval world – disguised as poets, yes, of course – leaving language that links into an irresistible testament to be revealed when it comes true. Was I eavesdropping on prophecy? I was further frightened, for predestination robs us of freedom, and I imagined instead a Christian heretic, familiar with dangerous creeds and banished here to this remotest shore of Europe. A deviant was banished to the moon, with nothing but a shovel to dig a shelter or a grave. He dug and dug until he scrawled a Word across the face of the moon, a profanity that could never be ignored again.

Whether Buddhist, Christian, or poet, the practical question remained; how had he written this? Had he levitated, or leaned from the deck of some mystical ship and chipped? Had he abseiled? I visualised it; a pole stuck out across the headwall, a makeshift pulley-wheel, a rope of hair and fibre. A harness like a trouser-seat. The monk lowers himself hand over hand into the weather, a rock counterbalancing his rope, and works all day at his cruel labour of love, of faith, of penance, all day through sun and wind and rain, pulling up hand over weary hand at night to sleep in a hole in the rocks. Prayer made manifest.

Perhaps – hardest, most desirable of all – he had accomplished it in his mind, trained to believe so deeply that it achieved itself. I spun on my rope and stared out to sea through, envious tears. Busy among the waves you swam by, and your wake made sense of the ocean . . . .

. . . I found it a healing concept. His readiness to believe the impossible uplifted me. He sought a greater role in human destiny than chance had allowed. The script was obviously Gaelic, not Asian, but I didn't tell him. I demanded the entire text. It was a spiritual order, not a request.

His strange eyes swivelled and bulged. The muddy irises glowed with golden mission. Perhaps his eyes weren't distorted at all, but sited for the widest range of vision. With all that lateral perception there must be a narrow ridge of blindness down the centre, so that he couldn't see what was in front of his nose.

Three days after the storm I swam past Aillanilla to view the text from below. In the centre of the grey wall he hung rapt as an artist, ten-foot sheets of print-out paper sellotaped across the rock. I saw no trace of writing, the distance was too great. Was he exuding something sticky from his own brain? The scrap he gave me was genuine, even to the extent of being innocently back to front – but it might have come from anywhere. He scrabbled sideways, unrolling paper, and I saw a fat arachnid spinning an arcane web.

No, he was a believer. I knew he was a believer, as I could never be – because he had missed the obvious detail in front of his nose; down the wall ran a jagged stain from top left to bottom right, so long exposed to the sea that it was almost invisible, almost the same ageless grey as the rock where he worked. Perhaps it was only visible from a distance, visible to an unbeliever, but there was no doubt that at some far-off time a pillar with ledges and flakes had clung to this cliff and afforded a stairway down the smooth wall. Nearby cliffs supported huge, leaning flakes, and on sea-level terraces I had seen the roots of pinnacles toppled by storms. Squinting, I thought the stain levelled out under his heels for about ten feet in a ghost of a ledge. It was very faint, the trace of an old shadow. The pillar had hung detached before it toppled. When they finished their script they had taken poles and levered it away from the wall. It rumbled into the sea, they probably raised a roar, but louder still was the thunder of the written word challenging eternity.

He didn't see me below. I might have barked like a seal, or tugged his rope to hear the cracked note of a hermit-bell. I swam below the wall. It was completely undercut. The deep sea nibbled a long way in. There was no plinth for a pillar. The first break was a hundred yards away, where the low overhang ended in a sea-level ledge. There, a deep cleft that looked almost climbable split the wall above the ledge.

After dark he came to the parochial house, excited, ill-at-ease. Despite my calculated aloofness we were conspirators. The paper was unrolled in strips across the linoleum. He had seen too many films; he called the letters hieroglyphs. After three full days we had half the text. The effort exhausted him; he got it back to front again. I was thoroughly irritated. I wanted a full version in decipherable form. Already I could feel the meaning stirring in my veins.

I goaded him; the monk must have been a hardier breed – three days wouldn't achieve much with a chisel. But it wasn't the work that bothered him. He needed to climb. Something was stirring in his blood too. There Were holds. They began with a foothold on the lip of the overhang. The rest were tiny, but they formed a sequence up the centre of the wall if . . . I knew what he meant; if you believed in them. In breathless, technical hieroglyphs he explained there was no protection, nowhere for another climber to belay, unless he stood in a boat, and he didn't have a boat . . . or a partner . . . .

'You expect *me* to hold your rope above while you fool around climbing?'

He was shocked, wanted no such thing. He intended to do without a rope. His eyes had that foolish, golden gleam again.

He would abseil to the overhang, ten feet above the sea, step off the rope onto the foothold and climb from there. If he fell he would hit the water . . . I realised he knew as little about the sea as I knew about rock.

'Can you swim?' No answer. 'What will you do – ' I was frigid with anger; ' – walk on water?'

That, as far as he was concerned, was my job. I wanted to punch him for his obstinacy. But a fist would sink to the wrist in him. I could have raised my hand in a blessing, that dismissive gesture only one move away from a slap in the face. He jerked his knees up towards his chest, a pulpy creature remembering violence, but within his softness there was a hard bargain; if I wanted the rest of the words I would have to swim.

A sharp wind blew against the swell and whipped up spray. Anger, salt in the blood, spurred me on. Long before I reached Aillanilla I saw him standing motionless on the rim. It was the silhouette of a standing-stone, a mooring-post, a permanence that could be marked on a sea-chart.

The wind and waves exhausted me. With numerous stretches like this I could not imagine swimming the island round. When I reached the wall he launched onto the rope and slid to the overhang, his feet compressed like a dancer's in tight, stiff shoes. The rendezvous was too strange for greetings; I, black and white, with rubber lips, red eyes and hoarse lungs – he, a hoofed spider disengaging from the rope. It sprang like elastic, out of reach.

Limbs spread he lay against the vertical rock above me, one foot on a marginal hold. I could see the full expanse of his rubber sole. Nothing else held him but the friction of danger. I had seen the others adhere like this; I knew it was possible. Some of them were louts, so it was neither miracle nor magic – just a skill. But they were strong and slender, adapted like rock-fleas to their medium. This one was short, round, fat. Instead of those little goat's feet he would have been better equipped for his immediate future with frog's fins.

He brushed the rock with his left fingertips, sifted options, selected. His right toe lifted, scuffed, engaged. It couldn't be more than a pebble. He stepped up. From beneath I saw what he was doing – what the others had done on the prow below the fort; he was flying close to the face, flying so close that he brushed it in places. A flutter of fingers, a flick of the limbs, he moved up again. There were holds. Blinded by spray I couldn't see them. I could only guess at the play of forces braced against edges and wrinkles, the tension plucking at tiny flakes. His feet lifted. Water-logged, unevolved, I couldn't judge their weight. Were they light as chamois, or were they armies marching up the alps? His body hung out from the rock, a sacrifice to gravity, then it soared from its slump with the mystery of rebound.

I wallowed on my back, shivering at the icy slap of waves on my belly. What I saw was more than skill; the intention, the belief, were so intense that he generated movement on blank rock, spinning progress within himself. The stairway was long gone – I couldn't even see the shadow – but he climbed as if it were still there. The act itself was not transcendent; he was a climber exercising experience and skill; as I accepted the progress I accepted the edges and flakes that made it possible. But the sea was black and hard as marble, he had no rope, and he could not have understood where he was going. *Om mani padme hum* . . . .

He reached an impasse. Antennae flickered, scanned the carving. I knew there were no holds there; any roughness would have been chipped away to smooth the page. Nothing there but the letters, and he knew they weren't holds.

Eager – a child's hand raised – he reached into the labyrinth for the meaning. *Om mani padme hum,* I should have told him. His fingers gripped, tightened on the invisible, he lifted the intent of a foot – and fell.

Fell? Falling, I thought he would drop feet first towards the sea. But he was thrown – hurled violently back by a jolt, a shock of incom-prehension. He spun sideways in the air; as he passed the overhang his head struck the blind blow of a hammer. Stunned, I didn't hear the splash. But there were two of us in the water. His black hair streamed towards me, staining the water red. A hundred yards away, the ledge; there was no rope hanging.

I had ordered him to place one in case of accident. I could leave him, unconscious, on the ledge while I swam off, or haul him up from above. He had his own means of climbing a rope if he was conscious. But there was no rope. It would have been a failure of belief, a safety-net? Perhaps he didn't have a second one.

I seized him under the arms, turned him over. His face was grey, and slack as rubber. Water dribbled from his mouth, blood bubbled in his hair. One arm clamped around him I flailed blindly on my back. He drooped against me like a corpse. A grim embrace. He dragged me down, down into the water. Sinking, there was nothing random in my memory; and no remorse. I thought of all the hours my arms embraced you, forbidden woman. Throughout that long, slow drowning my soul reclaimed you. It will never let go.

Inch by inch the overhang passed overhead. The cliff was opening to receive us. I kicked and fought until the ledge loomed alongside like a harbour wall and I gaped up into the cleft. Time and again I jammed him against the rock, willing him to float, climbed out to find he had drifted out of reach and was sinking. A final effort coincided with a wave.

I knew resuscitation, the kiss of life. Before I began that grisly embrace I heaved him into a sitting position, propped up his chin . . . *In nomine patris et filii* . . . I hit him a stinging slap across the face. He choked, dribbled, stared at me, one wild eye askew. The lid closed to shut out what he saw.

Fallen angel? Grey flesh quivering in garish garb he looked like a dissolving jellyfish. His failure confirmed the impossible. I would never swim full-circle now. Whether to survive or to escape, I climbed that fifty metre chimney, barefoot, naked. Gravity was a tidal current and I fought every vertical inch. He came up hours afterwards. I had transferred the rope from his abseil. I watched him climb the mouth of the groove, back and feet braced against opposing walls. I had squirmed as deep as I could within the cleft where the sharp rock bit into my flesh.

He stayed in the parochial house for a week. My housekeeper nursed him. I had never thawed her widow's chill, but she warmed to him. She called him Friar Tuck. I saw him as a half-drowned Buddha. Pale and bloated he squatted in an armchair while I chipped grimly at the text.

I extended two full-length mirrors edgewise on the floor and propped the tracing opposite. I worked from the reflection, distracted by my own unshaven face lurking behind the letters. Glossaries and grammars littered the floor. The outline of many letters was in doubt. If I copied down the text I seemed to define words in my mind. I avoided such concrete acts to keep the poem fluid until it hardened of its own accord. There was a constant feeling of energy frustrated, a fever like sugar burning in the brain. My temperature soared, I felt an overpowering urge to rip back my sleeves and cool my veins in the mirror, plunge to the elbows in its current where I would surely find the invisible shapes dropped there centuries ago. In the middle of the night I would start awake from a buzzing dream, drowned in sweat, and order – implore – him to go down again to verify. Some of the sketch-marks could be accents, or they might be incidental scratches. A dot or a stroke changed everything. The broad vowels floated in and out of shape like spots before my eyes. One accent and a flatter arc could make the difference between Bod and Bád for a serious example.

He was coarse enough to say that only a celibate would confuse those. Celibacy, I responded drily, is a moral intention, not an act of castration. We are normal men. I felt a near-irresistible urge to talk, to confess to this detached figure. But I knew that, without remorse, it is useless to confess. I could not regret a single embrace of our lost love; not one moment of our entire year stolen from my vows could I renounce. And I swear, Evelyn, if you would take me again, as you swear you will not, I would leave everything and go. The more I scraped at the mute surface, convinced that it could speak to me from the past, the more I needed to pour forth this language of my own. I shut my teeth against my tongue and laboured. I had to make a single chisel of my mind, but it rattled like a jackhammer.

He sailed on a stone boat and dreamed an island; that much seemed certain. It was an image of transcendence. I didn't quite translate it; it came like revelation. But he was pursued. By whom? By whom? The island turned to stone. Good or bad? Miracle? Disaster? He sailed alongside – to shelter? to hide? – leaned from the deck and carved. Why? *Faoíseamh ní gheóbhad* ... No respite from weeping rock ... or keening sea. Never? Not even light after darkness? I needed the final lines, for redemption or despair.

Buddha would not descend. He was finished with this – waiting to leave the island. He would wander east, to Asia. The mani-stones had laid a grip upon his soul. And there were mountains too. He was at peace with a new dream.

He taught me to abseil, gave me a gift of his rope. I learned on the fort, a twelve-foot descent. As the line poured slowly through the alloy knot

I walked down the prehistoric wall and felt no qualms. I was eager to begin the slide into the sea. At noon, my head full of translations and tides, without a whisper of prayer, I crossed the rim of the island.

He blessed me with farewell. I saw myself reflected in his mute appraisal; sea-plump and hairless, smooth skin blotched with blackened bruises, black togs, black rubber tight upon my skull . . . the brain and crotch were already seal, the skin was turning. Amphibious! Shock rippled through me as a shot explodes in blubber. But no one is fully human, no one is entirely man.

Below me, vertical rock, horizontal curve of the sea, severe dimensions for a distorted soul. Today I would swim around the island, thread that ellipse in the angle between cliff and sea. If anyone saw me now, a renegade, sleekly naked, striding down Aillanilla on a strand of coloured string, casual as a demon on a broom, I would be shot. 'We saw a seal at the salmon-nets, your honour'.

When I reached the centre of the wall I didn't recognise the inscription. I had an image chiselled in my brain. But these marks were not incut as I expected; the letters were carved in relief, a weave of bewildering ribs raised like Braille upon the rock. We had never discussed that detail. I placed my fingers on the first line and urgently penduled along. It made no more sense than a row of fossils. I swung back left, fingers still in touch. There it was:

I sailed on a stone boat . . . I dreamed an island

I found it, felt it clear as my own signature; thought too of the shipwreck – the Titanic's number in reverse reflecting Antichrist in code. Was it the boat that was made of stone? Or was it the sailor? Dully I probed for the real words now, not for images:

Adrift in a boat . . . made of stone . . . I dreamed an island

I knew how it felt to have a heart and soul of stone.

Around the raised letters the rock was natural – rough and weathered. It had never been chipped nor the level lowered to pronounce these words. Swinging wildly in mid-air I felt the cord tighten. The whip cracked. It was not reversed. It was written from within the cliff.

The final lines. I knew already. Written in darkness he spoke of sun. The last day sailed west and she went with it, crossed the horizon, and faded.

Aonraic. Oíche shíoraí
Solitary. Night forever.

JOHANN

The door opened. A figure in a shapeless tunic shuffled through. The long corridor was dimly lit. Johann guided himself by touch along the wet wall. After every dozen steps his hand scraped across another iron door. He added a name heavily under his breath. Some of the names were foreign but he pronounced them all with the same guttural resonance.

At every hundred paces a bulb shone in a wire cage. Lichens festered around the weak lights. He stamped his feet on the stone floor and clapped his palms roughly, applauding the illusion of heat. He breathed deep to prepare for effort.

Grey hair and beard fringed a thin, physical face. The straight nose, sharp jaw, jutting brows were reminders of aggression, but all the strength had drained away in the furrows of age and neglect. He stooped away into the shadows still naming absent names.

Johann smelled a hard, clear night outside the walls. The air had the dry sting of frost. No wind. Nothing to blind the sky. He was running out of names, or repeating himself – Wallenberg for the second time – Raul – pausing at the broken door; but that was years ago, and someone else had been there since, a man with a sharp, bitter language – English, he thought. He was gone too.

He turned a corner and saw the window ahead. Breathing quickened to a rasp and his palms skidded impatiently across nameless doors. The small opening high in the wall shed a square of barred light on the floor. He flexed his muscles and jumped clumsily to hook the grille. His bones vibrated with effort as he hauled himself up till his face was level with the light. It was night in the outside world and the stars struck cold and deep into his eyes.

He had timed it precisely. No watch, clock, or calendar, no sense at all of minutes, hours or days, but he could judge moonrise and sunset to within a hairsbreadth of the horizon.

He saw the blade of a crescent moon skimming exquisitely up the ridge of a mountain, slicing an icy arrowhead out of the sky. Once a year the image was immaculate, the silver scalpel paring the exact silhouette until it reached the tip of the icy triangle, and paused for the downward stroke.

He never stayed to see the moon escape into the sky. He had always dropped to the floor and returned to his cell to dream of the moon slicing back to earth along the other edge of the arrowhead. Others had brought him to this window when he needed a vision to survive. He recalled a line of men here on a clear night, queuing to celebrate an accident of beauty. Wallenberg had seen it first – the man with the power to interrupt nightmare.

The mountains endure. The first time he met Wallenberg – stumbling past the thin, pale man in a corridor – the Swede brushed aside his own guard, an obedient shadow, and laid a detaining hand on Johann's shoulder. The mountains endure. What shocked Johann, and drew him back to a kind of sanity where he questioned things again, was the sound of his own language, his own dialect, in the foreign mouth. It was as if he had spoken himself. The mountains endure. Afterwards, he was never sure if that was what he heard, or if he had simply understood by touch what Raul had meant to say. Perhaps nothing had been said at all. The mountains endure. The message carried an inescapable conclusion; in spite of this. In spite of suffering.

The guard materialised again and Raul Wallenberg moved on, but as always he was in control and it was the guard who was marched away.

There were windows for other seasons; dawn in the funnel of an eastern pass; alignments of Orion's belt.... But the men were all gone and Johann kept the vigils alone. They were the measure of his existence.

Sometimes the sky was sullen on this special night – it was a long time since it had been clear. But the past too was obscure. He could seldom remember who was the victim and who was to blame. The knife-edge of the horizon re-opened the wounds, and the cold night was full of revelation.

He knew immediately his strength had withered. He was shuddering with effort. Once he could hang by his bent arms, from the first phosphorescence to the final radiance. Now it had barely begun and he was sinking already, his feet scrabbling on the rough wall. Desire welled in his heart, a hunger for magnificence. Darkness slid inexorably up the mountain, and the windowsill eclipsed the moon.

Closing his door he lay on the iron cot, arranged the grey blankets to avoid the holes. Heels together his bony feet stuck straight up. He folded his hands across his chest and closed his eyes.

Johann concentrated on the midnight mountain. He plundered his dim resources to bring the shape to life. He summoned colour from distant meadows, olive uniforms, a blue-eye in a Judas-hole, to melt the long darkness into summer light. He tried to build a blaze from the brightest moments. Desire fanned the dull edge of memory. Colour was refused! His skull ached with effort. The bleak triangle of ice bulged within the bones. It was rooted in the glacier, locked into the pointed angle of the sky ....

... Five hundred metres above the glacier the ice funnelled through the first rock-band. From below they could no longer see the Major Icefield above the rock. They knew it was there, the upper half of the wall, swept by avalanches spouting from a rocky chute that might – or might not – penetrate the summit overhangs.

In the middle of winter they stood below the mountain, three young men on the edge of a first ascent. The icy wind was the breath of time and place. Two pairs of eyes, cold behind wire spectacles turned on him; your idea, lunatic. You go first.

Responsibility was the worst burden. It unbalanced Johann's heart in a way the heaviest rucksack never could. He stiffened himself. He was ready. His arms and shoulders, his chest, were powerful – swelling with strength. His booted feet were confident as hooves.

He looked up. Here, at its narrowest point, the bergschrund formed a shallow ice-cave. The lower edge of the slope jutted out across his head. He reached up with the heavy axe and struck a lazy blow. Sparks of ice flew from the glancing pick, and the shock of impact shook his bones. The others winced, shifted their eyes back down the valley. Snow-covered mountains stretched beyond the furthest limits of vision. Home was ten hours away.

Johann looked again along the great crevasse dividing the glacier from the face. There was no other way across. He removed his gloves, knotted the rope around his waist, threw the coils to a reluctant pair of hands. His fingers throbbed with hot, impatient life. They were immune to the weather. He was twenty-five, and ready.

Again he swung the axe. Anton and Boris ducked for fear of shattered steel, but the pick drove deep into the brittle ice. He released his grip on the singing handle, took a loop of cord and swung it high in the air. It dropped around the head of the axe. No one spoke. They heard the wind polishing the face. Johann beckoned and pointed. Boris stepped forward, handed him his axe and crouched on the narrow ledge. He clasped Johann around the knees and lifted. Seizing the buried pick Johann thrust his boot into the hanging loop. The axe jerked, tilted, the handle slammed against the ice, held by tension only. Johann's lips peeled back from his long teeth. Leaning backwards he swung the second axe at full stretch. It slammed into a tight fissure that split the rim of the overhanging ice. In the same motion he hauled on the handle and kicked off the loop below. He swung out, lunged for the second pick and heaved again. Crampons thrashed against the ice, his body lifted till he was level with the lip and pushing down on the buried steel. He jerked one hand loose and chopped a fist into the icy crack above his head, a salute to the unknown ....

That was someone else Johann watched from his grim pillow. He felt no connection with the brain and blood flailing against gravity long ago, pulling towards this future. He could not feel the force of being there. He might as well have crouched with Anton and Boris on the freezing ledge below, robbed of retreat, watching in horror as the rope twitched out another ten metres, then the blunt triumph of anchors in the ice – his voice coming down to them like a stranger's, stripped of feeling in the bitter air.

'Come up!' He hauled them onto the face.

The wind tore at their clothes, rejected them.

Sometimes butterflies were blown up from the valleys and plastered to the ice. Only the tides of avalanche, the explosion of a storm was worthy of attention here. The white triangle of the mountain billowed around them, the wind cracking in its frozen canvas. They were sailing into an unknown winter.

All the way up the ice, two days of hacking steps and hauling ropes, they pleaded for retreat. Boris short and squat with bristling hair, his bare face begging like a hedgehog; Anton strong and stocky, weak in the will, his eyes outraged, a student out of his depth. Johann ignored them, even when the cloud cleared and they imagined the chimney-smoke in the valleys. It was easier to go up than down, he said.

The gully did not lead to the summit. It died out among overhangs of rotten rock. He spent hours up there probing with frozen fingers while they sheltered below and begged him to succeed. Easier now to go up than down.

He failed.

He got them off in a day and a half, retreating down the face with a single axe between the three, ravaged by frostbite and defeat.

Anton and Boris never climbed again. They joined the army and went away to die defending two square metres of muddy snow.

Johann lost the will to try again; he had strained his courage in a single effort. No one suspected. His were pragmatic people to whom any success was an accumulation of attempts. They had problems of their own. War was coming closer.

For a while Anna seemed to cure him of defeat. Perhaps she drove the symptoms deeper. She arrived on holiday the summer after his attempt. The year before the war.

She wanted to climb while it was still possible. She could pay a little for the privilege. An old guide at the station said gallantly that he would take her himself if only he had the strength. He recommended instead a young man – a powerful climber – convalescing from a bad experience.

Anna stood firmly outside Johann's house while he stammered in the dark doorway. He was filled with confusion, unable to look her in the face, dimly aware of a woman almost as tall as himself whose smooth, brown skin was utterly exotic compared to the freckled complexions that he knew. At first her blue eyes and wide mouth were friendly, pleased to have found the right house. She explained her purpose in the cultivated accent of the lowlands. Her voice reminded Johann of the radio, the intelligence of far-off places and events. It was not the climbing that presented problems; what would he *say* to her all day?

He mumbled an excuse about farm-work and started to withdraw. She wore a yellow, sleeveless dress, one hand in a side-pocket clenching with annoyance. The colour shimmered before his eyes and her voice was distorted by a pulse thudding in his head.

She turned aside and looked angrily at the mountains around the valley. He looked at what she saw and the familiar view was completely changed, swimming in the sky, as if he was a child staring at it with his head between his legs.

'I was told you were available.' she said accusingly. 'I can pay. And I'm fit – if that's what you're worried about!'

She kicked the ground with impatience. Johann's voice shook, lapsing helplessly into dialect as he made the arrangements.

During the first day's walking in the sunshine her resentment relaxed, and gradually his shyness gave way. She was a little older than Johann but her manner was not superior. Her shirts, breeches and boots were well-worn and she seemed strong and independent. She had no need of a guide at all. Johann thought her perfectly capable of walking the mountains on her own.

'Walking!' she laughed. 'I came here to climb. When do we start?'

Johann had never climbed with a woman before. Usually they hired the older guides who patronised them and kept to easy ground. It had never occurred to him that anyone as striking as Anna would take the slightest interest in real climbing. He had always thought of it as an achievement of muscle and sweat. He had imagined beauty as meek and passive, self-protecting. He took the dawns and sunsets, the silent spaces, casually for granted. They were aspects of the weather. But it excited him constantly now to see these ordinary things through Anna's eyes. It was like a conversion of the senses, a refinement of reality. He realised he was deeply proud of the mountains, proud of his achievements. Proud and anxious. Everything was changing; under threat.

Anna sang, laughed, ran without losing breath, on the high tracks and easy ridges. She was fascinated by Johann's work and education. Her own urban background she dismissed as irrelevant. There were clashes. She seemed to think his dialect and accent quaint as if he had chosen them for effect. She laughed in disbelief at his rebel politics. To restore his pride he hinted at membership of the separatist guerillas. They would come into their own soon, he promised fiercely. He could not be drawn further on the subject.

After three days' walking he took her climbing. Rock, ice, ropes, pitons, a complete performance. She was easy to teach – hungry for a change of angle and elevation.

The dull earth reeled away beneath their feet. They entered an exalted state.

...Lying on the iron cot in the dark Johann leaned inwards towards the light he had released. His eyelids fluttered and the harsh breathing softened, fanning the dream to a blaze. Bright, sun-coloured days, red rock between the green valleys, the blue sky, and the white snow, came sliding up from the dark – from beyond the edge.

Holding his breath against excess desire he watched the radiant landscapes flicker, fade, and resume. He was waiting now, preparing to dissolve over the edge of disbelief into ecstasy, but already he was afraid of the horizon, of where he would arrive on the other side of memory. This hovering between delight and terror recalled the heat trapped in the colours, desire blazing in the blood. He remembered the rage for suffusion of the senses, stifled by dread.

The sunlight soured, laughter ripped through the dream. Beneath him, Anna's heavy hair swung loose. Sweat poured down her face. Her head was thrown back, smooth throat stretched, a pulse hammering below her ear. She looked up to him, pleading. She dangled from a handhold on a steep wall, emptiness below her, and he sat overhead helpless with laughter, ridiculing her reliance on the rope.

'Tight!' she screamed, and he pulled it tight until the line bit deep into her skin.

He could not stop the terrible laughter; it was strength asserting itself. He was still rocking back and forth, hating himself for it, as she collapsed weakly on the ledge, her confidence drained away in the reek of sweat. She allowed him his assertion as if it was a temporary right to be dealt with later. The breathless air was hard with light reflected from ice, water, mica . . . in the aftermath of cruelty Johann sensed his own transparency.

He helped her up, apologising, on the verge of strange language. Anna grimaced, looked at him, measuring his embarrassment. She leaned across and kissed him, in mockery, a salt kiss like a bite across the lips.

The climbing was easier above. They ran like partners in a dream, faster and faster for the sheer release of movement, the spirit flying while a conspiracy raged in the blood.

Days flared past. They scrambled on warm ridges and pillars, slept on starry ledges, dropped down to the village like parachutists for food and wine, and vanished again for a second week of celebration. Johann observed the code; propriety and safety. It was his last defence.

The villagers saw them wander in, hair bleached to straw, faces burned, the intimacy of height and silence in their eyes. They whispered to him that he deserved happiness but he must not get carried away. His eyes turned absently aside to search. Had he heard the news, they insisted – the armies were coming again? It was time to leave the mountains, to hide the harvest, to organise. His face lit up as she strode along the street towards him. The neighbours looked at her and shook their heads. They were afraid for Johann. He had endured pain and hardship, he was a special young man with great strength – but he was too single-minded to understand loss.

Crossing a wide stream in the mountains Anna slipped on a wet stone. There was no danger. Cursing, she floundered in the icy water. Again Johann was overcome with involuntary howls of laughter. She was helpless, falling again and again, unable to keep her feet. Her clothes clung to her body. He stumbled across to help. She wrenched powerfully on his arm and dragged him in. The water was glacial, agonizing.

Shocked to hysteria they crawled out on the grass, and wept with laughter, their eyes locked together. The sun was plunging into evening. Anna sobered suddenly. Started to shed her soaking clothes. A moment of hypnotised silence and Johann began to strip. The wind quickened, she moved towards him. He recoiled . . . . The smooth legs, the brown face and neck, were part of a stranger's body, ice-cold, unknown, pale as snow from the shoulders to the thighs.

Trapped in the dream, approaching the dark shore. Memory swept him along. He struggled to withdraw but he was caught in the grip of the truth. Johann was running slowly through his brain on rubber legs pursued by Anna's terrifying laughter. The laughter was hurt and childlike, sharpened by the shrillness of betrayal.

Anna went home. She wrote immediately, preoccupied with the chaos in the south. Life in the city was under siege.

Johann didn't answer.

He no longer knew what was restraint and what was failure. He stalked alone in the mountains balancing his future on his finger-tips, testing fragile rock with the weight of his existence. He caught glimpses of the White Sail brooding remotely, threatening the return of winter.

Work forced him back to earth. He reaped acres of grain single-handed, refusing assistance, and stored it in the foothills. Within two months war was underway, conscription in the plains, the disaffected fleeing to the mountains. The population swayed like seaweed with the tides from the west and then the east and back and forth in the ebb and flow of influence. But resistance hardened in the mountains. The separatist movement gathered strength. Patriots from all over the country – some of them mountaineers – flocked to join the partisans.

Johann hurled himself furiously into the organisation. He was admired for his accomplishments and courage, to his secret shame. He burned to justify that respect within himself. Overnight he became leader of the local unit, arms and men – some of them climbing comrades – at his disposal.

On a wet September evening just before dark Johann stood at an upstairs window waiting to hold a meeting. It was as if he had been posted there. The weary shape approaching in the street must be imagination – but his heart was thumping so hard he couldn't breathe. He jerked back out of sight.

Cropped hair, wet and plastered to her skull, face thin and white, shadows in the eye-sockets. The shoulders were slumped and she wore grey, anonymous clothes. The difference proved her real.

But it couldn't be! Wild evasions sparked. Her sister . . .? He saw the real Anna lying in bomb-debris, blood in the corner of her mouth; 'Find Johann. Tell him I . . . .'

He slammed his back against the wall. As if he was stalking terror.

Anna knocked at the old guesthouse across the street. Her knuckles hammered among his heartbeats, and went on hammering when she stood back. She squared her shoulders to the closed door with sudden authority. Aunt Zelda opened it a few inches, shook her head through the gap. Anna's hands lifted towards her. Reluctantly the door opened wide enough to admit her.

He knew he had seen her, but he could not believe it. Johann watched the house till midnight. Even in the dark he could imagine every detail – the ornate woodwork he painted for his Aunt Zelda, the bowed roof that might refuse another winter, the split grain of the front door, the hinges he replaced last year. His mind clung to the shapes of things, fought clear of meaning. The outlines of the ancient village sagged together in the dark. Pain creaked beneath the surfaces of objects and events.

That night he lay entirely sleepless – Anna, the movement, mountains, Anna . . . .

The eiderdown smothered him. He knew Anna would have no trouble sleeping. She was like that. He threw off the cover and lay shivering in the cold.

On the iron cot in the cell Johann's knuckles clenched in the same frenzy of desire and rejection.

This was not memory. It was re-experience!

As always he had broken from the dark into brief sunlight, and then crashed on into deeper darkness beyond.

He saw exactly how Anna's hair had swept up from her clear forehead, curling and twisting thickly, and the tiny scar below her right cheekbone where a mole had been removed. He saw the long lobes of her ears and the way her top lip clung to her teeth when she was tired or thirsty.

But Anna was no longer in a room across the street. Anna was thirty years away. And her eyes – looking up as she climbed towards him – were not the soft blue of alpine flowers. They were the colour of icy water reflecting the sky.

He was headlong on his way to learning everything he had always known.

In the morning he hurried along the street. Worn cobbles, cracked black timber, houses decaying with their occupants. The whole village crumbling into the earth.

She carried Zelda's egg-basket. Accepted already.

'Johann!' she bubbled with unreserved delight, 'Johann! I thought you'd be away! My God, I didn't know you. It's the . . . it's the beard!'

Emotion thundered towards utterance, but the words froze. His hand jerked up to the hair itching his face. He had lost control of expression, his mouth smirking and his brain helpless to stop it.

'I don't have time to shave now . . .' he mumbled idiotically.

'So I hear! You must be very busy . . .' her voice dropped, '. . . organising . . . .' She gazed at him in admiration.

He gave a sharp, melodramatic frown. 'What do you know about that?'

'Zelda told me of course. She's very proud of you. You're going to save the whole country it seems . . . .' She was laughing at him.

'Zelda remembers me from the summer,' she continued happily. Johann caught a flash of the closing door, the imploring hands.

'She says I can stay awhile if I work for my keep. My money's no use to her, and anyway there's nothing to buy . . . .'

Johann said nothing. He sensed a hollowness without knowing what it was. She chatted away gaily, flashing glances at him, then lifting her head to the clouded mountains beyond.

Sudden determination focused her. She looked around quickly. An old man smoked in a doorway, gazing at the weather above the rooftops.

'Johann, I came to help! It's – nothing to do with you – you'll be glad to know. I just want to be part of whatever's going on up here . . . .'

Her tight hair was greasy. There were blemishes on her skin, and the sunken cheeks emphasised an awkward nose. He had never seen her plainness before. Deep creases of fatigue between her eyes. The mystique had vanished. She was ordinary now, like a local woman. Less, even. They had substance behind them.

He saw Zelda's basket again. It was heaped up with precious brown eggs, worth a fortune. She was carrying it exactly as Aunt Zelda did, exactly as his grandmother had carried the same basket, looped over an arm and resting loosely on her hip. He had never been trusted with it. He would break an egg at every step. Anna was at home already.

'Why did you come back?'

He meant it to sound curious, flattered even, but it came out as an insult.

Her chin lifted under the impact. He felt the force that distinguished her.

'I like it here. That's all. It's beautiful. I feel I know the mountains – ' her eyes dropped and he suspected mockery, ' – thanks to you, I suppose.'

But she looked vehemently south. 'I had to get away – as far away from all that as possible.'

She faced him, just as she had faced Zelda at the door.

'Don't make me unwelcome, Johann, please. I have nowhere else to go.'

Anna could not be kept out of the resistance. Nothing balked her determination to belong. Within weeks she was attending secret meetings, sitting quietly at the back in a long, black coat borrowed from Zelda. She was careful not to offer opinions, though Johann could sense her mind working like a hidden clock in the room. She had regained her colour and her face was keen with a nervous urge to serve.

Her presence hypnotised and horrified him, like mountain roses swarming with bees; absorbed, seductive, dangerous. When she was in a room, no matter how crowded, Johann felt isolated from the others, as if – between them alone – they shared a powerful mystery; but when emotion surged forward he found the barrier again – the very idea of her. She was beyond him. He did not know how to reach outside his limits.

Anna was only one of the new faces. Some had been frequent visitors but they remained outsiders. Those who remembered her from the summer idyll saw her at first as Johann's girl; they were amused by the distance at which he kept her, as if he was trying to disguise the fact. When they teased him he showed a vicious streak of authority and stunned them into silence.

Johann believed passionately in the need for revolution and an independent mountain-state. It was the only way to preserve their lives from dilution. The mountain-farmers believed not only in defending their land but in reinforcing private ownership. They let the idealists say what they liked as long as their speeches added up to that.

There was very little they could achieve yet. The military had not penetrated that far, and showed no sign of doing so. There was a comfortable suspicion among the local men that the area would be ignored. It was too awkward, too poor. Who wanted it? The visiting partisans were happy to keep it that way. They saw no need for provocation. They were fed and sheltered. They spent pleasant days in the mountains storing food and weapons against the day when Johann's plan might come into effect.

He was determined to make that day happen. First they would provoke an all-out attack. Then retreat into the high mountains to fight on their own ground. His strategy was to lure the enemy through key passes to be ambushed by pockets of guerillas overhead. Calculated explosions would cut off retreat and reinforcements. Avalanches could be arranged. The campaign was planned to act as a flash-point, rousing a passive people to widespread rebellion.

Anna was in the mountains every day building up the supply-dumps. Good-humoured, resourceful, she was becoming a popular focus in the village. Her reputation as a climber grew and she was careful not to challenge anybody's pride, She was indistinguishable from the others, even in the rowdiness she cultivated to hold her own. Scornfully Johann thought that, if she could, she would have grown a beard. He never missed a chance to deny her hold on him.

He was living on the run – from his own imagination more than any threat – bearded and spectacled, moving from house to house with a rifle and a box of books. He suppressed his passion and it tormented him. His zeal for revolution grew as the winter hardened. It was the mission his life hungered for. He stood for hours above the village, staring out towards the valleys and the captive plains. Behind his back the mountain leaned over the horizon.

Weekly briefings became harangues. Revolution must be taken seriously! It demanded secrecy and discipline. His lean face had become hard and drawn. He raged that the police knew every single move they made. Why not invite them to the meetings to save the trouble of informing?

He organised a number of ambushes to capture arms, detonated some explosives; suddenly, two of his men were killed in an attack on a barracks. One was a bizarre outsider who had been certain to kill himself anyway, but the second was a neighbour, dull and slow-witted, whose death hung over Johann's head. The others were even more convinced of the need for caution. Thoughtfully they continued training and stockpiling in the mountains. When the village ran low on certain provisions these were carried back down again. There was little else to do in the winter snows. Events developed a strange quality, somewhere between farce and nightmare, fuelled by quantities of potato-spirit.

Another ambush, another death. The taste of resistance was turning sour. Anna confronted him in a candle-lit attic where he sat speechless with obstinacy. She stormed in wearing the long, black coat and an air of delegated challenge.

He was alienating the community that supported him, she began.... Johann jumped to his feet, shouting. Whose community was it? His skin tightened to an ugly ivory.

She tried to argue. What was the point in attacking with inadequate weapons and numbers? Was it violence for its own sake?

Johann was enraged. They understood nothing that was going on. It was the evidence of guerilla presence that kept the military out.

Anna retorted that the only evidence was three dead comrades....

The plane droned through the darkness, turned abruptly as if it had strayed north and realised its error. A parachute drifted towards the snow. As he watched it drop like a foreign seed on their moonlit mountain Johann chilled with premonition. He had received a rare, coded briefing in advance. His men ran forward and bundled up the silk. Johann strode stiffly towards the stranger.

Jean brought greetings from the separatists of Western Europe. His contacts were impeccable and he came with the warmest recommendations from Johann's superiors further south. He was being lent to the movement because of his experience in alpine combat. His mission was to liaise with local groups and instruct them in new techniques.

To Johann this was evidence on the one hand of the importance of his area; on the other, it was interference with his command. Jean could neither be ignored nor absorbed. His manner had the wide-awake ease of self-sufficiency. He stood inches taller than Johann and his spare frame was wiry with muscle. A ready grin invited acceptance, but without the smile his face was hawk-sharp with a hard, energetic mouth and eyes hooded against speculation. His age was uncertain – the weathered skin too tight to wrinkle, too hard for youth. Only the clear, grey eyes gave a clue; when measuring Johann's welcome they cooled and hardened with old experience.

But his arrival galvanised the flagging group. Some members had lapsed, discouraged by Johann's emerging politics, others had disappeared to join the army. Now the faithful felt an official sense of purpose again. Recognising the hungry urgency of their mood Jean quickly made it clear that he did not deal in impetuous action. He was here to help with long-term strategy. And to learn the language: – he grinned agreeably through his mangled phrases. He believed, not in outnumbered defence, but in undermining occupation. He understood from his previous briefing that it would come to that – if enemy expansionism continued, Johann noted the easy grasp the stranger had of complex terms despite his language problems.

'Our aim' he contradicted bluntly 'is to prevent occupation in the first place!'

Jean's eye wandered, without any obvious sense of irony, around the room taking in the numbers present, dwelling on them individually with abstract assessment. Johann was about to explain hotly that they were only a fraction of the available support, but he realised the other man knew all the details already and silence knotted between them.

Jean wore an emblem composed of ice-axes on his lapel. He had been a mountain-guide at home before the war. Comp-limenting the local mountains he asked about the prominent face he had seen in the moonlight of his arrival. His fingertips met in an elegant point and his palms leaned apart at the wrists enclosing a sharp triangle of air.

It was climbed of course? he presumed delicately. – Often? – implying that it would be a slur on local talent to think otherwise.

Johann ignored him, continuing to list items in an inventory.

Jean pressed again, deliberately.

Embarrassment forced others to answer together.

No, they admitted with unexpected shame – it was not actually climbed ... the ridges yes, of course, but that face ... well, it was probably impossible! Rubble falling down it all the time! And bloody steep – far steeper than it seemed!

– But Johann here – they smiled at him hastily, patching the atmosphere – Johann tried it once. He spent three days on it in winter – and if that wasn't enough ....

The explanation faltered again. Jean flashed a smile of approval at him, but Johann wasn't fooled. He smelled the superiority behind the respect. The gallic tribute of those tight jaws meant nothing. The tall man was sitting easily on the edge of a table, his tunic open, one leg swinging affably, thick black hair with startling flashes of grey pushed back from his aquiline face. He was waiting. Johann felt his skin grow clammy in the cold room, frustration forced out through his pores; he wanted to say coolly; quietly, 'the rock up there is rotten, too rotten to climb!' and dismiss it then. At once an excuse – and a challenge. But in spite of himself he growled abrasively 'You'll have to wait till winter to find out!' Smarting with resentment he turned back to his notes. 'If you're still here!'

Jean showed no sign of departure. He was as captivated as a tourist by the pretty villages and the wild mountains. Everything here, he said, reminded him of his own area before it was developed. Billeted at Zelda's he told stories of the war at home – over now and won – marvellous stories, livid with blood, ice and courage, tales of ambush and attack, of white eagles and silver foxes skiing down the mountains to decimate the enemy. He took no credit for gallantry, reflecting instead a wry sense of self-ridicule. When they wondered breathlessly why he wouldn't stay at home and savour the peace he laughed and admitted he preferred the excitement of a just cause. The movement, he said, was world-wide now and his war would not end till theirs did. His listeners felt the warm fraternity of struggle.

But for the time being it seemed Jean was more interested in exploration than resistance. One shoulder was hunched slightly higher than the other, sharpening the angular attention of his head. He was recovering from a bullet-wound and he needed a lot of exercise to restore his strength.

'No use getting into a fight without the strength to win.' he shrugged.

Apparently unaware of the effort they had cost he dismissed Johann's hoarded weapons as 'catapults and spears.' He had a trick of relying on language difficulties to offer innocent insults. He would organise an air-drop of arms as soon as supply-lines were set up. Meanwhile lie low and keep fit! There were comrades abroad eager to help when the time came.

Keeping fit meant climbing everything that had not yet been done in the mountains. Jean hardly ever repeated an existing route regardless of its excellence; he was interested only in pioneering, even if the new line was inferior to an established climb.

Johann knew the name of this attitude from his textbooks; it was imperialism! To his utter fury Jean innocently handed him details of every new route, neatly written out with the date, the grade, and the time taken. The standard of difficulty was consistently high. He obviously inspired confidence because none of those who climbed with him ever mentioned fear when they discussed the routes, maliciously he thought, in Johann's hearing. He was the only one who resented the agreeable foreigner. The others were confused by the vehemence of his hostility. It couldn't be on account of Anna; Johann went out of his way to underline his total detachment from her. He answered her frigidly when necessary, never using her name or looking directly at her. Sometimes it seemed to the others that she was teasing him, tricking him into confrontations.

They competed eagerly among themselves to climb with Jean. There was glamour in a first ascent, even if it was an unappealing couloir they had never noticed before. But Anna was his preferred partner. She was the only one who spoke his native language and had an international sense of events. And she was talented – lighter and faster than most of the others. She would never challenge for the limelight either, for Anna had compromised her independence. Fearing to antagonise the men she had become an habitual second. This had developed into an assumption of inferiority. Anna had let it happen as the price of absorption into a male community.

Johann spent the year doggedly trying to build up his support. He became increasingly politicised and caused a split in local feeling. He argued now that independence would not be sufficient in itself. They must aim towards a state that was absolutely true to the traditions of the mountain people, a state impervious to corruption by outside cultures. Exclusive nationalism.

He was not alone in his ideas, neither locally nor on a larger scale, though he was unaware at first of the echoes. Soon covert rallies were being held in an effort to build a political wing to the movement. Johann and others travelled widely, urging the need to break with the neighbouring country that had diluted their history and identity for so long. Only through national freedom could they find the strength to resist the totalitarian invasion already devouring their neighbour!

For a while Johann found relief in his new crusade. He was standing on a rough platform at a village festival on the far side of the mountains listening to speakers of his own persuasion arouse the audience when he first became aware of opposition to what he thought was absolute – almost genetic – truth. The hard blue sky, the festive costumes, the dark mountains, clustered farms, and the intent listeners, were identical to the features of his own home. Character was shared like a language, a unique identity, by that small select group – his people! And though a long way from home Johann was known here, both as a partisan and a mountaineer. He was astounded therefore to hear voices heckling a local speaker – it was as if they contradicted the rhythm of his blood, challenging the very nature of his feelings.

How, the hecklers demanded, did the platform think a handful of mountain-farmers could maintain a separate existence without the support of that country which virtually subsidised them at the moment with employment and trade? It was pure fantasy, they yelled, a fairy-tale, an impediment to progress.

Thunderstruck, Johann saw many of the audience nod and smile with furtive complacency as if their own ideas were being voiced. A moment later he found himself at the front of the platform shaking with fierce conviction. He addressed the objections, denouncing them as treachery. He sketched the evils of invasion and tyranny, the subjugation of a proud race, confiscation of the tiny fields, collectivisation on behalf of factory-workers in foreign cities .... Had they no pride, he exhorted, no will, no sense of destiny? Did no one realise there were more important things at stake than material wealth – which would be robbed from them as soon as they succumbed to it?

The true issue, Johann asserted, was national identity, the noble spirit of the people. It was a cultural value which could only be preserved in determined isolation. And its propagation was their sacred charge.

'Without identity,' he challenged fervently 'without soul, without language, without the old and tested way of life, the way that is hard but simple and pure, our children will be impoverished beyond slavery, beyond starvation!'

Johann's harsh voice ignited the emotions he had aroused. The crowd flared with patriotic passion. He offered them answers; discipline; courage; self-determination! They must stand now and fight! Fight for the future in the name of the past!

He raised his arms in the fascist salute, his eyes rose fervently above the tumult, and the barrier of mountains blocking the whole horizon echoed their isolation from the outside world.

But the opposition at home to the new doctrine was not so easy to quell. Johann was no longer a hero or a prophet there. The force of his faith made it impossible for him to understand how anyone but a traitor could attack it. It was as if he discovered poison in a mountain-stream. In the intervals between his travels he tried to increase the guerilla activities of his unit. The response was sluggish – there was an uneasy cohesion now between politics and militancy. Johann knew they badly needed weapons for the coming struggle, but there was no further mention of the promised airlift, and Jean contrived to be away when Johann was at home.

The older people favoured his politics – but not his violence. Resistance was fine when it meant firing off the odd shot from a safe ambush to preserve their self-respect. But they were not willing to be sacrificed for a lost cause.

There was raw dissatisfaction among the younger men.

Tradition robbed most of them of any rights to the land that passed from patriarch to eldest son. They sought a focus for their discontent. The neighbouring army, already at war, was an uneasy option. It was hard to decide whether or not they were actually occupied by a country of which they had been part for centuries.

But surely, they had a common enemy now in that totalitarian expansion threatening to engulf them both?

The Movement, popular at first, was losing its grip on them. They had no place in its emerging politics, and there was no clear direction for guerilla action. In the intervals between seasonal work they enlisted their frustrated energy in the mountain-cult. Jean and Anna were the focus of this disaffection.

The summer passed in a blaze of inflamed emotion and autumn brought the first high snows.

Rationing increased the disillusion in the villages. Suddenly there was harsh resentment of any mouth without a justified claim on food. It became apparent to Johann that people cared more for bread than brotherhood. He denounced the failure of patriotism. Some of his men were forced out of their billets, and he had to impose authority for the first time over his sullen neighbours.

On a freezing afternoon in midwinter footsteps hurried up the ice-encrusted stairs to the loft where Johann was studying. He glanced up impatiently, expecting the woman who brought his food. Anna stood in the doorway, the promise of a smile offered in exchange for a welcome. Behind her the outside world was a blinding rectangle of snow and icy light. He smelled the cold air invading the room, withering the quiet shadows.

Anna's cheeks were rubbed to a bitter glow by the wind, and her eyes were bright and nervous with excitement. In spite of the savage draught ruffling his papers Johann felt his cramped heart expand towards a source of warmth and instinctively he tightened his limbs against the urge. He noticed that as usual his feet were numb with cold. His eyes returned to his book. The print was meaningless and he shut it slowly with an imitation of reluctance that appalled him. Giving her no chance to speak he rose unsteadily to his feet.

'Anna' he ordered heavily, 'you will have to stop this nonsense in the mountains. There's work to be done here! You're giving bad example ... making it impossible for me ....' Anna recoiled in angry surprise. 'Don't blame me,' she snapped. 'You create your own problems!' Then she laughed and rolled her eyes at his idiocy, refusing to take her own anger seriously either. The old fashioned, local clothing she wore should have placed her firmly under his command, but her expression repudiated him. His knuckles clenched with anger and the realisation that she would never respect his authority. Without her approval he had no respect for it himself.

'What do you want?' he snapped frigidly. 'I'm busy.'

Anna glanced at his books with ironic disdain. Following her gaze Johann flushed. He felt how precarious his world of intelligence and inspiration must seem, balanced on a few battered, uncertain texts.

'I came to tell you something important!' Anna burst out. Her voice shook with excitement, animosity forgotten. She pointed through the black, timber-beamed wall, her finger stabbing the shadows with determination.

'Johann, tomorrow we're going up ... to climb *that*! The Spearhead!' The whimsical name spat at him from her glistening lips. She stamped once on the dusty floor then looked him straight in the eye with tense anticipation. Her lips stayed open in a fixed smile full of white teeth.

Johann heard himself laugh. It was the first time in months. It scraped from his throat and fell helplessly into the room like a dry coughing. The absurdity! He felt the weather – the deep snow, the abysmal cold – tighten in his head sharpening his defences. The impregnability of the mountain was assured. 'Who ...' he demanded contemptuously '... is WE?'

Anna ignored the insult but the tension in her jaw increased. Without changing her expression she was no longer even faintly smiling. She put strong, roughened hands on the table and leaned towards him. Johann saw her knuckles trembling, almost felt the vibrations through the timber. It was the nearest he had been to her since they climbed together and he was shocked again by the difference in her face. She was never what he expected. The constant shifts, not just in style but almost in substance, bewildered him. It was impossible to know her. He saw the hard, naked flesh of a face from which romance and luxury were pared away. It was not a woman's face – to be calculated with emotion – but the cold visage of an antagonist.

She swallowed deliberately before she spoke, determined to carry out some intention though the reason for it had already deserted her.

'We wanted ... we *decided* ...' she corrected coldly '... to ask you to come with us, since you had the ... the *courage* to make the first attempt. We thought it *right* ....' She was underlining words to whip him with the absolute failure of the idea.

Johann's breathing locked in his throat. He floundered in angry confusion. Were they mocking him? He knew Jean would never have thought of asking. The gesture was entirely Anna's. Did she mean something by it, or was she trying to make a fool of him? She must have known he would refuse. He had no idea what to think, but he was already answering with grating sarcasm. 'It's madness! Dangerous lunacy! He will not succeed!'

He thought of the gaping bergschrund, the ice stacked above it like a limestone overhang. His lip curled. 'He won't even – '

She was turning on her heel, the heavy dress flaring with fury.

'Anna!' his voice barked impulsively, 'Wait!'

She turned, charged with hostility. Seeing the expression on her face he was terrified by what he had achieved. The shock detached him briefly. As his mouth struggled for the truth he felt – for an instant, within himself – a dark, silent opening. It was a displacement between feeling and words, and within the gap he felt a poisoned response flicker towards emergence. It belonged neither to emotion nor to reason. It was beyond his control. If he could hold the awareness long enough to ....

Hoarse and bullying a cry broke from him.

'Anna! Don't go!'

Not what he meant. It was an order, not a plea.

'Why not?' she sneered scornfully, tossing her head. 'What is it to you?' The moment closed over, sealed with an instant scar.

'There's a *war* on, Anna!' he retorted furiously. 'A war! ... Out There!' He stabbed his finger in the opposite direction.

'We must dedicate ourselves to Resistance. We can't take any other risks. The mountains will wait – ' He stumbled; mountains waited for destiny, not for individuals.

'Don't you understand?' he demanded desperately.

'I understand *fear* when I see it!'

It was said with the contemptuous clarity of the obvious. He knew what she was going to say in advance, and knew she was right. The real shock came from this sense of foreknowledge.

'Fear?' he raged. 'Fear!' His fingers tore at his face in denial.' The long, wooden word gagged his tongue, '... responsibility!'

Choking with fury he glared at her. 'I have nothing to be ashamed of.

I did my share in these mountains when that was the thing to do! Anyone will tell you that!'

The need to hurt was naked on Anna's drawn skin. 'Not any more, Johann,' she hissed. 'Your reputation has run out. I'll tell you what they're saying now –

' – That you've lost your nerve and you won't admit it. That you're trying to hide behind politics. That you want to be a hero but it's always someone else who has to pull the trigger – ' She stamped her foot viciously with each accusation, 'And they're right! They say it would be better for everyone if you gave up playing politics and went back to climbing mountains. At least you knew something about that – once.

'I've just offered you a chance to prove them wrong. It wasn't easy to come here like this – but you turned it down. Like everything else! I thought if you took a break from your . . . your *patriotism* you might recognise it for what it is!'

She took a bitter breath and plunged on, enraged by an echo. 'You dare to tell me there's a war on! Me! As if I didn't know more about war than you ever will.

'What do you think drove me back here?' She pounded the table furiously. 'When I got home after that self-indulgent . . . *holiday* with you I found out all about war, very quickly.

'And it's got very little to do with discipline and sacrifice! And plans, and patriots, and guns.' She snorted with outraged contempt. 'You ought to have joined the real army, Johann. You'd love all those games. They'd have made you an officer – you're fool enough. Maybe there's still time!'

Johann said nothing. He didn't move. He knew he was seeing Anna clearer than ever before. And with a sharp, almost sensual pain he saw himself too, reflected in her contempt.

'. . . But that isn't war, Johann. That's only the sound of it. War is invisible. It starts long before the armies face each other. Real war is a disease . . . a civilian disease.

'It's hunger, curfews, disappearances, midnight arrests, torture, people too frightened to talk to each other. The kind of terror that power, and death, feed on!

'That's what I found when I went home. Maybe it was the same before I left, but I didn't notice it until I felt the peace up here. Then I saw war raging like an epidemic – a fever – in the people around me. They were rotten with disease. I knew it would take bombs and guns and soldiers to burn it out. And death!

'It was incurable by then. Too late to do anything. Either get infected, or escape.

'So I came back here! I thought it was cleaner in the fresh mountain air. The disease hadn't reached here yet, and *you* dreamed of keeping it out. Such an innocent dream! – I laughed at it first when you told me – then I had to come back and help, in spite of ... of everything, including you. But whatever innocence you had here is dead now – and you've strangled it, Johann. You've strangled it!'

His mouth opened to protest, a black gap in his silent face.

'You don't believe me, Johann, you don't know what I'm talking about yet. But it's you! – you and your disciples who did it. You're full of hatred and fear, and it's infecting everything you touch. Look at the people around here! Your people!

'All the warmth and humour and trust is gone. They're at each others' throats now. They don't even know why. It's all disguised in slogans – who's a fascist, who's a red, who . . .' she blessed herself sarcastically '. . . who's descended from a Jew – It's a dirty little war of ugliness and suspicion and you're fanning the flames in the name of freedom! You don't even see it yet, you won't recognise it till the blood spills. And it will be the blood of your neighbours, and they'll get nothing for it – not even pity or respect.

'It has to come to that now, because the disease is gone too far. Maybe even then you won't understand – you'll think people should be sacrificed for principles – as long as you're around to enforce them afterwards.

'Listen to me, Johann! You were born here, but you've forgotten everything. There's a world of difference between dreams and reality and everyone else knows it. You don't!

'They think first with their blood, their bones, and their bellies. You're thinking with a box of worm-eaten books before you even use your brain.

'They don't give a damn for an independent mountain-state. A ghost republic bathed in blood. They know they'd starve if they tried to stand alone. That's all that matters!

'Listen to them if you still don't believe me. Listen to them – when they don't know you're there. They can't say it openly. You've got a few fanatics behind you now Johann, and it's dangerous for anyone to contradict.

'The only supporters you have are men with a grudge against reality like yourself, and that's the most lethal support of all –

' – That's the disease!'

The final words came as fiercely as if she tasted blood and spat it back. Johann remained motionless. His only hope lay in the dignity of silence. Between the phrases of the attack a cold internal voice advised him to have her shot. To do it himself. He shivered with desire and revulsion, imagining his comrades in the Movement, dedicated men, strong and peremptory. They eliminated opposition before it interfered. They were committed to an ideal and fierce in its pursuit. There was no other way.

He saw them now as they had assembled the week before – the national revolutionary committee – himself the youngest member, and a sudden, sickening jolt of distrust questioned the row of heavy faces and the sharp, shrewd eyes. They lived on a constant level of violence. For the first time Johann understood he would not choose to be involved in an ordinary world with any of them. He examined the faces individually with bitter disillusion. Some were there for the thrill of reckless conspiracy, some were honing private ambitions to settle on the day. The rest, like himself, were puppets of their own emotion.

In an awful, undermining way Anna was right. There was no support. He felt the confused and suffering weight of the people dragging down his dreams like paper flags into a mess of blood and snow.

Johann stared back into Anna's glowering eyes.

'Are you finished?' he asked quietly. He knew she was not. The sharp teeth were ready to rip him again.

But he had recognised with a shock of identity a familiar echo in Anna's voice. It was the resonance of hysteria and it came from the same dark displacement he had discovered in himself a few moments before. Anna too was on the very edge of control, torn between opposed convictions. She had come back here to fight – now she had lost her nerve, and taken refuge in mountaineering with its imitation of courage. And she too hated what she had given up. Johann had gone the other way; briefly they had passed each other by, their voices were entangled and still tearing apart. Johann found himself transparent with bitter lucidity. Anna's attack, fired by her own crisis, had exposed him to the bone. He felt no temptation to argue his case, to justify himself. There was nothing to say. Anna had echoed his own hidden awareness with unerring accuracy.

He knew he had chosen impossible politics, and used violence to punish reality when it did not conform. And yet – despite the absurdity – he had no choice. There would be no alternative soon except to lie down and rot into their own soil. He felt dimly that struggle was still a valid end in itself – but only for the undivided, the incorruptible.

'. . . at least you knew something about that, once!' Briefly the echo reassured. But he had reached a point in mountaineering when his nerve would take him no farther. He had to live with failure at that point, or else push himself – and his luck – farther than he dared. He did neither. He turned his back and hoped the mountains would have changed before he looked again. Johann admitted all that. It was obvious, and he brushed it impatiently aside.

But passion was a different thing. It was a constant crisis. It bulged within him, livid, unmentionable, a physical condition. He could never come to terms with that.

Anna waited, unappeased. When he fell in love with her, tumbling into an impossible obsession, he had feared her sophisticated standards and refused to face them. He had cut himself off, agonizingly, rather than risk any further failure.

He knew now that that was the ultimate defeat. Self-inflicted! Beyond anything else, he hoped she did not guess what he had done to both of them. He was determined to keep that secret at any cost. He had never given the slightest clue to his feelings.

'Are you finished?' he asked again, unsteadily. Anna shook her head slowly, deliberately.

'No! I came to tell you something else. I'm leaving, Johann! As soon as that climb is finished. Jean is right; it's the only thing left here, and I'm going as soon as its done.'

She was leaning towards him – not to approach, but as if to push him away. And yet he heard her words from a long way off. He felt her hot breath on his face and smelled a faint sting of alcohol. Awful certainty stabbed him, jealousy before any emotion. 'You . . . you're going away with Jean!' His voice wailed and broke.

'That's none of your business!' Anna retorted angrily. 'Don't play the wounded lover with me, Johann. It's too late for any of that. You had your chance!'

He was staring at her in open-mouthed anguish, his face unmasked. Anna laughed harshly. 'Oh yes, I know what you're supposed to feel, though sometimes I doubt it. Zelda told me about you months ago.

'I suppose I was meant to come crawling to you on my knees again. Well, if you couldn't tell me your own feelings – whatever they were – I didn't want to know. You killed mine deliberately anyway. Whatever inadequacy you're cursed with you took it out on me.' She drew a deep, vindictive breath. 'Let me give you a bit of advice, Johann! What you feel is not love. It's self-pity!

'Well I'm sorry, but I can't waste any more sympathy on you. You've done too much damage already.'

She drew further away in distaste, shaking her head at the stricken face that gaped at her, bone-white and betrayed. Her voice dropped to a cold, even tone of withdrawal. 'You disappoint me Johann, and that's the reason why I'm going. But you've disappointed a lot of others too, and they have to stay here. That's why I'm telling you this; I'm trying to do something for them before I go!'

Stripped of secrecy Johann's resistance collapsed. In its place there was an eerie, detached calm – pain stretched to a pitch that his mind could not admit. He felt his heart hammer loud and loose in his hollow chest, as if it had torn away from a powerful enclosing pressure. The released heartbeat was so strong he felt his body twitch and jerk. In a moment the shock would diminish and the overwhelming pain return. In the interval disembodied reason functioned coolly. He could not let her go, or existence would always feel like this, unendurable, inescapable.

He backed unsteadily into the dark loft, retreating before Anna's hatred. Shards of plaster crunched beneath his boots. Reaching the solid resistance of a wall he focused painfully on the waiting face blurred by silence and shadows. He had watched her from this distance at every meeting. He could not remember a single thing he had ever said or done that did not revolve secretly around her presence.

She was still there. Waiting. A question stirred in him. It was almost a joke the way it crept into his numb vacancy and he felt his horrified lips twitch. Did she intend a miracle of reconciliation? or was she bent on his total destruction?

The two possibilities were the furthest extremes of optimism and despair – and though he knew which was true he knew also that an illusion of hope was essential to him.

The light seeping through the snow-banked window was waning fast. The loft was thick with shadows. Anna's white face drifted in the darkness. The anger on the dim features was indistinguishable from grief, or pain, or loss ....

Johann was convulsed suddenly by guilt, as if he had struck her brutally. It passed and left a sense of clear, tragic pity in its wake. He was not the only victim! She was waiting because she had nowhere else to go. Obviously Jean only wanted a second, a temporary partner. He would be gone as soon as it suited him, and gone alone. The mountain was not a destination for her either – it was an act of defiance. She thought that if she reached the impossible summit she would come down somewhere else, somewhere completely different.

But the notion of the mountain terrified him. He saw the pointed roof of the loft rear above her, the apex lost in shadow, a prophecy filled with threat.

If she simply went away he would still have hope, but he knew with certainty that departure to the mountain was final. _It had happened before._

He moved impulsively towards her. Anna straightened and jerked back but his hands beseeched her.

'Anna don't. That mountain is not . . .' he struggled for words '. . . not what you think! Leave it alone, Anna! Let him take someone else. It's too dangerous!'

The warning tumbled passionately from his mouth – but she heard him say plainly: You're not good enough.

Her pale cheeks reddened and she threw back her hair furiously. 'How dare you tell me what to do . . . .'

Johann ignored her protest. He knew where he was now. He felt the wound in his consciousness opening again, a blind gap widening quickly as memory pushed through the darkness towards recognition.

He was breathless with urgency. It had happened before. He had to stop her. How to begin?

'Anna – remember the medal I had . . . the International Expedition! I gave it to you!' His voice was quick and impetuous, almost a wail. He had never spoken like that before. Crying for attention.

'Everything went wrong.' His hands were close to his face, hovering.

'I couldn't believe how big the mountains were. These – ' he shook his head fiercely at the walls ' – these are only miniatures!'

'What are you trying to say?' Anna broke in impatiently, 'You did nothing, did you?'

'No,' he admitted, 'I did nothing, – but not for the reasons you think. The expedition was cancelled. It was a disaster.

'No,' he rushed, forestalling her, 'I wasn't involved. They wouldn't let me . . . .'

'They wouldn't let you? What kind of nonsense is that?'

Johann spread his trembling hands, his voice was tired, incapable of anger. 'Anna, four women died in a blizzard a week after our arrival. Is that enough for you?'

He saw furious resistance on her face but he went on flatly. 'The first female team to try anything so high. They couldn't wait to hurl themselves at it. I was in base-camp all the time. They wouldn't allow me on any team because I was too young. Not even the easy ridge-repeats.' A sullen shadow passed across his face.

'It was my own fault. I was sixteen, I passed myself off as twenty and they found me out. It was too late to pick someone else from our province so they put me on base-camp duty. Kitchens and latrines – working with the porters – it was a punishment.

'The other climbers ignored me. Some treated me like a servant, especially since I came from here. They pretended they never heard of our mountains, they made stupid jokes. But the women understood. Especially Vera! They understood why I wanted to be there – no matter where I came from.'

He put his hands to his face and spoke through his fingers.

'I think I knew beforehand that something had to happen. She was the best person there, and she was living those days at an incredible pitch of anticipation.

'She used to show us pictures of her children. She had a daughter my age, she said I'd have to meet her. . . .'

Anna's eyes were narrow with suspicion. 'Don't give me a sob-story!'

'No. No! It's the truth. I didn't feel . . . . It's not what you think.'

'They went up in poor weather. No one else was doing much, just acclimatising, but Vera and Arlova were full of confidence. It wouldn't be a hard route – just an enormous snow-climb.

'I was with them when they left for the walk-in. I helped Vera put her rucksack on. I couldn't believe the weight of it! I couldn't have carried it to seven thousand metres, or even five! But she just shrugged it on and walked away, waving to everyone.

'She was walking backwards, laughing at us all, waving for a camera, and I tried to imagine they were coming down to meet us after the route shouting in triumph. But she was getting farther and farther away and the laughter was growing thin, and she stumbled a bit and had to turn her back on us.

'The weather broke two nights later and it never really cleared again. It snowed right down into the valley, into the summer meadows where the flowers were growing the day before. Every night was like another door locked behind them. The porters said they were the worst storms in twenty years. Even in base-camp the winds were so fierce that tents were completely destroyed.

'We wanted to go up after them – not just me, but most of the others. Maria's husband was in the camp, but the authorities wouldn't let us move. They said it would be suicidal, the mountain was avalanching over and over again and the winds were impossible. I don't know. I would have gone anyway, and so would the others. Everyone loved them. We knew there was only one hope – that they might have reached the summit and dug snow-holes before the worst of the storms. Tents would be useless in the winds. If they were in snow-holes they might survive to traverse the mountain in a lull and descend the west ridge. But they couldn't have enough food to endure the storm and then the long descent. I remembered the weight of Vera's sack and I wasn't so sure.

'There was almost a mutiny and a rescue-team was allowed to leave base-camp. They crawled along under the storm for two days and then began the ascent of the West Ridge to meet the women on their way down. I begged to go, but they wouldn't listen to me.

'The weather cleared a little and they were able to climb. But they met nobody on the ridge. The higher they went the more hopeless it was. Finally they knew they were just a recovery-squad.

'You can't imagine what it was like for the rest of us below, no word, no hope, nothing to do but wait for the worst, and all the time inventing some impossible escape. I still couldn't get the weight of Vera's rucksack out of my mind. I told everyone she was carrying spare food. I was determined to believe it. But they said if she was carrying that much weight then she was in even greater danger from exhaustion.

'It wasn't food . . . .

'The rescue-team found them on the summit. They had to dig. They were wrapped together in one tent, buried under thick snow. The whole bundle was already frozen into the ice, and the rescuers had to . . . to hack it loose with ice-axes.'

Johann paused. Looking over Anna's head he confronted something invisible, '. . . and do you know what they did then? They were too exhausted to bring the bodies down. Do you know what they did?

'They wrapped them in the tent again, tied them with a rope, and . . . and pushed them over the East Face. I still can't believe it, but that's what they did!

'They thought the bodies would disappear . . . like a burial at sea, but they came all the way down to the lower slopes. Three of them. The canvas ripped and three of them came down. 'They sent me out with another team to help bring them in. I don't know why they did that either – my God, we were all too young!

'And Maria's husband . . . he came with us, and examined them one by one as we lowered them onto the glacier. But she . . . she hadn't come down. He was hysterical with grief. They had to restrain him physically from starting up the face. He wasn't even a climber. He blamed himself for letting her go . . . .

'Vera was the farthest away. She almost looked alive. Asleep or something. Her skin was so cold and hard it was unmarked. Her rucksack was there too. It was still heavy. I opened it. There was a big camera in it – an old-fashioned one – to prove they'd been on top I suppose. It was smashed to bits.

'All the pictures of her children were in there. And a picture of her husband. He was much older than Vera. And there were flags . . . from her club, her city, her province. But there was no food.

'I found a diary in the top of the sack while they were carrying her down. There were entries for every day of the climb and they got shorter and shorter as time ran out. Pages with no dates, no times, just a clumsy scrawl as if she had gloves on – or her hands were numb. Messages for her children and people I'd never heard of. She didn't know where she was towards the end, no mention of the snow or the storm, just vague things she wanted to do. And then – a last page that said the others were all asleep, she had done everything possible for them and . . . and soon she would sleep herself. It was like a lullaby, as if she were singing a lullaby!

'At the bottom of the page the writing cleared with a great effort – the pencil dug into the paper – and she wrote

'We are sorry we have failed you'

'Can you imagine that?' Johann whispered to Anna. 'They thought they had failed us, US!'

He took a shivering breath and exploded. 'It was OUR failure! They were too important . . . We should never have let them go!'

Anna flinched. Her head jerked back fiercely. 'What right have you' she hissed 'to decide what anyone else should do?'

Johann was jolted brutally into the present. He stared at her dizzily, tears blinding his eyes. The rage of loss was so bitter he could have struck her to release it. He could say nothing. Nothing! The air was frozen finally between them, his heart ticking towards explosion. In five seconds, four, three . . . he would shatter. She turned abruptly and left the room. The door slammed. Boot-heels hammered down the wooden stairs.

Johann stood in the darkness. He held his breath, straining for footsteps returning on the stairs, like heartbeats from a dream of death. But there was silence everywhere, and he exploded in slow, unbearable grief.

He followed them when they quit the smothered valley for the white mountains. Away from the village Jean and Anna clasped hands briskly and swung along together oblivious to the extra shadow they cast in the early light. Anna was teaching Jean a song and she laughed helplessly at his total elision of the guttural. Their voices chimed thin and faint in the muffled landscape. They moved fast on the frozen snow-crust, skimming across the drifts as if on skis.

Johann struggled grimly to stay in range. His muscles were weak and stale, and the icy air burned in his throat. He knew every step of the path, knew exactly where he could move unseen and when to hang back. But he was invisible to them; they were sealed in their own rapport. It was exactly how Anna had been with him at first.

Soon they left him far behind. Already his boots, stiff from disuse, were gnawing his heels. The heavy rifle slung across the rucksack chafed his shoulders cruelly. He carried it for –

Certainty burned in his brain. Last week three of his best men had been ambushed in action by the military police. They had barely escaped with their lives. A pattern was finally exposed. Johann had worked it out grimly last night, grief and humiliation hardening together into revenge. Someone was spying. Informing! He stalked Jean, like a wounded hunter.

He lost them in the afternoon when the memory of tracks had faded away, and the rocks, the streams, the great reefs of moraine, were sunk without trace under frozen waves of winter. He stumbled to a halt at times, against a bank of snow, to gnaw some bread and cheese, churning it around in his mouth. His stomach rebelled against it, and finally, after struggling up a steep slope he threw it all up and left himself utterly raw and empty, at the mercy of the landscape. The sky, the ice, the crackling air, the rock-scars like chipped enamel on the white faces, closed in to crush him in the grip of a monstrous, mineral world.

Traversing the endless plateau, skirting its ridges and rifts, he no longer thought of where he was going. He would travel until he dropped. He was conscious only of a determination to go on – on to some conclusion. Not to be beaten by default.

The pain of betrayal, the rage for revenge, were dimmed by exhaustion and cold. But there was never any doubt of his direction. He had not seen the mountain all day – it was hidden by intervening peaks – but it drew him with irresistible force.

There was no twilight. Darkness fell like an abrupt decision. It seemed to come from within his brain, a dismissal of the white wilderness.

Hours later a stark moon rose and lit the glacier. The way stretched wearily on, up into the shadow of the spear-crested cirque. Once he saw a light twinkling cheerfully ahead, but it was a bright star rising over a ridge. He climbed a buried ice-fall to the upper glacier, and a grunt of relief acknowledged the easy step. It was normally a steep, unstable obstacle; but now the heavy, solid snow made everything possible. It would have been a good time to climb . . . .

There were familiar peaks on his left and right. Thin, tapering spires, dizzy junctions of rock and air, he had climbed them all before, addicted to their altitude and grace. Now they were stony shadows – scraping sparks off the black sky.

He could not recall warmth under a blue heaven, could not remember sunlight blazing on bright rock, nor remember a time without this dark taste of ice and pain in his mouth. He was drunk with displacement. Someone he had known – close and lost as a dead twin – had revelled in those jubilant walls and kept the memory when Johann fell away into confusion. As if he had slipped from some golden, forgotten morning far down into this hideous dark he flashed past all his attachments, saw how they were linked and lost; he had loved these mountains and been rejected, had loved Anna and been displaced, had loved an idea and left it in ruins behind him in the valley.

Jagged splinters of the past tore his memory from within. And the cold weight of the rifle dug deep into his back.

Casually he broke through a crust of snow into a hidden crevasse. Instinct jerked his body into a whiplash and he saved himself. As soon as he was secure on the rim of the chasm he cursed his recovery. Then the hallucinations began. He stumbled into villages of sérac and shadow that returned to ice with such poisonous derision that he doubted whether reality existed anywhere. All he wanted now was sleep; isolated houses – some with doors, windows, smoking chimneys – drifted up from his subconscious, jutted cruelly into the landscape. And for a long time the traitor was behind him, pursuit reversed, and Jean was filling in his footprints to erase him from the surface of the snow, so that the further Johann walked the less he existed. He dodged, weaved, and sometimes he doubled back to shake off his invisible pursuit. But Jean was deadly. He had a year's practice in trailing Johann!

When he reached the little hut on its rock-island near the head of the glacier he almost dismissed it as another mirage. It was caked with frozen snow – only the shape was visible in the shifting night – an ice-enamelled box drumming with silent tension. Together they were asleep inside.

The logic of arrival returned him to his senses. He saw a grotesque image of himself shambling through the dark towards inevitable contempt. He could not bring himself to approach the door and whimper for shelter. He had rights here. He remembered the building of the hut fifteen years before, the first time he had come this far into the summer mountains riding a mule with a load of planks, then trotting behind his father's long steps across the glaciers. The hut was hammered together from pine-planks. His father and his uncle were two of the carpenters who finished it, hanging the heavy door at the end of the third day's work. The following year they were conscripted and never returned. Now the hut looked as if it had absorbed its origins. It seemed to have grown from its own powerful root under the snow, and the door and windows were indistinguishable from the dull bark of the trunk.

He thought of kicking the door briskly open, announcing he had come to join them on the climb . . . .

An image of two drowsy heads on one mattress regarding him with horrified contempt dragged an atavistic grunt of humour up from his bowels. That he should come to this!

It was obvious that he couldn't climb tomorrow – he could barely walk. He was at the limit of endurance now, but it would be a greater humiliation to reveal that jealousy had driven him there. He had no faith now in the moral superiority of revenge. Guilt was too complex to be resolved by execution. He dreaded the icy cave, the old bivouac nearby. It was like deliberately entering a grave, but dignity forced him down. There was a flat space there under a boulder. He had cleared it himself long ago, and built the overlapping walls to shelter it on the first day the men were erecting the hut. He crawled in now and spread out his coat. He pushed the frozen rifle down through a sleeve and dragged a heavy sleeping bag on over his clothes. The gun lay awkwardly beneath him, but he fell instantly into an icy sleep.

. . . Under the blankets on the iron cot Johann lay wide awake in his cell, dreaming, dreaming. The details were perfectly clear; the heavy boulder crusted with icicles; the black hole in the snow-drift. And the wooden box nearby, containing all that anyone could ever desire – shelter, warmth, food. Jean was inside with Anna.

And he, was outside.

How much was true, how much reserved by memory, no longer

mattered. Reality had no witness except himself. He was outside.

But there was a quickening of cold new emotion in the old man's brain this time. A trickle of judgement. Clearer than revenge. It stirred like blood released from a long freeze.

He knew that somewhere guilt must emerge this time, like the bones and the rags, the buttons, the teeth, and the rotting leather that dribble out at last from the snouts of glaciers . . . .

Voices outside the hut woke him slowly. Consciousness drifted up through drowning waters. A gulp of icy air. Self-discovery sharp as nausea. Cold shudders racked his body, convulsions racing through his frozen limbs. He clenched his teeth against the spasms, and all the shivering came to a rattling focus in his jaws. He opened his eyes and felt the black weight of the boulder pressing down inches above his blind face. He almost cried out in choking terror.

They were leaving for the mountain. It was still pitch dark and he had slept at most three hours. If he had lain unconscious any longer he would never have recovered. Footsteps rang past the bivouac. Not the faintest crunch of snow under the boots. Anna's voice was strained and brittle. She spoke the foreign language but her fear was obvious. Jean's response was low and toneless, like water running under ice.

Johann crawled from the bivouac and stumbled towards the hut. It was a desolate sanctuary, the blood-heat had leaked away, and the bare walls and roof enclosed a solid cube of night.

He shook with advanced exposure. Heat was crucial. An ashy spark in the woodstove! He built it up into a reckless furnace, plundering the emergency firewood, splintering the wooden spoons and breadboard.

He rooted frantically for food. They must have left him something! He refused to believe he was invisible to them; they must be as involved in his presence as he was in theirs. Not a crumb! He boiled a jagged lump of snow-ice. The hot water seized his stomach with violent cramps. Blood returning to the frozen toes and fingers brought the agony of amputation in reverse. At this stage of exposure he knew revival was harsher than decline. He writhed before the stove, an animal in crisis.

The mattress lay neatly rolled against the wall, feathers sprouting from its cover. He rocked back and forth moaning with recovery and stared at it in a desperate attempt to ignore the increasing pain. When he lost control he beat his frenzied fingers into its limp, unresisting bulk forcing it to absorb his anguish. The coarse texture and rusty pattern responded with a gush of memory like an explosion of feathers. A matrimonial mattress long ago – dangerously close now to the source – it had slipped down the scale of comfort until finally exiled here. He remembered it swaying up the track, outrageously loaded on a mule's back, firewood slung across it, and they rushed to tilt the mattress every time the mule's tail lifted. Deeper still he seemed to recall it – not this one but exactly the same – in the vicinity of childhood, in a hushed dark bedroom, before it went down to Aunt Zelda's house after a funeral.

He hurled it flat on the floor fumbling and tearing for its secrets, as if something might reveal how close they had been last night. Feathers drifted up around him like snowflakes, but the past was silent and absorbed. With detached horror he saw himself crouch in wild unreason over the battered mattress, cursing, and clawing – and yet he knew that somewhere behind the pain he was bitterly, irreducibly sane, like a man driving himself into a drunken frenzy to blind the unforgettable.

Long after dawn he left the hut and followed the last curve of the glacier. The mountains were carved out of solid daylight, with smears of darkness where the rock showed through. He turned the foot of the final ridge and looked straight in at the blank triangle.

Impossible breath seized his throat. Three hours at most and the two black dots were one third of the way up already. Johann could measure them moving – the white bulge of the rock barrier sliding away below them. It was time accelerated; seeing an hour-hand move. He shook his head in stupefaction. It must be an illusion – choughs flying up the face. They could never have got so high!

A second shock! They were moving together. No belays! Thirty feet of rope between them as if they were walking up a snow-slope. But this was an ice-wall . . . . Insanity! At that angle if either slipped they were both whipped off instantly.

Johann had spent a whole day's climbing to reach that height – three hundred metres – on the face. He had bivouacked on a rognon just above it. Every metre gained had meant a step cut, holds hacked in the glassy ice with the blunt axe, a ledge chopped at every twenty metres, ice-pegs battered in, the others dragged up skidding and scrabbling on the grey, winter glaze.

His stunned brain slowly absorbed today's conditions – eyes dazzled from within as he understood the glowing face. Instead of winter water-ice – the colour of lead and as hard as glass – he saw breathless, fresh brilliance clinging to the face. Fresh snow . . . . Snow! The huge triangle was lightly, evenly plastered.

Johann gouged his incredulous eyes, The north-facing ice was too steep, too smooth! to hold snow like that. It sloughed off in powder-avalanches immediately after a fall.

But Jean and Anna were still moving. Even as he gaped the rock-barrier slipped another ten metres below them. They had stepped up through it on a rib of snow, as if bare rock had never existed there . . . . The recent weather flashed through his mind. A storm three days ago. But the effects of that should have avalanched immediately! Then the temperature had dropped to an abnormal low. The day of Anna's visit the village was creaking in the grip of a savage freeze. Then bitter, windless weather. Yesterday evening the temperature had seemed beyond the extreme – he had put it down to his thin blood, the loss of heat from a raging heart. But he understood now! Extreme conditions had frozen a crust of snow to the ice-face overhead. Crampons and axes bit firmly into it. But it was no more than inches thick and already thawing. The temperature was shooting up this morning! Johann broke into a frantic sweat at the consequences.

He realised he was watching something new in mountaineering – new by local standards. A gamble on opportunity and speed! Where he had waited for stable conditions, however hard, and then inched his way upwards, Jean had seized transition and was flying towards the top. He had a few short hours between the snow-ice and the avalanche. But surely he had misjudged it. Surely he was a day late!

A thousand metres, angle sixty-five degrees, temperature minus ten and rising, eight hours of daylight left. Three hundred metres climbed. Johann worked it out numbly. They could do it. Barring accidents!

But an accident was guaranteed. Inevitable! He could not believe the mountain would submit to calculated treachery.

Standing on the smothered glacier looking uselessly upwards, Johann saw his last ambition being cheated from him. He had meant to climb the mountain when the war was won. It was a pledge to self-respect, made in subconscious silence in case it could not be redeemed.

Barring accidents! The insistent thought had the conviction of evil in his brain, a primitive mix of curse and prayer.

But if Jean failed, Anna was doomed. That rope was the ultimate intimacy, even more than the mattress.

The face was angled away from the heat of the day – until this afternoon, when the last rays of the setting-sun would breach the summit-cornice. They must reach the top before the thaw if . . . .

A rush of awful contradiction squeezed venom from his heart. They . . . Must . . . Fail!

The deliberate curse echoed around the silent cirque, gathering force and resonance as it hurtled from wall to wall, crashing and booming between the summits, a brutal, voiceless roar hammering at the frozen lid of the sky.

The vengeful breath retracted and sobbed in his throat. There was one thing stronger than hatred. He could not bear to lose Anna. She was a hostage on the mountain. Jean had robbed him now of his last resorts – of hope and of revenge.

Helpless rage ignited him. He dived against a smothered boulder and dragged the rifle from his back. Trembling, white-tipped fingers clung to the icy steel. He screwed a telescopic sight onto the barrel, a clumsy range-finder – two lenses and a focus. No, he did not intend to shoot! He could not execute Anna. In the valley a traitor had betrayed the Movement. That was Jean! It had to be Jean, the foreign agent! It was either him, or . . . ? Panic exploded in mid-thought.

The weapon gave a vacant sense of power, something to control. And through the powerful lens he could watch her crawling up the face. Towards what conclusion?

Weaving with weakness the cross-hairs searched the shining snow. The smooth stock against his trembling jaw, the solid rock and ice under a sliding elbow – he knew he was the only weak component in a hard machine. The sight lurched, picked up a blurred figure, long and thin as an insect, limbs working busily. His fingers stumbled against the trigger and withdrew. The rope led downwards. He lowered the barrel to find her. A terrifying thought kicked from the polished wood into his skull. Bullets would not be necessary! The sound of gunfire alone would trigger an avalanche on that shivering face.

She was unrecognisable in helmet and bulky clothes. For one exultant moment he thought it was someone else – a legitimate enemy on his terrain. But her movements, the angle of her head, the action of her arms, were undeniable. Anna had not adapted to ice with the smoothness she showed on rock. Ice took confidence beyond technique. Johann felt a stab of simple surprise; there was something wrong. She was fumbling, climbing without rhythm. He had expected to witness excellence. Instead she was visibly slowing Jean.

He felt his tension release a surge of sympathy. He understood the fear she felt up there, making her kick too hard and flail the axe into the ice behind the snow. It was not just fear of avalanche and the frail snow-crust, but a sense of the overwhelming enmity of that wall. The exposure undermined the imagination. Jean knew nothing of that, the inhuman vacuum sucking at the soles of the feet. There was nothing in his head but time and motion.

Still Johann couldn't believe they had climbed so high – a third of the face in three hours. The bergschrund alone . . . ? He whipped the barrel down the face, found the black crevasse and followed it. Magnification was unnecessary. With the naked eye he could see the mass of old debris heaped up on the glacier below, ice-blocks supporting a tongue of snow that bridged the bergschrund and reached onto the face. He remembered the bare, overhanging ice, the rattling axes, his skin sticking to the steel, the wildest thing he had ever driven himself to do. He focused on the spot. A ramp of ice-blocks loomed through the glass. The myth was buried and Jean had strolled across it, stripped Johann of his main achievement.

Barring accidents!

The telescopic sight crept up along the snow, found Anna again. Her legs continued to kick and lift, arms threshing like a swimmer caught in a current. He made an effort of will and attached her to himself – focusing the glass carefully to increase her safety, as if he were tightening the rope around her.

He opened the other eye beside the barrel and reeled with the strain of split vision. She was still there, working jerkily upwards, safe within the hazy cameo that pinned her to the face. But there beside her, far, far away on an unbearable expanse of white, two tiny black spots crept beyond control against the rising light. He felt the sun swinging south, rolling towards the rim of the cirque, blazing already onto the glacier behind him. His heart pounded in panic and Anna dissolved in his sweating eye-socket, distance sucking her away into its vacuum.

He shut the murderous eye of exposure and drew her back into the rim. The tense cross-hairs meshed against her body like a safety-net.

Through the long, melting morning he lay flat on the rock, his head on his rucksack, rifle pointed at the face. When he blinked his eyes stayed shut and he fell instantly asleep for seconds at a time. Waking, he caught her again and again as she faltered, the rope twitching impatiently at her waist.

Trickles of snow were pouring down the face now. The southward slopes creaked and settled behind him. When he glanced fearfully at the sun-clogged snow, it shone with a slick, creamy gloss. But the face was still in shadow.

They were over two-thirds of the way up. Anna rested frequently, slumped against the steepness. He breathed slow and deep, sent strength along the line of vision. Sometimes she was lost in spindrift – streams of powder sliding from above. Once she disappeared for so long that he screamed and waved his arm clawing the curtain aside.

And there were stones – he knew – shooting from the summit as the ice peeled away from the rotten rocks. He could not see the missiles but the air around her was charged with menace. She was difficult to pick out now, even through the lens, a limbless dot on broken ground.

The great rock-bulge below the last ice-field glowed ethereally as the sun swung towards the west ridge. Light trickled softly onto the face down the ramps and gullies from the summit. The mountain gleamed with a vicious grace.

He knew Jean thought nothing could stop him now, ladders of sunlight lowered to lift him to success.

What did Anna feel? Pain and the futility of pain? Doubt and dread? If she knew the stories of the first attempt then she was expecting the real trial overhead.

Johann had never explained what was up there, on the rusty tip of the spear. The rock was steep and rotten, the ridges beyond reach and impenetrably corniced. He offered no excuse beyond his own weakness. Conditions must be worse today, a treacherous scum of snow on the crumbling rock. Squinting, he saw the cornices foaming in the sunlight.

Jean was starting the crux now. He was at the foot of a gully, halted at last while the second dot crept up to him. What did they say to each other? He strained to understand. Anna was beyond speech. They were taking a belay at last, where there was nothing solid enough for support or attachment.

Johann saw the position as if he stood there with them, crowding for space, Boris and Anton slumped weakly on the ledge beside his feet, black lips and burnt-out eyes. A rough groove reared out of the ice, splitting the last rock-step. It was full of congealed rubble, fragments of red rocks stacked overhead, shifting and smearing at the touch.

The poison on the point.

He had hammered an ice-piton straight into a loose seam in desperation and still there was no security. In a moment of lucid fantasy he saw himself climbing on sea-shells and broken crockery.

Twenty metres higher, out of sight of the belay, an overhang sealed the groove. To right and left bloated red rock bulged. No way of knowing what lay above, how much climbing, how hard or dangerous. The one thing he knew for certain was the function of this gully.

It was a snow-spout and a stone-chute!

Johann leaned out below the overhang. A fall must drag his comrades off the ledge; they could never hold him now. He was entirely alone, surviving for three men. He mustered a surge of courage, a snarl of faith. Stepped up and leaned out again, fumbling below the rim of the overhang ... a jutting block to grab; if it held, swing free and launch, lunge for something secret behind the lip ....

His mouth moved, inventing holds, cementing them in place. A foothold shifted under his sagging weight. He had found the crux of his existence and it was a gambler's choice. The wrong decision now and he would be dead and a double-killer. Johann backed off.

Jean had no such choice. The slopes below him creaked and rippled with tension.

Anna swayed at the foot of the gully. She was invisible to Johann at last, but he knew exactly where she was, her head bowed against the rubble, wet rope useless in her hands, her face transparent with exhaustion. She no longer knew who was climbing above her, why she was condemned to be here.

Johann rubbed his eyes in anguish for her. He heard the rumble of his fingertips against his skull. Under a rush of pressure the eyelids burst open again ....

... White light burned into his brain, rebounded through his mouth. The summit was erupting in a storm of powder, the cornice pouring white lava down the gullies. The mountain shivered softly, brilliance seething and streaming down the blind triangle. The snow-slope burst in billowing waves, surging, sliding, sweeping .... A huge pulse drummed in Johann's head, darkness screaming from his mouth. A wooden club kicked against his jaw, butting and recoiling over and over again. He squeezed the frenzied trigger at the serene avalanche, and the rifle hammered tiny nails into the thunder.

The old man closed his eyes. Barely breathing he lay in darkness. His memory was empty. The white wave had erased the black pinpoints of pain and cured the long, sharp scrape of their ascent.

The past hung within him, a clean, grey triangle, steep and uninhabited. He lay at the apex, looking down. Levitation was as simple as desire at last; no ambition to impede or challenge it, no emotion, no witness.

He saw the great spillage fan out from the base below. Like milk boiling over, a pleasant stir of recognition. It flowed out towards the glacier and slowly seized solidity – swelling the river of ice. Shimmering clouds hung in the air awhile, then cleared like morning mist.

Johann was in no hurry now. He had thirty years at his disposal.

He embarked on a rhythm of cold content, allowing the rubble to settle softly in his mind. The snow merged with the underlying ice and slowly melted into the glacier to make room for the next avalanche and all the falls to follow. He almost slept on the cot, turning sideways and drawing his legs up under the blanket.

But try as he might to retain the ease of passion spent he could not erase the two small mounds together on the ice below. A thin cover of snow persisted over them, a blanket on a distant accident.

Later, there were voices near him. The gun was levered from his hands. He was lifted roughly and carried against his will. He had no desire to be taken down, jolted across the ice on a rope-stretcher. He lay sprawled in warm darkness then and molten liquid filtered down his throat. He was aware of his hands and feet being massaged, but it seemed as senseless as polishing timber. When he opened his eyes he found the woodstove floating in a haze beside him, the wooden floor, the striped mattress under his cheek.

He looked up into ambiguous eyes. His lips struggled to offer the most important truth. His tongue was useless, but the words slid up from his chest, already shaped like nuggets of ice.

'... they got nowhere ... just over the bergschrund when the cornice fell .... Madness!' He buried his face and dissolved in genuine grief.

He was carried down to the village. And two days later soldiers swept the valley. Their information was precise. The hardline partisans were hunted down. Some were shot on sight.

Johann was held for interrogation. There was no attempt to save his fingers and toes. They were amputated in case he died too soon.

Deranged with pain, torture revealed nothing but hatred. He was obsessed with one thing only – Jean's treason! He had the final proof, too late; as soon as their agent was dead they had moved in and cleaned up.

A thin, sharp-eyed officer with weak hands and a lateral approach took over the interrogation.

'Marceau?' He raised his eyebrows coolly at Johann's ranting –

'No, no, you've got the wrong spy there.'

He crossed his boots with polished satisfaction, smiled and knifed him with her name.